THE PROMISCUOUS PUPPETEER

THE PROMISCUOUS PUPPETEER

*To: Steve + Laura
Katie, Sarah*

Walter B. Biondi

TATE PUBLISHING
AND ENTERPRISES, LLC

Published by Tate Publishing & Enterprises, LLC
127 E. Trade Center Terrace | Mustang, Oklahoma 73064 USA
1.888.361.9473 | www.tatepublishing.com

Tate Publishing is committed to excellence in the publishing industry. The company reflects the philosophy established by the founders, based on Psalm 68:11,
"The Lord gave the word and great was the company of those who published it."

Book design copyright © 2014 by Tate Publishing, LLC. All rights reserved.
Cover design by Joseph Emnace
Interior design by Caypeeline Casas

Published in the United States of America

ISBN: 978-1-63268-175-1
Fiction/General
14.07.29

Vancouver, B.C. ·

Kingston, WA

Seattle, WA

Nez Perce
Elk City, ID

Port Ludlow, WA

Boise, ID

Washington, DC

Carlin Trend, NV ·
Elko, NV ·

Salt Lake City, UT

Sacramento, CA

Denver, CO

· Hopi Reservation
· Tucson, AZ

Tonopah, NV

Las Vegas, NV

To all my loved ones

ACKNOWLEDGMENTS

I am grateful for the encouragement and suggestions given to me by Mike Rhodes and Bill Jackson. Their interest in my efforts to create this novel is greatly appreciated. Mike Rhodes helped introduce me to the geological aspects of some of the subject matter in this book. Bill Jackson's intuitive and optimistic interest in the precious metals mining field helped fuel my interest in a portion of the book's area of focus. They, and others, were a constant source of motivation for learning and researching far ranging aspects of geology, the exploration and mining industry, lapidary, and other related subjects.

I'd also like to thank certain current and prior shareholders and employees of Premium Exploration, Inc. My experience with them, and others in the exploration and mining industry, served immeasurably as a partial background for my writing. I wish them every success.

My three years of research and experiences led me to many places and gave me the opportunity to make valued new friendships with people in Arizona, Nevada, Idaho, Oregon, California, and Washington state. Among them are certain people associated with the Royston Turquoise Mine in Tonopah, Nevada, who, I must add, never said a single derogatory word about their hometown.

My thanks go to the many new friends I made while researching some of the details used for the purpose of writing this book. Among them are the members and geologists of the Old Pueblo Lapidary Club in Tucson, Arizona, and the Port Townsend Rock Club in Port Townsend, Washington.

Dr. Donald Grybeck, PhD (Geology) was a former Chief of Mineralogy for the US Geological Survey Service and a professor of Geology for the University of Alaska. Now deceased, I can only posthumously express my gratitude to him for the exploration work he had accomplished during his lifetime, for the inspiring benefit I received as a consequence, and for the mineral collection I acquired including samples containing various very small amounts of precious and base metals from Alaska, Colorado, Washington, British Columbia, Peru, and Russia.

I'd also like to acknowledge my acquaintanceship with, and express my personal thanks to, several Native American law enforcement officials I came to know in Arizona. I also thank retired California District Attorney Bob Ebert for his advice and counsel regarding certain legal nuances which I applied to this novel.

To Mark and Li Salopek, I thank you both for your time and effort in helping me with your insights, observations, concepts, and encouragement. Mark's extensive experience in undercover and investigative law enforcement work in Nevada and Li's cover page art work talents emanating from her being a Doctor of Industrial Art and a Professor at an international university were of significant help to me in evaluating many aspects of this novel, including the hard and soft-edged heroes and villains.

For all of the above, please allow me to underscore my gratitude by adding the words "emphasis added."

CONTENTS

Part 4

PREFACE

I wrote this novel after having spent nearly three years researching some of the many facets of the world of geology, minerals, prospecting, exploration, mining, related finance, and the precious metals market.

The deeper I went into the various subject matters, the more intrigued I became. Although one could study any one of the industry-related categories indefinitely, my crash course included "kicking at the soil," personally mining for minerals and gems, becoming involved with an exploration and mining company, marketing, "rock hounding," and various other related lapidary pursuits.

My research included obtaining "hands-on" experience in finding semiprecious and precious rough gemstone material, some of which I cut, shaped, faceted, and polished. The world of lapidary arts and "rock hounding" was an experience that taught me much.

At one point during my research, I visited with Mr. Dean Otteson, the owner of the well known Royston Turquoise mines in Tonopah, Nevada. While there, and while digging (hand mining) for turquoise at one of his mines, the thought occurred to me that what I was experiencing about turquoise and Tonopah, Nevada, could become a part of this novel. Ultimately, it became the place where this story would originate.

Importantly, as a portion of my research, I visited with Mr. Delbert Steiner, the then CEO of Premium Exploration, Inc., and his senior staff at their exploration site in central Idaho. It was a unique experience to realize that I was literally walking on top of an untold wealth of gold and silver while we visited old placer and adit tunnel mines on their Oro Grande Shear Zone patented and unpatented land claims stretching well over twenty miles in length.

The story you are about to read is fiction. Although much of what I wrote contains some factual information. The one thing I constantly have wondered about is the existence of a geological feature, a gold formation, perhaps worth trillions of dollars. Does it really exist? I think it possible, to some varying degree. But that is only one opinion. It seems to my unprofessional eye that such a feature may indeed exist. The issue is already drawing a lot of quiet attention, especially in Idaho, in particular by Midas Gold, Inc., and Premium Exploration Inc., among other companies.

I'd like to make a distinction here which will aid the reader. There is a difference between "visible" gold and "invisible" gold." Visible gold, obviously is that which one can see and what early gold miners sought when they superficially surface mined, placer mined, or tunneled, following a seam of visible gold or looking for nuggets large and small. Those early miners only scratched the surface, so to speak. Their back breaking efforts, while using hand tools and comparatively primitive mining methods, resulted in the finding of perhaps only a very small portion, a mere fraction, of the surrounding gold that remained undiscovered and untouched in those very locations. Such small and inefficient mining endeavors, often resulted in finding hundreds of thousands of ounces of gold. These former small mines were sign posts as to where to look for the remainder of the gold that had been missed.

THE PROMISCUOUS PUPPETEER

Among such yet to be discovered gold is what is now called "invisible gold" which is usually not apparent to the naked eye. Yet, it is often found in sufficient concentrations to be considered economical to find, process, and retrieve. Mining for such invisible gold was the reason for the success of the world-famous sixty million-ounce Carlin Trend formation in northeast Nevada.

Please read on and enjoy.

PART 1

CHAPTER 1

Tonopah, Nevada

Some things are better off left to die a natural death.

Dalton Trindall's day's work was coming to an end. It was late August and the sun was noticeably rising later each morning, and setting earlier than it had since the summer solstice, on June twenty first, a time when the sun was at its most northern point in the northern hemisphere. Now the sun was setting and the sky, with wide ranging colors of orange and wisps of crimson to the west, faded to a purplish gray hue toward the east. He saw movement just in front of him and glanced down in time to see a scorpion hesitatingly advancing toward his one boot. Cooler evening air had brought it out of its burrow in search of something to feed on. Just before the scorpion reached Dalton, he lifted his boot, bringing it back down squarely on the poisonous arthropod. The crunching sound he heard assured him that the scorpion was no longer a threat.

Dalton turned and looked eastward towards the direction of Utah to see an early evening three-quarter-sized moon rising above the distant horizon. In the desert, a person usually had an unobstructed clear view for dozens of miles into the distance, in all directions, and this evening was no exception. He thought about the secret mission he was on and the life-changing possibilities that could result to the benefit of an untold number of people. The question was, could he help prove what others had dismissed as fantasy? He thought it increasingly likely, in theory at least. And evidence was steadily mounting that supported his, and others', theory. He had to know with some degree of finality. He had to try. He was restless and eager for some conclusion, some resolution. The question had haunted him for decades.

Some of the abrasive and irritating dirt which made up the desert's surface had found its way into Dalton's hiking boots. His sweat-stained clothes were caked with the high desert wind blown soil and his blue jeans now appeared almost tan in color.

The desire to take a nice hot shower was overwhelming but his camper didn't have one. A quick sponge bath out in the desert air was all he could look forward to. Earlier that morning, he had placed on the ground outside of his camper several gallon-sized clear plastic jugs. The containers had been filled with water to be heated by the hot sun. The warm water would be used to wash up with when he returned to his camper.

Dalton swung his backpack over his one shoulder and a loaded canvas bag over the other. They were both filled with soil and rock chip samples which, by the end of his day, were a burden to carry. He had marked the location of where each rock or soil sample specimen had been retrieved on his handheld global positioning system (GPS). He had then placed each soil or rock sample into a cloth bag and wrote the GPS's indicated longitude and latitude location along with a special coded number to help identify where each specimen had been found. He had also written into a logbook the same information plus any notes he thought essential. The logbook would serve to help remember why he thought each sample could be of some possible importance. This method would allow him to find any of the sample's original locations in the future should it become necessary.

His muscles ached as he headed for his nearby truck. He was fifty-five years old, yet still trim. He was reminded of his age each day as he accepted the fact that his physical endurance was less than what it had been when he was younger. He intended to drive into Tonopah and later to his camper several miles away at a location where he wouldn't be subjected to the prying eyes of curious townspeople.

As he drove toward Tonopah, he glanced off to the right of the road towards the town that once was vibrant, exciting, and full of laughter, life, and dreams. The town was now a decaying version of its former self. It had gone into decline when the Promise Land Mining Company shut down decades ago. *Promise Land*, Dalton thought to himself. *This was a town once characterized by its people as a financial paradise. Maybe they should have called the place "Paradise" instead of Tonopah. Then the mailing address for the former mining company could have read "Promise Land Mining Company, Paradise, Nevada.* Dalton smiled to himself as he continued driving.

Indeed, the real Promise Land in Nevada, so far as mining went, was the ongoing mining of the Carlin Trend. It was a rich sixty-mile long gold-bearing fault line stretching northwards, from the more northern town of Elko, Nevada. Many gold mining companies had staked out their claims along this stretch of desert land and just as many had made their fortunes, and made some of their shareholders rich.

Dalton parked his truck and walked a block to a restaurant he had come to favor. Once inside, he ordered his meal and daydreamed as he looked out the window from his booth.

Tonopah had once been a rich gold and silver mining town a century ago just as Elko was today. Now it was dilapidated and seedy in many respects. The town's landscape had been scarred. Any indication of the town's former success and wealth were all but gone. In its place were aging structures, sagging roofs, rusting unusable old vehicles, and some small struggling service businesses. A couple of makeshift unglamorous casinos punctuated a certain kind of depressing resignation of the town's reality.

One cemetery in the town was populated with wooden grave markers, many of which had weathered and had fallen to the earth where they had once been planted. Each place of rest had been merely outlined with the abundant rocks that could be found everywhere one looked. The gravesites seemed untended, a fate that eventually was the result of the incessantly blowing desert dust, the hot summer sun, and the cold winter nights of its five thousand-foot elevation.

Dalton got the impression while taking a picture of the cemetery with his camera that few people likely had cared much for those who had been buried there. He wondered if most of the deceased had likely been people of little fame, recognition, or consequence. Perhaps many had lived and died on the brink, people who were born with nothing and died with little more after decades of digging. More than a few, he thought, had likely been people who, by and large, were friendless and had been merely tolerated at best. He wondered if, upon their passing, they had been missed by someone, or perhaps no one at all. It seemed, from the looks of the cemetery, that those whose remains lay buried in it were probably soon forgotten by those who still lived, those who perhaps had the good fortune, or misfortune, of remaining behind, above ground.

The Pink Elephant Motel at the edge of town sat strategically on the only two-lane road that led into, and out of, town. Its sign unnecessarily announced its gaudy presence while flashing its neon light on and off in carnival-like fashion, advertising "Bikers and Hikers–Welcome." Yet, the parking lot was nearly empty. Paint was peeling from the motel's exterior. Dalton imagined the same was true of the motel's unseen interior.

Dalton had spent too many nights in such places. There had been many motels with leaking faucets whose dripping sound caused sleepless nights, rooms with rust-stained tubs and toilets, air conditioners that didn't cool, and lamps with burnt-out light bulbs. He had come to favor his own camper to sleep in. It was sparsely appointed, but it had the advantage of being mobile when hitched behind his pickup truck.

He recalled that this was the remote and isolated place where fate had led the infamous Charles Manson and his gang to live for a short while. It was a little over a dozen miles from town. Once discovered, the Manson gang had been unceremoniously chased out of a small structure built by the famous Tiffany Jewelry Company of New York. In the early 1900s, the stone structure had housed a couple of Mr. Tiffany's turquoise miners. They had been employed to tunnel a small hillside for the rich sky blue and varying shades of green turquoise used by Tiffany's artisans to make turn-of-the-century jewelry. Then, some seventy years later, Manson tried to claim the place for his drug den and hideout. He and his followers then went on to murder the wealthy La Bianca family and Hollywood actress Sharon Tate, among others.

Tonopah had many unfortunate stories associated with it. The Charles Manson episode, Dalton thought, was probably but one among many other stories comprising much of Tonopah's unrecorded, if not long forgotten, notorious past.

After eating, Dalton paid for his meal, left a tip, and stepped out onto one of the few decent sidewalks in the town.

He walked down along the street away from his truck, wanting to see a bit more of the neighborhood he was in. After turning the corner and walking a short distance, he turned to his right again and continued walking down what could pass for an alley behind a long row of rundown one-story houses to his left. The structures, such as they were, had been originally built, and occasionally added onto, by miners who had long since passed away or who relocated before time took what was left of their lives.

Once the mine played out and closed, signs of success were replaced with signs of growing despair, aided in time by the termites that infested the wood structures. "*The town is not a pretty sight,*" he thought to himself.

Decades earlier, when some of the town's miners workday was completed, they would come back to their homes where they would resume their digging and tunneling around their small plot of land and under their homes. They had hoped, prayed, even begged to strike it rich by finding a thick vein of gold on their very own piece of hell. Piles of rock chip "tailings" and desert soil, which had taken the form of large mounds of rubble accumulated from digging, had been deposited by the miners in the front and backyards of some of the neglected dwellings. The manmade hills on many plots of land were often high enough to obscure part or most of the unsightly structures. The mounds of tailings often hid neighbor from neighbor and neighborhood from neighborhood, where many of the town's residents still lived.

Some effort seemed to have been made in recent years to restore small parts of the town—to tidy up the place, the yards, the structures, and the infrastructure. There was no visible indication that the rubble had been moved so that some of the sidewalks and road sides could be restored or paved. The whole town seemed to have pits and tunnels everywhere. They were evidence of failed dreams, desperation, anguish, lost hope, and eventual acceptance of fate, followed in time by the inevitable trip to a newly dug plot of land at the local cemetery. Digging up the desert landscape, it seemed, was a necessity for both the living and the dead.

"*The town,*" he thought to himself, "*could have been revitalized if the town's residents, those who still remained, had resurrected Tonopah by recreating itself based on its past. Perhaps the town could have been rebuilt in a western motif so as to create a new industry for vacationers and tourists to enjoy. They could have created a gold mining town once again, but in a Hollywood stage-like fashion, as entertainment, anchored by a classy casino.*"

Leavenworth and Winthrop, Washington, had been reincarnated in the image of its old self. So had Bisbee and Tombstone, Arizona, among many others, surviving on their restored town's historical appearance and reputation. But Tonopah remained an eyesore, a place out in the desert that deserved better. It remained a reminder of what happens when a one-company town's business goes bust, and the town's luck and good fortune vanishes almost overnight.

Dalton stumbled on a stone in his path. The debris was everywhere and unavoidable. Dalton rounded another corner to his right, having circled what was supposed to pass as a small city block. In the distance he saw his pickup truck. He picked up his pace as he passed a sorry looking mom and pop-sized combination casino, restaurant, and coin-operated laundry.

Through an uninviting window, he saw a few disheveled looking retirement age people playing the slot machines, still hoping to strike it rich. The casino had become one of the few sources of local entertainment for the residents who remained. It was what survived from the gold and silver mining days in this once proud, rambunctious, and prosperous town, a town that had at one time been characterized as having a well-deserved lofty opinion of itself. Now the town was worthy of little more than pity. The gamblers in the casino, Dalton thought to himself, were living a kind of cruel mocking fate as some fruitlessly tried their luck to no avail, in a new era, one which was worse than the previous one.

"You having any luck today?" asked an old man from up ahead at the corner. He had been hoping to learn of some news from Dalton Trindall. Many of the townspeople were aware of his gathering of soil samples outside of the town. The gossip made for what passed for some of the local news at each new morning's local coffee shop gatherings.

"None," Trindall replied. "I've had better days."

He knew better than to mention anything revealing, pro or con, about his work. He also knew better than to denigrate the town, to remark about its glory days or to overstate what little could be said that was positive. Saying most anything was usually met with a contrarian view which was said merely for the sake of being argumentative. The townspeople were understandably cynical for the most part. He had drawn some attention during his three-day stay around the area. Some folks had been friendly to him, some had been curious, and there were some who had been less than hospitable or inviting.

As a geologist, he knew that the miles of tailings all over the town likely contained minute traces of silver mixed with lead and or zinc, called galena. But it was an open question, until assayed, to think that the quantity of precious metal contained in his soil and chip samples could be deemed possibly economically feasible to extract. Whatever traces of gold or silver existed, it wasn't yet known whether it would be worth the cost to process the material containing it.

Dalton, like many others, had often pondered if the precious metal found in this area was a southern extension of a rich metal-bearing fault, one that connected with the world-famous Carlin Trend further to the northeast above Elko, Nevada. He knew that he may soon be asked for his professional opinion by his employer. There had been some evidence that the wide and deep gold-bearing fault line continued north well into Idaho under its high desert, its central rugged mountains, and on into its northern hill and lake region of Coeur d'Alene. One of the continent's largest silver fields had long since been discovered in northern Idaho. There was seemingly growing evidence that this fault line could also continue in a southerly direction away from the Carlin Trend, southward to the Mexican border.

But that was not his focus today. He had hoped that he could find certain minerals, in desired grades and quantities, within the samples he had "tagged and bagged." The samples could be assayed and studied more closely in due course. Meanwhile, Dalton had other things to think about. Some of his samples seemed promising to the eye. A couple of them displayed barely visible gold, or at least what he felt sure was visible gold, as opposed to pyrite, or "fool's gold" as it was known.

It was almost dark when Dalton reached his truck. He unlocked and opened the driver's side door and saw that his backpack was in the same position he had left it in on the passenger side of the truck. He took a swig of water from his last remaining water bottle and started his truck's engine. It was a little slower than usual in sputtering to life. The air had been bone dry and his truck's air filter was partially clogged from the dust his truck had kicked up as he drove it through the desert trails, washes, and hillsides.

Dalton put his transmission into drive and as he began to move forward, he flinched at the sound of a loud bang. He stopped, heard a hissing sound, and instinctively knew that he had a blown tire. Not an old tire, but one of the four new ones he had bought just a couple months previously.

He got out of his truck and circled it, inspecting each tire until he found the one that had been punctured, now nearly flat, from what appeared to be a "jack rock." A jack rock is a four-pronged metal device, where three of the prongs rest on the ground while the fourth prong pointed upwards. Jack rocks were once used to keep unwelcome horses, and their riders, away from land claims and mine entrances and tunnels. Dalton had heard of them being used to keep deer away from prized apple trees, to keep shore-based fisherman away from favorite fishing locations, and they were used in more recent times to puncture the tires of unwelcome vehicles and their occupants, for whatever reason.

He changed the flat tire with one of his two spares he kept in the truck's bed. Driving out in the desert required being prepared for flat tires because of the often treacherous ground surfaces that had to be driven on.

Dalton got back into his truck and looked around the immediate area. "*Some things are better off left to die a natural death, to be mourned by few people, if any,*" he thought. "*This town would have been better off bulldozed and tunneled from end to end as an open pit or underground mine. Dynamite would help to expedite the process.*" He imagined low underground rumbles, as the earth and rock was loosened, from calculated explosions, making people's dishes rattle in their cupboards.

The townspeople, for the most part, had little imagination or even less determination or inclination to save their little town. "*If the town had been bulldozed and tunneled,*" he thought, "*then the laborers who returned to their glory days of tearing up their property could rejoice in being able to do so once again.*" They could repeat history, finish the job their forefathers had begun a century earlier, until the town remained no more. Then Tonopah could have found its place in history, its rightful destiny once no brick remained on top of another, no window remained to be opened or closed, and the mounds of tailings had been all loaded up and hauled away and processed for their precious metal. The pathetic existence of the once-proud town would be extinguished by the very gold fever that gave birth to it. Instead, having found little precious metal under their homes with which to start new lives elsewhere, today's townspeople had long since given up their gold fever. They had settled in for the remainder of the prior and the beginning of the new century in a town whose continued viable existence was in question as evidenced by the town's neglected cemetery and the landmark Pink Elephant Motel.

The cooler desert night air blew into the truck's open window. As a precaution, Dalton turned on his headlights, exited his truck once again and looked carefully a few feet forward of his truck while inspecting the ground for signs of any additional jack rocks that might be in his path. Finding none, he started his engine, made a U-turn in the street, and headed north out of town to his camper.

Dalton noticed headlights in his rearview mirror as he traveled out of town. Upon turning onto a one-lane dirt trail where his camper was located, the car that he thought might have been following him continued on past his turnoff. There were few towns within easy driving distance at this hour of the evening. Dalton assumed the vehicle was driven by some local person who lived out in the desert far from the ugliness of the town they both had just left. It was a welcome escape for both himself and likely the car's driver that had been behind him.

The high desert landscape stretched in all directions. It was not mountainous, nor was it flat, but from the many hilltops one could see a hundred miles of the same kind of terrain, seemingly endless, from every vantage point. It was a place made up of thirsty raw land with sparse vegetation to provide shade for what little could survive the severe conditions. As dry as the surface was, the ground beneath it was just as dry, yet cooler than the surface in the summer and warmer in the winter. What life existed learned to use the subsurface as a moderating counterbalance to the harsher conditions that lay above. Yet, it did occasionally rain here, although not much when it did. It seldom was enough and never lasted long.

The winters at this elevation were usually cold, windy, and dry. The occasional snow that fell quickly evaporated into the dry air.

In warmer weather, micro wind vortexes were a common sight. In the heat of the summer's sun, hot air rose from the baked desert floor to meet lightly blowing crosswinds, creating interesting, harmless, miniature tornadoes. The surface-to-skyward funnels were made visible from the dust it drew up into what was often referred to as "sun devils."

The desert surrounding Tonopah was mostly uninhabited. It was a place of lonely solitude. At times the desert was noticeably quiet. When the wind blew, one could hear the dust making a tinkling sound as it found new footing on the desert surface, a sound oddly much like snowflakes falling to the ground when the wind was not blowing. The desert is a life sapping place for life unprepared to survive its challenges. Circling vultures, often seen riding hot air updrafts, capitalized on whatever life failed to measure up to the desert's harsh living conditions.

The desert had seen many men and their mules crisscross its seemingly lifeless terrain, searching for one thing or another. Wandering prospectors had come to make their fortune. Most had departed with less hope and enthusiasm than when they came, as they continued to live their self-imposed kind of fruitless nomadic torture.

To the northwest of Tonopah lay the Monte Cristo range, which consisted of hills, compared to the mountains found elsewhere in Nevada and Dalton's home state of Washington. He had parked his camper within view of the more distant hills. He turned off of State Route 6 onto a dirt two-lane road at the southern end of the range, which consisted of a series of hills known to contain several one-man, family-owned, turquoise gemstone mine sites. After driving a short distance, he turned and drove parallel to a wash which would take him to where he had parked his camper on US Bureau of Land Management land.

His headlights lit up his camper as he approached. Then, he stopped and turned off his truck's engine and headlights. He sat in his truck for a moment, taking in the partially moonlit landscape. Dalton got out of his truck and began to walk towards his camper. Suddenly, a cold chill went up his spine when he smelled the odor of tobacco smoke. He stopped as his eyes hurriedly searched the dimly lit surroundings. Dalton subconsciously gripped his backpack's shoulder straps tighter as adrenalin surged through his veins.

"Hello, Mr. Trindall. Not to worry," said a voice some ways away, "I'm a friendly. I've been waiting for you to come back so I could meet you."

Dalton was speechless and his mouth had gone dry with the suddenness of his alarm. He instantly turned in the direction of where the voice had come from.

"My name is Rodrigo Black Coyote," the voice said. "I wanted to introduce myself to you, but not in the presence of others. I live a few miles west of town, off of Route 6. You drove past my driveway on your way here."

Dalton found his voice, and in an unusually deepened tone, so as to make himself seem surly and brusque, he asked, "What do you want?"

Rodrigo Black Coyote stood up from Dalton's folding lawn chair, dropped a lit cigar to the ground, and squashed it under his left boot. He could see in the dim moon's light that his approaching visitor was of average height and build and was perhaps in his early thirties. He quickly sized up his uninvited guest as one who could easily overpower him. Dalton was an even six feet tall but older by perhaps a generation. When Rodrigo reached him, Rodrigo stuck out his hand, to shake Dalton's, while saying, "I am aware that you are prospecting the area and I want to offer you my help." He shook his visitor's hand and he relaxed a bit as Rodrigo backed up a step and continued talking.

"First," said Rodrigo, "we are almost neighbors out here. I invite you to my home tomorrow morning, say seven or eight, for a hot breakfast and fresh coffee. You can meet my family. Then maybe we can talk for a few minutes before you leave. I don't mean to make a mystery out of it, but it's late and I didn't know how else to meet you other than to be here when you returned to your camper."

"Talk about what?" asked Dalton.

"I have some information that you might want to keep in mind, I think," said Rodrigo. "I don't know how long you plan to stay, but in case you do, please consider me your neighbor. There are things here that you might want to be aware of and to be careful about. We can talk tomorrow. Listen, Mr. Trindall, I know a little bit about you. I know you are a geologist, and that you seem experienced at what you do. I had one person tell me that they thought you worked for a mining company near Elko. My friend had been a miner at a neighboring mine. He said that you were a part of that Carlin discovery, the one that resulted in mining what they call 'invisible gold.' It turned out to be more gold than anywhere else."

"Invisible gold," Dalton repeated.

"Yes, that's it. And I think you are doing research here. There are people who you need to know about. I'm a small-time miner and jewelry maker, and I know all the Bureau of Land Management agents, and others you might have to deal with. But, tomorrow morning I will be of help to you by telling you more. Will you be my family's guest, at seven or eight? I'm about five miles west of town. Look for the mailbox with 12466 painted on it and turn down the driveway, about a quarter mile, to my small ranch." Rodrigo handed him a piece of paper with the mailbox number written on it.

"I enjoy going to various places and discovering whatever the geology has to say to me. It's in my blood," Dalton said with emphasis. "I enjoy camping out in the desert and spending my time digging up rocks."

"You underrate yourself," said Rodrigo.

"You overrate me," he replied.

"One of us is right, Mr. Trindall. Perhaps in my mind I see you as something more, and in your mind you see yourself as something less. It doesn't matter. I look forward to seeing you tomorrow morning."

Rodrigo Black Coyote smiled, again shook hands with Dalton Trindall, turned without waiting for a reply, and walked off into the desert a short ways. In the dark behind a large tumbleweed, a motor came to life and his unexpected visitor rode off back towards Route 6 on his four-wheel all-terrain vehicle (ATV). As he drove off, his headlight bounced over the landscape and his vehicle created a faintly visible growing trail of billowing dust behind him as he disappeared on the other side of a small hill.

As the four-wheeler's motor faded in the distance, Dalton continued looking in the direction Rodrigo had driven. Then, turning towards his camper, as his heart pace slowed, he prepared to shower with the plastic bottles of warm water he had set out in the morning sunlight nearly fourteen hours earlier.

The next morning, as the sky lightened, Dalton's cell phone woke him from his sleep. He had made sure he had parked his camper in a place where he could make and receive phone calls via the Tonopah cell tower at the edge of town. Reception from his location was good.

He answered the call to discover it was his brother calling to tell him that their uncle had passed away during the night. Dalton's Uncle Lloyd had never been fond of him or just about anyone else in the family. Dalton had found it easy to return the favor by keeping his distance through the years. His brother wanted to know if he could be back in Seattle in time for their uncle's funeral. Dalton told his brother that he had an appointment that morning and would have to get back to him later. After hanging up, he thought to himself that it was hard to have to attend the funeral of a loved one. It was even harder to attend one for someone whose dislike for him had been unequivocally mutual.

So as to not be either too early or too late, Dalton drove his truck up to Rodrigo Black Coyote's ranch house at seven-thirty the next morning. Immediately, Rodrigo came out the front door, smiling broadly, to welcome him as his family's guest. He met Rodrigo's wife, young son, and his mother who had been widowed for nearly three decades. He was also met by the aroma of freshly-made tortillas. Rodrigo's wife, Susan, and his mother, Emelina, busied themselves in the kitchen preparing scrambled eggs and bacon which would be wrapped in the tortillas, along with traditional Mexican sweet bread. Rodrigo and Susan's ten-year-old son, Xavier, brought Dalton a cup of coffee on a tray with a bowl of sugar and a cup of milk beside it.

Rodrigo's home was average in size but well furnished with a mixture of Mexican folk and Native American possessions. In the corner was a traditional beehive Mexican fireplace, unused in the summer season, with a stack of mesquite firewood in a cradle next to its hearth. The walls were decorated with a mixture of paintings made by Susan and blankets hung from strip boards which had been the creation of Rodrigo's mother.

Dalton was made to feel welcome. The warmth Rodrigo and his family showered him with was palpable and Rodrigo's mother, Emelina, had given him a brief hug, in a kind of European manner, upon their introduction. Susan, more reservedly, shook hands with him but with a smile that spoke her sincerity. Xavier brought his hand-carved wooden desert collection for Dalton to see. Included were carvings of a snake, an owl, a crow, and a pickaxe, a historical hand tool used by miners to this day.

During their meal together, Rodrigo talked about his small mine up in the Monte Cristo hills to the west of where his father had built the family ranch. His father had filed a claim to mine the land over thirty years ago. His father died when a wall of rock, under which he had been digging, gave way, crushing him. The thought sent a chill down his spine as Dalton briefly reflected about his own father who had spent his life working in a mine in Montana. It was sad, Dalton thought to himself, that the very gemstone Rodrigo's father was mining had brought his father's life to a sudden end. It was a common story in the mining industry, one which was more prevalent in underground tunnel mines than small open pit surface mines like the one that caused Rodrigo's father's death. His eyes turned from item to object as Rodrigo talked about the turquoise mine he still occasionally mined today. He noted a large turquoise nugget on the sofa's end table enclosed in a glass showcase.

Rodrigo's father, a Native American, had married Emelina, a mix of Native Mexican and Native American heritage whose gracefulness caught Dalton's eye from time to time as Rodrigo talked about his family heritage. His father had carried on the Indian tradition of finding turquoise and making it into jewelry. Rodrigo, in turn, had learned to set his gemstones in sterling silver and had established a steady customer base.

Dalton summarized in his mind the family's artistic tradition in weaving, painting, gemstone cutting, silversmithing, and wood carving. While doing so, Rodrigo completed his family history with an explanation as to how he had taken over where his father had left off. He explained how he had been supporting the family, mining the turquoise and making jewelry for various retail outlets both in and outside the state. Rodrigo lit a cigar and drew on its smoke, seemingly showing great pleasure in doing so. Emelina brought Dalton a cigar and offered to light it for him but he declined while thanking her. With a smile, Emelina took a seat in the chair next to the sofa where he was sitting.

"Will you be here in Tonopah for long?" she asked him slowly and softly.

"No, I have to leave for home today," he replied.

"And where is home?" she asked pleasantly.

"Near Seattle, Washington, in a small waterfront village." Dalton thought it better to not mention his hometown's name. "Oh, that's such a beautiful area. The city of Seattle was named after an Indian chief back in the late 1800s, who lived further to the west across the waterway. Anyway, you chose a pretty place to call your home."

As Emelina finished her thought, Dalton's cell phone rang. His immediate reaction was to think that his brother was calling to see if he had packed up his camper and was on the road heading north. Instead, when he answered, the voice he heard was his employer, Wayde Ramsley in Denver. He excused himself from the Black Coyote family and stepped outside their home so he could talk in private.

Dalton had known Wayde Ramsley from his former career. They had met at a mining convention in Toronto many years ago when Wayde had been the president of an exploration company based in Quebec. The new shell corporation that had been formed for the ongoing venture was given the unsuspecting name of Mining Engineers, Inc. It was a privately-held company with shares divided between the corporate consortium members who were financially backing the mammoth-sized exploration initiative. When, and if, a decision was made some day to go public with the company's intentions, a new, more appropriate corporate name would be carefully chosen. Then the company's backers could get financed and reimbursed for their expenditures by selling shares through the public marketplace, while becoming listed on one, or more, stock exchanges. But that was a ways off, Dalton knew, and there were a lot of hurdles that needed to be crossed in the interim.

Progress updates, to his employer, had been done on a monthly basis. He had spent most of the past year researching and soil sampling primarily in Nevada, a state he knew well from his prior job helping to mine part of the Carlin Trend. It was that very gold field that had made his career successful and which financially secured his future.

Over sixty million ounces of gold over a sixty-mile length had been mined so far from the Carlin Trend and the termination points in both directions had not yet been found. Dalton's, and his employer's, theory was that the gold could be ubiquitous, seemingly everywhere along the fault line. Included in the host rock was turquoise, a gemstone revered by Native Americans. The potential for Project X's gold discovery initiative were unfathomable. If economically mineable gold was found in the one thousand miles of terrain stretching from Canada to Mexico, the potential value of the gold could approach trillions of dollars some day if ever recovered.

The numbers were mind-boggling, impossible to wrap one's head around.

The turquoise primarily found in Nevada, Arizona, and to a lesser extent in New Mexico, Colorado, and California, had different meanings to different tribes. Some saw it as having special healing powers. Others believed that if turquoise was attached to a bow, an arrow would find its intended target. Some thought the mineral brought good luck. Others sought it for trade, and some for further enhancing their appearance. Tribal shamans used the mineral for medicinal purposes. The turquoise found on the Carlin Trend was being sacrificed. It was literally being ground to dust, in preference of the seemingly endless precious metal-bearing fault containing the more desirable invisible gold. The rich microscopic ore was processed for its gold and, to a lesser extent, its silver. It was weighed and measured for its economic viability, by the grams per ton, or fractions thereof, and was generally so minute in size that it was invisible to the eye. Extracting the gold under such conditions required pulverizing the host rock and then leaching out the tiny dust-sized particles of gold.

Interestingly, in a direct line north of Nevada's Carlin Trend, in Idaho, two explorer companies had found enough gold, on a per-mile basis of drilling, to possibly qualify for becoming another Carlin Trend. Further north and east, silver and palladium was found to be abundant. The connection between these, and other discoveries, and the Carlin was a part of what the geologists were attempting to make. To the south, other gold discoveries had been made in line with the north-south direction of the Carlin. Dalton had wondered if these discoveries were anomalies. Or, were they all a part of one long gold field? If so, this field would unquestionably become the most significant gold discovery in the history of the world.

Dalton's first priority was to keep his mission, and its potential, secret. Although exploration is always a costly risk, his employer knew that the work being done by him could result in the filing of thousands of individual twenty acre claims by anyone who could be the first to do so. The secrecy required would possibly give his employer the upper hand in surveying and filing land claims with the federal government. It was an advantage that his employer thought only right since they were paying for all the ongoing exploration being done by geologists who were well-noted and respected by the mining industry.

After Dalton finished briefing his employer, he paused outside the Black Coyote home to reflect for a moment that he was but one of a dozen others, not unlike him, who had been ordered to fan out from northern Idaho, generally in a line, to as far south as the Mexican border. Their job was to review all of the findings made by previous small and large exploration efforts, over the past decades, north and south of the famed Carlin Trend. Additionally, they were to perform their own on-site geological research and to incorporate those results with everything else that was known and learned. He was being well paid for both his work and, equally as important, for his silence.

His employer had formed a shell-type corporation for this very purpose. Their hope was to proceed with their under-the-radar efforts, to go unnoticed for as long as possible, until the evidence being developed justified a massive claim filing. It would be unlike any other similar event ever attempted. When the time came, if it came, it would require the hiring of hundreds of surveyors. They would have to survey an unfathomable length of territory winding its way through desert and mountains.

Dalton went back into the ranch house. He felt that it was time to ask his host what he had meant by what he alluded to the night before outside his camper. In doing so, he asked Rodrigo if they could go for a short walk around the ranch alone for a brief conversation. Before leaving the house, he thanked both Emelina and Susan for their gracious hospitality and gave a few words of encouragement to Xavier to continue with his woodcarving.

Once outside the home, Rodrigo said in a soft voice, "So, do you know that there is a small family of Native Americans who are from many separate Indian Nations? Their purpose is to work together to make money. This band of Indians, and I use the word band for historical purposes, want to recover some of what they feel is rightfully theirs. No, not just the land, much of which, in and of itself, seems useless, worthless, barren, and uninhabitable, but to illegally obtain a portion of what others have. They ignore the law. If they discover what you are doing here in Tonopah, they may want to pay you a visit to ask you for money for protection. Whether you find anything important in your research or not, they may assume that you did. So, know that they can stay out of your way or they can stand in your way, so to speak."

"I'm not—" Dalton tried to respond, but Rodrigo continued talking.

"If that day comes when you are paid a visit, they could approach you like I did. I can help you by letting you know who is who around these parts. If someone approaches you, you let me know and I will try to tell you what I know about the person. There are some people around here who prey on others. They have formed a group and established themselves in many places in the southwest. Try to stay away from town. Get your supplies elsewhere. And, keep what you are looking at, and what you are doing, to yourself."

"You make it sound like there's some kind of an Indian mafia," Dalton stated.

"They have eyes and ears everywhere, certain people who will tip them off with information in exchange for a little cash. But I have friends here too."

Dalton felt unnerved as Rodrigo finished by saying in Spanish and then in English, "El diablo mira a mi nuevo amigo. Tenga cuidado. That means the Devil is watching, my new friend. Be careful."

CHAPTER 2

Kingston, Washington

Nevada plates are common here.

There was a cool breeze coming off of the Puget Sound's fifty-degree water as Dalton Trindall drove his truck and camper onto the Edmonds to Kingston ferry. It was the final leg of his journey back to his home. He had attended his deceased uncle's funeral with family members in Seattle. Not surprisingly, none of his uncle's friends were in attendance, he mused, probably because his uncle didn't have any. What few family members who attended the funeral used his uncle's passing and funeral as an opportunity to get together, catch up on things, and to feel good that they had gone to the trouble to see the sorry old bastard off.

Dalton's home was on the west side of the Puget Sound overlooking the water, the skyscrapers, and the old World Fair Space Needle in downtown Seattle. He parked his vehicle on the ferry and climbed its inside staircase to the first deck where walk-on passengers were lounging, napping, reading newspapers, making cell phone calls, and checking their e-mails. Many of the passengers had taken seats at tables and benches that lined the outer windows. They were among the first seats taken so that the riders could watch the passing fishing and pleasure boats, daydream, or to do some last minute work before arriving home at the end of their day.

Dalton went to the vessel's small cafeteria where he bought a cup of coffee and a Seattle newspaper. Then he walked back down the staircase to his truck to wait for the vessel's arrival at the Kingston dock in a little less than thirty minutes.

He noted the presence of a woman he had called and arranged to meet earlier while in Seattle. Sharon Bivens, one of the first female special agents hired by the US Secret Service, had retired and worked for a national security and investigations company. He had hired her, out of an abundance of caution, to discreetly follow him home and to ascertain if anyone was following him.

When Dalton retired, at the early age of fifty-one, as the VP of geology at Continental Mining, he sold his home in Elko, Nevada, and moved to Kingston, Washington. After an amicable divorce a few years prior to retiring, he lived alone. He met and dated several women who he, for one reason or another, failed to fall in love with. He had long conceded, to himself at least, that a reciprocating enduring relationship with his former wife, or any other lady for that matter, just was not in the cards for him. Women's attitudes had been changing. He was "old school" and found it hard to accept change—at least the kind that related to love and marriage. Women were more independent now. "One night stands" or "weekend hookups," as some people referred to unattached, non-committal, part-time, recreational romance, were commonplace but not what he wanted to engage in. He was not at all opposed to women having their own careers, he just didn't find the all-consumed career-minded women he had dated as serious love prospects or "marrying material."

Soon after Dalton's divorce, his son graduated from the Massachusetts Institute of Technology in Boston and settled into a job at a solar panel manufacturing company in Indianapolis. Dalton discovered that his son's attitude about relationships fit the new modern way of living. "Live alone, except on weekends." The word "dating" was not in his son's vocabulary. Instead, a night out with a romantic prospect meant that each person paid their own way. It was considered normal for each to ask for separate checks at a restaurant or each buying their own ticket to see a movie together. Gifts to each other, on the other hand, were considered favorable or perhaps, to tone it down a bit, welcome.

Dalton wanted to find someone he could love but it seemed marriage, or remarriage, even among people in his own age group, was becoming less common place. Not marrying was seen as being less complicating. Less restricting. No combining of assets. No consolidation of two residences into a shared single home. No strings or commitment to one and another made more ironclad by ceremony or license. "*Perhaps it wasn't meant to be*," he had thought more than once to himself. Going home to an empty home was better than going home to one occupied by someone who did not love him, or to someone he did not love in return.

Dalton regretted taking a leave of absence from teaching his mineral course in Seattle. The university had been gracious in granting the leave. It wasn't the money, surely, because it didn't pay much. But he enjoyed the teaching, and the interaction with students and other faculty members, especially one new female professor who had drawn his attention.

When the ferry docked, Dalton drove to his home. He usually tried to get back home for a couple of days at least once every couple of weeks. He had hired a lawn service to keep up with the chores outside of his home. Little else needed to be done when he was away. As he pulled into his driveway, he backed the camper into a special graveled nook he had the landscaper create in between some shrubs.

After unhitching the camper, he reached inside to retrieve a laundry bag containing his dirty clothes. The numerous cloth bags containing his soil and rock samples would be moved to his garage later. Each sample had to be divided into two. He would keep one half of each sample in a smaller bag so he could forward it in batches to his counterpart in Denver. Then, as was his routine, he would send the other half, all marked and cataloged, absent the GPS location from which each came, off to the designated contract assay laboratory in Vancouver.

The results of each assay report were mailed to both him and his corporate office in Denver. The company's head geologist's assistant would marry up the assay results with the GPS locations, and the other half of each sample which had been sent to him for each assayed item. The Denver geologist would place the results into a special computer program and store the results in a secure facility for future reference. In time, a series of maps would be updated to show the results of all the geologist's exploratory fieldwork. It was an expensive and time consuming endeavor, one which was referred to by all who were involved only as "Project X."

As was his routine, once inside his home, Dalton checked for any new e-mail messages. There were the usual routine ones, and one from his son, and then there was one from Alice Harrison, the vice president for administration of Mining Engineers. It read: "Dalton, come to Denver on Wednesday for a meeting with the other geos at 3 p.m. See you then, Alice."

Dalton's cell phone rang. He read on the phone's ID caller feature that it was from his private investigator, Sharon Bivens. He was told that the covert surveillance had revealed nothing unusual other than there had been a car on the ferry, a few vehicles behind his, with a Nevada license plate. Bivens said she had a friend run the plates and found the car registered to an owner from Las Vegas. Inside the car was a man and a woman who didn't follow his vehicle once off the ferry. The car had then been discreetly followed to a casino owned by an Kitsap Peninsula Indian tribe, one which Dalton knew well and had visited many times since moving to Kingston. Bivens wanted to know if he wanted her to continue the surveillance, and if so, for how long, and whether he wanted to know more about the two people who had parked and entered the casino.

"What did they look like, I mean how old were they?" Dalton asked.

"Both seem younger than us, but I was too far away to see much about them. I know what they are wearing and probably could find them in the casino, if you want," the investigator said.

Dalton thought for a moment and then asked, "Do you think they'll check into a motel? It's getting late and I doubt they'd travel back across on the ferry tonight unless they're already staying somewhere on the other side of the Sound."

"Only way to find out is to follow them some more," she quickly responded. "Nevada plates are common here. They come up to the Pacific Northwest to get away from the summer heat. Seventy degrees here is a lot better than a hundred down there."

Dalton decided to terminate the investigator's work but asked her to try to learn more about the two people who had been in the car and to get back to him the next day if she discovered anything noteworthy. Sharon Bivens had replied that she could only learn more about the car's "owner of record" if continued surveillance revealed something about the two people. Dalton was not overly suspicious as a result of the information he had been given. Yet, Rodrigo Black Coyote's words of advice still clung to him as something to be careful and worried about.

———— ⁓⁓⋄⊙⋄⊙⋄⊙⋄⊙⋄⊙⊙⋄⁓⁓ ————

Sharon Bivens, on her own initiative, decided to go into the casino to try to get a better look at the two people she had been surveilling. She wandered around inside the football field-size main parlor going from one end to the other without seeing anyone dressed in a manner similar to the two she was looking for. Nearly a hundred cars had been parked in the parking lot and she calculated that perhaps there were one hundred and fifty people at the gambling machines and gaming tables. As she headed for the front doors, she glanced into the casino's restaurant where she saw them. They were sitting at a table talking with two men who appeared to be Native American.

Bivens went back outside through the casino's grand front entryway and sat on a bench a short distance away from the doors. In less than twenty minutes, the man and the woman from Nevada departed the casino, apparently without having stayed long enough for a meal. They were followed by the two men they had been talking to. The four of them stopped in the casino parking lot and continued conversing for an additional twenty minutes. Sharon Bivens wrote down what she had observed and waited, hoping to remain unnoticed, as if just another casino guest getting a breath of fresh air.

It was almost dark outside and the parking lot overhead lights silhouetted the four people well enough for Bivens to see clearly. As the four split up to go to their individual cars, Bivens slowly got up from the bench and went towards her car. She noted the license plate number of the vehicle the two men got into. Then as both cars headed out of the parking lot, she followed behind them at a safe distance. The two men in the one car turned off the street into the casino's reservation

residential area while the man and the woman she had originally been watching proceeded to the ferry that would take
them from Kingston back to Edmonds. Once on the other
side of the Sound, the man and the woman proceeded towards
Interstate 5, headed south through part of Seattle, and eventually headed east on Interstate 90 in the direction of either
Idaho, Eastern Oregon, or Nevada. Sharon Bivens turned off
at an exit and returned to Seattle and then on toward her home.

—————✺—————

A fog was forming over the Puget Sound. The evening air had
become much cooler. Dalton checked his window thermom-
eter and saw that the temperature had already fallen to fifty-
eight degrees. Needing a blanket for sleeping was an appealing contrast to the hot desert he had just left behind.

Outside, he heard a distant fog horn sounding its warning
to vessels still out on the water. The sound was often comfort-
ing, soothing, and at times gratifying. But on this evening, it
seemed to have taken on the sound of something less than
reassuring somewhere off his backyard. The fog horn's sound
carried with it the intended warning of unseen danger.

After opening a can of chili and pouring its contents into a
sauce pan, Dalton set it on his gas stovetop and lit the burner.

He then placed his dirty clothes in his washing machine
and added an extra measure of soap before turning it on. He
retrieved a cold bottle of beer from his refrigerator, a box of
crackers from the pantry, poured the pan of hot chili into a
bowl, and sat down at his kitchen table.

After eating, he went out his side kitchen door to his
camper and took the few five-gallon buckets containing his
bagged and tagged soil and rock chip samples into his garage.
After that, he went back to his camper and retrieved a small

gym bag, locked both truck and trailer, and went back inside his home.

Dalton turned off any unnecessary lights, closed what curtains he had previously left open, and locked both the front and back doors. He unzipped the gym bag and unpacked and unholstered his .357 semi-automatic handgun and a box of cartridges, which he usually took with him in his camper while away on his field trips to Idaho and Nevada.

Upstairs, after a refreshing hot shower, he opened his bedroom window and crawled into his oversized bed. As he drifted off to sleep, he heard the calls of seagulls settling down for the night, the never-ending sound of gentle small waves lapping at the shoreline, and the discomforting, eerie, low, monotone sounds of multiple fog horns, taking their turn in succession in issuing their warning, each one more distant from the other.

Soon after he had fallen asleep, what he could not hear was the sound of the ferry whistle as it embarked on its last trip of the day from Kingston, headed across the Puget Sound, back to Edmonds.

CHAPTER 3

Denver, Colorado

What if these were not merely coincidences?

Early the next morning, as light first appeared on the horizon to the east, Dalton got up and started making preparations for his departure to Denver. He thought he would drive the distance with his trailer in tow so he could do some work in Nevada while on his way back from Denver.

After having retrieved his mail, he methodically sorted and packaged all of his new soil and chip samples and took them back to the post office for mailing.

Upon returning back home, he carefully went through each room looking for any notes or correspondence that might reveal to a possible future burglar anything about his ongoing work. He gathered what he could find of importance or value and took the items to his bank's safe deposit box for safekeeping.

Then Dalton gathered certain personal file folders, containing various personal records, statements, and identifiers, from his desk and credenza, placed them in a box which he took to his basement. He wrote on the exterior of the box "Obsidian samples from Burns Paiute Indian Colony region, Oregon" and covered the files with a few inches of small pieces of the commonly found shiny black volcanic rock material which he had gathered for his own use on one of his many trips to and from Idaho and Nevada. By doing this, he hoped that any intruder who might venture into his basement would see what appeared to be but one sealed box among dozens of others being warehoused for no essential reason. The many boxes, stored against a basement wall three boxes deep and four boxes high, would give the impression that he was merely the typical homeowner hoarding items that probably had been untouched for years.

Dalton planned to depart Kingston on the 3:35 p.m. ferry that would go from Kingston back to Edmonds. He busied himself drying the laundry he had washed the night before and packed his truck and camper for his trip to Denver. He made a reservation at a camping ground outside of Denver, added a topped-off tank of propane gas to his camper for cooking and other requirements, and gassed up his truck for the journey east.

While waiting at the ferry dock to embark, Sharon Bivens telephoned him on his cell phone to bring him up to date on her surveillance observations since their last conversation. She also advised that the license plate on the vehicle containing the two local men was traced back to the owner of a tribal commercial fisherman, a Dungeness crabber, who was also the owner of a thirty-year-old twenty-seven-foot fishing vessel. Bivens also described that the owner of the ten-year-old Ford SUV vehicle was a charity organization from Las Vegas which also owned a newer white Lexus.

Dalton asked Sharon Bivens to try to ascertain what she could about all four people and to get back to him before his meeting in Denver.

While driving through southern Idaho, he decided to park his camper at a campground near Salt Lake City, Utah, instead of outside Denver as he had originally planned. He thought it best to not overburden his truck with having to pull the added fifteen hundred pounds of weight the rest of the way over the Colorado Rocky Mountains.

He arrived in Denver a day early and wanted the extra time to learn how the slumping precious metals market was doing and to get up to speed on how the mining sector was reacting to gold and silver prices. He knew that most exploration and mining companies were hard pressed to obtain financing for ongoing unprofitable exploration. Those companies that were mining precious metals, he knew, were able to sell their products but at a reduced profit. Conversely, explorers had nothing at all to sell because they produced nothing. All they essentially had were claims that potentially contained economically mineable gold.

Changes were occurring in the mining sector, in general, and those companies that were not flush with cash on hand or income were in danger of gradually going broke. Some who were creative found ways to obtain needed operating cash to keep the lights on. Some sold timber rights to the land claims they held. Others sold grazing rights on their claims to nearby ranchers. Striking private financing deals with investors for short-term cash was a more routine way of keeping their heads above water while waiting out the precious metals correction and a return of needed positive retail investor sentiment.

Dalton allowed his mind to momentarily wander while he pondered how many of the dozen or so Project X geological experts had been invited, or would show up, for the next day's meeting. He looked forward to seeing and hoped to spend time talking with Wayde Ramsley, Alice Harrison, and their home-based vice president of geology, Stuart Bergman, in their small suite of offices at Mining Engineer's, Inc. He had been amused when Bergman once told him that Bergman's German last name meant "miner."

After checking into his motel, Dalton turned on his motel's television set and gave an audible sound of disgust as he pictured in his mind the room he had once stayed in at the Tonopah Pink Elephant Motel. He recalled how the television in his room had no cable reception and how the "bikers and hikers" had to rely on a fuzzy picture and a nearly undecipherable sound of what few channels could be received from an antenna on the motel's rooftop.

Dalton found the cable channel he had been looking for. It was a regional cable business news station that sometimes broadcasted opinions and interviews of leading business and industry leaders. Within moments he saw an old schoolmate of his giving an interview. He had been working towards his doctorate degree at the same time Dalton had pursued his. Now the old acquaintance was a professor of geology at the Colorado School of Mining. He was saying,

"...although a larger or smaller concentration of precious metals, including copper, might be discovered at any time in the western states, there is little to indicate that deposits of high-grade ore will be found than that which has already been discovered and was being exploited. Large areas still remain thoroughly unprospected and future exploration could one day reveal ore bodies comparable with those now known. In that case, if such discoveries were pursued and made, mine industry-related employment opportunities would be significantly enhanced in the region of such discoveries..."

Dalton listened to his old school acquaintance talk about the mining industry's recent doldrums. He followed with how to rank the best miners from the worst to the best and what the criteria was for establishing an economically profitable mining operation. Last, his old schoolmate addressed the important role investors played in the chain of events leading up to profitability. The professor stressed the risks involved in such prospecting, the costs involved and the rewards for the small percent of companies that were lucky enough to be able to take their precious metals discoveries to production.

These were all matters, the details of which, Dalton knew by memory. They were the bread and butter essentials of the industry he had been so much a part of. They were the requisites he had to live or die by to help his company succeed not unlike those he had to help ensure were met in his former management role at Continental Mining in Elko, Nevada. Dalton had invested as much of his earnings as he could afford in Continental and he made a small fortune as a result. Additionally, his insights, instincts, professional demeanor, and his knowledge all helped him to progress quickly to his final senior management role.

Dalton reflected for a moment how he had labored in a mine in Idaho while pursuing his bachelor's degree in geology. Then, using what funds he had been able to save, he paid for some of his higher education in Colorado not far from the motel where he was staying. He knew Denver well enough and was well aware of how the mining industry had established itself in the city and how it tapped graduates from his old alma mater. It was how he landed his first job as a junior geologist, a trainee, for an internship that would pay off what remained of his school loan.

After the professor's interview had concluded, Dalton turned off the television and checked for new e-mails on his laptop. There was one from his private investigator, Sharon Bivens. It seemed to raise more questions but also could be a partial explanation to the series of incidents he had encountered in recent days.

The e-mail said: "Dalton, my husband is a retired criminal investigator from the Bureau of Indian Affairs, the BIA. He said he recalled something about a fairly new, possible organized crime element from within the Indian community at large, something he had heard about. He can't recall who he heard it from."

Bivens also wrote that there had been a rumor mentioned by a tribal police officer somewhere that some element of the Native Americans had formed an organization to extort money from individuals and businesses by forcing them to pay for protection, among other criminal activity of a more substantive and violent nature.

Bivens further wrote in her e-mail, "More than that, it was rumored that one of these people may have recently shaken down a developer in Nevada to get money for not interfering with the developer. It had something to do with Indian ancestral burial grounds, kind of like the method used by those who do the same thing in the African American community. It was seen as legal if done a certain way. The African American civil rights leaders would approach a company and accuse them of racial discrimination. They would offer to put on sensitivity training to a company's employees in exchange for a significant donation to the proposing organization, which in turn, by the way, paid millions of dollars to those who ran the organizations. If the company refused, the civil rights organization would threaten to smear the company's reputation and the reputation of its senior executive and board.

"Just a thought," Bivens continued in her e-mail. "Sounds far fetched I know. The vehicle license plate check I made on the car driven by the man and woman was registered to a charity called The Indian Plight charity organization. That's TIP, for short. Strange, huh? Too little is known. Do you want me to continue digging?"

Dalton e-mailed back to Bivens to hold off on doing further inquiries until he had an opportunity to explain the whole matter to his people in Denver. He also wanted to know if they would foot the bill for the work she had done so far and for whatever work would be deemed prudent or necessary in the future.

———✦———

In an office park on the outskirts of Denver's south side, Wayde Ramsley met with his board of directors, which consisted of people who were CEOs of companies that owned an interest in Mining Engineering, Inc. A debate had been raging over whether to concentrate all of their geologist's efforts to the south or to the north of the Carlin Trend in northeast Nevada. The thinking by a couple of board members was that they had spread their geologist resources too thinly over long distances and that to continue to do so would mean that Project X would take longer to preliminarily explore. Others on the board felt that they were getting close to decision making time as to whether to shut down the initial phase one effort or to decide to go all out and implement their massive phase two claim-filing campaign. If so, it would be a region-by-region effort until all the pieces of the supposed possible gold-bearing fault had been staked out and were controlled by the consortium.

"We can't keep funneling tens of millions of dollars a year into the effort with no end in sight," said one member.

"We need to either 'shit or get off the pot,'" said another.

Ramsley asked the others who were present whether they felt confident at what the company was finding as a result of their geologist's work, saying "…along the whole thing, from one end to other."

Their in-house resident lead geologist, Vice President, Stu Bergman, busied himself scurrying from board member to board member, handing each a photocopied package of updated charts and maps showing the assay results of their field geologists' work. The charts showed various markings depicting both the quality and quantity of the mineral substances that had been identified as of the last assay reports. The overall map was punctuated in a way that made all findings show up as being compressed onto one small sheet of paper, making the results look significant. The following pages in the handout were enlarged charts of regions showing smaller segments of the overall map shown on the first page. The enlarged regional maps made the results appear far less significant than had been first shown on the first compressed chart.

"Look at all the places we have yet to visit and document," said one of the attendees.

"How can we cover the rest of the ground in so short a period of time?" asked another "Perhaps we need more field geologists."

"Some of this ground has already been sampled and staked out by other companies' explorers," said one. "We can have someone feel them out for possible interest in selling their claims to us. Have them sign a nondisclosure agreement so we can get a look at their detailed geo reports and their resource discovery math."

"That's probably less than ten percent of all the land we think could be part of the overall fault line," said Ramsley. "We'll have to move our people to just one area and finish our soil and chip samples, do some geomagnetic airborne tests again, make a decision on that parcel, and then move on to the next."

"That would draw too much attention," said another board member. "People would know that something big was going on. No, we have to remain discreet and make it look like our occasional individual geologist is just roaming around like prospectors of old, nothing fancy or flashy. Keep a low profile."

The debate raged on for almost an hour. The board meeting was set to end by the close of business that day and each of the attendees had their own corporate aircraft waiting for them at the Denver Stapleton International Airport. There were no commercial airline schedules that had to be accommodated.

Ramsley picked up on the comment made by the one board member regarding the issue of funding the contracting of additional geologists so as to help expedite the preliminary exploration process. Again, there was significant disagreement between board members. Some saw the need to finish Project X within the next year. Others were in no hurry and figured that if their plan ever became known by their industry competitors, they could then decide how quickly they wanted to complete whatever work needed to be addressed. Besides, a couple argued, the more people they hired, the more they risked that Project X would become known. The conversation seemed to be going in a circle, becoming repetitive.

"Our geologists are recognized industry experts in their field," one said. "They know a lot of people, have a large network of contacts, and one or more might decide to bail on us in favor of a better deal with someone else. Someone might spill the beans if the salary was right. Or they could accidentally mention what they had been working on."

Wayde Ramsley leaned back and let the "bags of wind" pontificate, strut, and flap their lips. "*Assholes,*" he thought to himself. "*Too many egos in need of placating. Too many who were used to having their own way.*"

———⁓〰〰———

On Wednesday, Dalton arrived at 2 p.m. to meet privately with Wayde Ramsley. The meeting was scheduled for half an hour to be followed by the general meeting at 3 p.m. with the company's field geologists. Dalton laid out his series of incidents starting with the one in Tonopah, including the flat tire and the car that seemingly followed him to his camper that same evening. He told Ramsley about the surprise of having Rodrigo Black Coyote waiting for him in the dark at his camper and the equally alarming conversation he had with Rodrigo the next morning. Lastly, he explained the information developed by the private investigator about the possibility of having been followed while in Nevada, and in the Seattle and Kitsap Peninsula areas in Washington state.

Ramsley sat back in his oversized leather chair, put his hands behind his head and put his feet up on his desk. "These could all be just coincidence," he remarked as if both a statement as well as a question.

"Maybe so," replied Dalton. "But, just to be safe, maybe we should learn more without anyone knowing that we are suspicious of something. I guess my concern is what if these were not merely coincidences?"

Ramsley agreed and told Dalton to submit his investigator's bill for reimbursement. But, he admonished, he wanted the investigator to reduce all of her spoken communications into an e-mail as well. "Let's think about this for a while," he said in concluding the meeting with Dalton Trindall.

———⁓⁓⁓———

The general meeting with the geologist staff was attended by ten of the twelve geologists. One, it was said, was resigning for personal reasons and the other reported being sick and was unable to attend the meeting.

Stu Bergman conducted the meeting with Alice Harrison sitting in. The meeting was essentially formatted in the same manner as the board of directors' meeting the prior day. Bergman felt that putting the same issues before his esteemed group of expert geologists would get better results than it did with the group of directors. The geologists were among the best they could find and Bergman thought to himself that he "preferred working with the geologists because they were people who had no corporate egos looking to be massaged, no heads looking to be crowned, and no asses looking to be kissed."

Wayde Ramsley joined the meeting while it was under-way. He sat quietly, mostly listening and observing, wanting Bergman to show the geologists that his leadership role was more than a mere staff position.

At about five o'clock, Ramsley wrapped up the session and instructed the geologists to return to their homes, take a paid week off, and wait for instructions from Stuart Bergman concerning any modifications to their assignment locations. Then he adjourned the meeting and asked Dalton Trindall to remain behind for a moment.

Once the room had cleared, Ramsley said, "I've been think-ing about what you said about the coincidences. Does this private investigator outfit have an office they can liaison with here in Denver?"

"Yes," said Dalton.

"But she's in Seattle?"

"Yes, she lives and works there. But her firm has peo-ple in many of the major cities including Denver," Dalton explained further.

"Contact your lady PI friend and ask her if she can arrange to have someone do an anti-electronic surveillance sweep of our offices here, you know, see if we are being bugged. Also, ask if they can do your vehicles and your house, and mine as well, while they are at it. Perhaps to do it once a month. Do you have any kind of security system at your house?"

"No," Trindall replied.

"Get one installed and send the bill to the company. In thinking about it, I also sensed one too many coincidences lately and your briefing made me realize that we have to be more careful, more then ever. Maybe one of our people has been yapping about what they do. Maybe word is getting around. Then again, maybe I'm just getting paranoid. But we can't take any chances. If someone really wants to know what this company is up to, they may spare no effort in finding out. In that case we should spare no effort in making it difficult for them."

Dalton departed the Mining Engineer's, Inc., offices, drove his truck back to his motel, and made a telephone call to his investigator, Sharon Bivens. She told him that her husband had been unsuccessful in confirming the incident about the Nevada developer. She said that her husband also confirmed that the local US Bureau of Indian Affairs was aware of the TIP Charity in Las Vegas, knew nothing untoward, knew that they had distributed funds to a couple of the local reservations, and they had no knowledge about an Indian organized crime ring. He then related to Bivens his boss's wishes. After getting assurance that Wayde Ramsley's instructions could be accomplished, he ended the call and then proceeded to make a few other unrelated calls and to check his laptop for any new e-mails.

CHAPTER 4

Las Vegas, Nevada

This guy was eyeing up all the women.

The headquarters home for The Indian Plight non-profit charity organization was located in a low-rent part of Las Vegas close to the mega casinos that lined the famous Las Vegas Strip. Its office consisted of three rooms. One was a small reception area, the second room was a meeting room with a table that could seat up to eight people, with the last being a bathroom. The office and meeting room was sparsely furnished with cheap plastic chairs and discount store furniture often found in low-rent neighborhood store front businesses.

Seated behind the lone desk at the front of the rented space was an overweight elderly Native American looking lady, perhaps in her late fifties or early sixties, dressed in Native American clothes with bright traditional colors and patterns. She wore turquoise earrings and a reddish looking coral stone in a silver cuff bracelet. While she busied herself reading a book in the absence of a visitor, a phone call that needed answering, or paperwork in need of being processed, she sipped on a cup of coffee oblivious to the meeting going on behind her in the charity's executive board room. She was a receptionist who said little but looked like she knew plenty.

In attendance at the meeting in the board room were two women and three men, all of whom were, to varying degrees, middle age. They were leisurely dressed like any other person who walked the streets of the city. The leader in the room was officially the vice-chairman of the not-for-profit charity and was conducting the meeting. All appeared to have some Native American facial feature and skin tones that fit with the charity's image. All were officially listed as members of the board of directors of "TIP."

The chairwoman of the organization was conspicuously absent, as usual, but she could electronically audibly monitor such meetings from some other location via a conference call connection to the board room. If she wanted to interject her thoughts, she would call the vice-chairman on his cell phone to do so. She was a busy woman, often driving back and forth between Las Vegas and Native American reservations in various parts of the western states doing her charity work, meeting with people, and always soliciting donations for various needs of the various tribes she tried to support. She had become well known and was well received by various tribal council members wherever her travels took her.

Often, she would meet with her contacts and then hand them a check for whatever request had been made of her charity organization. She had a condominium in downtown Las Vegas and it was believed she stayed for periods of time at various other locations. Aside from the charity's three-year-old white Lexus, she also drove what she liked to think of as her charity's more discrete, well-used, ten-year-old Ford sport utility vehicle (SUV), used for times when she wanted to blend in more with her surroundings such as when she visited a reservation. She knew that she needed to create an austere appearance when representing her charity organization to certain people. The Lexus was usually for her personal use. She lived in a manner that, by all outward appearances, most people would consider average.

The vice chair and the hand-selected group at the meeting were the chairwoman's lieutenants, so to speak. They were the field coordinators, the people who she relied on to capitalize on opportunities for adding sums of money to the charity's coffers. In turn, the charity's funds, controlled by the chairwoman, were dispersed to accomplish the charity's mission. There were payments that had to be paid for a variety of other people and purposes, sometimes nefarious in nature. The board members were all full-time staff, receiving salaries plus 10 percent of the legal, or questionable, contributions or payments they could acquire through their people who worked for them.

Vice-chairman Tony Rappaport was talking to the "board" members who were present when his cell phone rang. The chairwoman called to tell him to not tell those who were present at the meeting anything about the possible new donation prospect, named Dalton Trindall, and those who the prospect might work for.

One of the charity's contract "rovers" who was always on the lookout for opportunities to make money, had contacted Tony Rappaport the week prior, to tip him off about some "'meth-head" teenager who carefully broke into Dalton Trindall's camper out in the desert near Tonopah. He had found some notes indicating that some of the rock samples stored in the camper, appeared to be "galena" in nature, containing silver and other metallic minerals.

On another slip of paper, there was a reminder of sort, saying, "Call Larry-Boise-switch locations-call HQ for approval." The note contained a phone number with a Denver, Colorado, area code. The chairwoman had called the Denver number and a receptionist had answered by saying "Mining Engineering Corporation, may I help you?" The chairwoman merely said, "Sorry, I have the wrong number."

There was also a note that seemed to be a reminder of a dozen other geographic locations heading northwards from Tonopah, Nevada. Many of the locations on this piece of paper also had the initials "Au," "Ag," "Cu," and sometimes two or all three of them in sequence. The symbols were known by all who made the desert their home as standing for gold, silver, and copper. Beside each noted location were initials, perhaps for a name, each different from the other.

The teenager had also found a loaded semi-automatic handgun in a fabric bag. He used his cell phone to call a friend who called one of the charity's contacts to see if they were interested in the information. If not, the meth-head teenager had planned to steal the firearm and several other items and sell them for drug money. If they were interested in what he had stumbled onto, he would write down what he saw including the camper license plate number and exchange the information with his contact in Tonopah for a hundred dollars.

Tony Rappaport discussed with his cohorts a just completed "donation operation" of a businesswoman who had a momentary affair with one of "their" ladies after meeting at a casino in California. The eventual donor was a representative for the Brittany Software Company in London.

"Our own lady had been recruited by our charity's local representative. He found her on a website advertising her availability. Our guy had her work the reservation's casino looking for either a man or a woman to cozy up to," Rappaport said. "After their eventual intimate liaison, we confronted the Brittany Software lady for a donation. She wrote a check to the charity. Our guy looked at it and in disgust and said 'Two hundred dollars?' The lady looked at him for a moment and then wrote another for a thousand."

Smiles broke out on the faces of the meeting's attendees.

"Our guy said 'Lady, that's what our people usually get. You can do better.' 'Oops,' she said. Out came the checkbook for another thousand. Twenty two hundred dollars total. Not good enough, but our guy had to let it go. Hitting her up again would have been pushing his luck."

Rappaport asked one of the meeting's female attendees to brief them all on her success at another casino in Oregon.

"This guy was eying up all the women. Our lady saddled up next to him at the video poker machines and started playing. She did right. She made some small talk. He began to answer her back. She told him if he was interested she'd meet him in the parking lot in thirty minutes. We got her the casino transport van. No windows. In they went, like a couple of rabbits. Then our guy opened up the door, and acted shocked at what he saw. The mark paid off with a four thousand-dollar check. He was told three thousand but he added an extra thousand as insurance, I guess. Nice guy. He was a local dentist. He wrote the charity a donation on one of his dental practice's business checks. I guess he didn't want his secret found out by his dental hygienists and family. He was so interested in supporting the Native American cause he couldn't write the check quick enough. Our guy told him that the charity was nonprofit and he could write it off on his taxes."

The room of attendees broke out in laughter. Two of the attendees high-five'd each other as the laughter subsided.

"We share these stories with you to help you with ideas for what you can do in your own areas," Rappaport said. "We had a developer who wanted to build something out in the desert. He starts to get the license approvals. We instruct our local reservation guy to tell the developer that the land was a Native American ancestral burial area, and that many Native Americans considered the land sacred. The developer contacted his lawyer. The lawyer asks a lot of legal gibberish stuff. He says we need to file this and that. Our guy said he'd show up at the building permit hearing with a dozen Native Americans to protest the license and to ask that the land be donated to the reservation. Or," he continued with a smirk on his face, "the lawyer was told that a financial donation to our charity would be used to search the land by our own people. The lawyer said he would contact the reservation's tribal council. Our guy said go ahead, but we we'll still be there. We won't go away no matter what the council says or does. The lawyer asked how much it would cost to make this problem go away. We never said a price. We told him to search his soul for the answer. The developer developed a conscience, I guess. He forked over fifty grand. To the charity. We have ninety days to search the land and then we'll gladly sign a waiver agreement with them."

One of the board members explained how he succeeded in shaking down a contractor who was building a new addition to a local shopping center and adding a gas station. "I approached him, saying he should tell the shopping center owner that Native Americans would hold a demonstration on the sidewalk out in front of the existing stores. The demonstrators would be unemployed Native Americans carrying signs saying they were being discriminated against by not having been hired. I told him that he had not hired one Native American who applied for jobs for the project. I got a call from him, after he presumably discussed the matter with the shopping center's owner. He said they would hire three Native Americans. I said make it five and write our charity a consultant's fee check. He hired five and the charity got a two thousand dollar check."

Another attendee volunteered a "complicated" scenario in which a business agreed to pay a "finder's fee" to the charity for locating qualified Native American applicants for some new positions.

"What kind of jobs?" asked Rappaport. "The usual kind, minimum wage?"

"No, they paid better than that. They were for bill processing. It was for some computer work that needed some familiarity with computers," said the board member.

"What was the complicated part?" Rappaport questioned.

"Finding enough applicants who had sufficient skills and then getting them trained," the board member answered. "We negotiated with the business to agree to pay for the training of the Native American applicants because Native American computer expertise was at a disadvantage compared to the general population. The finder's fee, for the charity, was a thousand dollars per applicant. The charity was also paid to do the training through the reservation. Native Americans got jobs, the reservation got paid to provide the training, and the charity got its finder's fee."

Rappaport finished the meeting by handing out an envelope with a pay check for each person, a check done properly, with tax deductions, as required. Then he said, "Remember, if you don't make it to the next meeting you don't get paid. Tell your contacts to stay loyal and clean. No crossing the line. No drugs. No violence, not ever. What they do wrong reflects on you. I always remind you to tell your people that our chairwoman is the one who pulls the strings here. She's the boss.

"Some of our funds come from people who go to Native American casinos to try their luck," Rappaport continued. "We help them 'get lucky.' Then they want a free ride and we remind them that they just got lucky." His comment brought more laughter. "We remind them that it is far better to be lucky than to risk becoming unlucky. Right? No threats. No promises. Just a donation, in the right amount, of course. Keep all of your people out of the casinos unless we assign them. Here is my point. We need to keep all casino-related activity as clean as possible.

"We try very hard to break no laws. Laws governing shake-downs, blackmail, extortion, sex, etcetera, are not broken if we say and do things in a certain proper way. Soon, we hope to have other ways of fundraising. We want to benefit the reservations. We will not victimize our own people and we want to avoid using their casinos. They need to have good reputations. We can't risk hurting what they work hard to make succeed. They are benefiting their people through their new businesses and casinos. We should try to help that and not hurt it."

After the attendees departed, Rappaport's cell phone rang. It was the organization's chairwoman Tiponi Isaw, the one their staff used to call the "Madam," but who was now affectionately referred to as their Promiscuous Puppeteer, the woman who pulled all the strings. She had been a "legal" Nevada prostitute in her younger years, and had saved enough money to open her own brothel. Then, she had the misfortune of not paying enough taxes to the IRS. The result was the seizure of her business to pay back taxes. The IRS ended up owning and running a brothel until it could be sold. There had been many jokes made about the IRS running a house of ill repute, something they were said to be expert at when it came to their reputation as a government agency.

The "Madam" had lost a piece of her net worth in the process. But she had learned a lesson. Since then, she had found a new way to earn a living, while doing some good in the process. She wanted to be as legal and as clean as possible, but she wanted it to be her organization, with her making the decisions. She wanted to couple her former expertise with a nonprofit, non-taxable business.

The chairwoman had her faults, some would think, if they knew what they were. She wanted to pay her people well. One rule she had insisted on, among many, for example, was to never demand any kind of payment and to never meet with a mark a second time so as to not have a "reverse sting" scenario unfold on their people involving the authorities. No violence. No arm twisting. No demands. No coercion. And no threats.

She had maintained her distance from all that she orchestrated from behind the scenes. She seldom was seen. She never directly gave instructions. And, importantly, no one knew most of the time where she was or what she was doing. They knew little more about her, or her background. On occasion, when she did appear before her lieutenants, she said little, smiled and thanked them for their work and handed them cash, a sort of commission, in whatever amount she felt was appropriate based on the amount of the donations they acquired for The Indian Plight Charity Organization.

CHAPTER 5

Boise, Idaho

Jackpot indeed.

Dalton drove from Denver back to Salt Lake City, Utah, and retrieved his camper and spent the night at a local motel. The drive was uneventful and he had thought about continuing with his work in Tonopah. He also weighed the offered week off and the possibility that the promised instructions as to where each geologist was to work could result in his being reassigned elsewhere. The next day he could drive in a direction that would take him towards Kingston, Washington, via Boise, Idaho, or he could take another route towards Tonopah that passed by Elko, his former home for over twenty years.

Dalton didn't need a map in Nevada because he knew all the highways and primary state roads. After all his years of living and working in the state, he was tired of Nevada and he wanted a change, yet a small part of him wanted to head back to a place he had come to loathe.

He knew the winter months further to the north would be harsh and that the deep snow and the constant subfreezing cold would prevent him from being able to work for much of the winter, and thus being paid during the "downtime." Being in south central Nevada, even if it was the high desert, would allow him to see the ground he needed to work on. No snow cover. The occasional snow that fell there usually melted quickly. He could work further south towards Death Valley,

California, where the winter weather was warm and more favorable. He'd also be much closer to Tucson, Arizona, where he had wanted to visit in February during the world famous Tucson Gem and Mineral Show. He was a geologist and, as such, he found the annual Tucson event interesting to visit.

While in route to Tonopah the next day, and while near Elko, Dalton got a phone call from one of his fellow geologists who was working a geographical area north of Boise, Idaho. He was asked if he could meet the geologist at a motel just outside of Boise along the Interstate on his way back to Kingston. The geologist gave him the name and the location of the motel where he was staying for the night. Dalton agreed and said he would arrive later that evening.

Dalton stopped at a gas station and then went to a nearby shopping center in Elko where he bought a cup of coffee at a place that had WiFi internet access. He located the website for a restaurant he knew in Tonopah, found their phone number, and then called the restaurant on his cell phone. He then bought a restaurant gift certificate for Rodrigo Black Coyote and his family, paid for it with his credit card, and asked that it be sent to Box 12466, RT-6, Tonopah, Nevada. Dalton was grateful for Rodrigo's words, and for sharing his home, his family, and a breakfast meal with him. The gift certificate was a way of saying thank you in the absence of being able to reciprocate in person.

Dalton drove on towards Boise, found the motel he was to go to, got a room, and immediately called Larry McGray to let him know that he had arrived.

Larry was a former US Geological Survey (USGS) geologist from California. He had specialized in minerals and did considerable research in neighboring Nevada. He had fresh new students each year when he taught an evening class at a local university and many wanted extra credit in their attempt to brown-nose their way toward a better grade. Larry would assign them research projects on a wide variety of geological interests pertaining to the Carlin trend. Over the many years, he acquired extensive new information from the USGS, but the students sometimes found something new that had been overlooked.

After retiring from the USGS, he sent out a resume to over a hundred precious metals explorers and miners hoping to be hired as a contract geologist. The response was reasonable enough to afford him choices. One particular CEO of a significant mining outfit had forwarded his resume on to a new company whose board he was a member of in Denver. McGray choose to work for Mining Engineers in Denver when he learned what the work would be like and, importantly, what the job paid. It had been over a year since he had reported for work and he was one of the original twelve geologists hired for Project X.

Larry McGray had spent much of his first year in Idaho doing the same kind of work there that Dalton had been doing in south central Nevada. He wanted to meet with Dalton to talk about Project X and its potential.

The two met in the motel lobby and went together to a nearby restaurant to eat and talk. Larry seemed excited about what he was finding. In short, he related that there had been some serious and successful exploration in segments of Idaho. Things had been heating up there with new exploration announcements that he had read about in various trade journals. There had been a couple of new substantial claims filed tying up land that Mining Engineers, Inc., would have been interested in.

Aside from the well-known silver deposits now being mined in the northern part of the state, he had reviewed what records he could get a hold of from the corporate exploration activities that had been done in recent years. His geographical area of interest stretched from south of Coeur d'Alene in the foothills and mountains down through the mountain ranges of central Idaho and into the high desert of the southern part of the state.

He believed that there was a northern extension of the Carlin Trend and that pieces of it, in a generally north-south line had already been discovered, particularly by two exploration firms. One was soon to begin a mining operation and the other was waiting out the precious metals market correction to obtain the necessary financing to expand the exploration of their extensive discovery. The company intended to prove the presence of additional potential ounces of gold and silver in addition to the noteworthy numbers they had already announced that they had discovered. The potential was seemingly limitless. Larry thought that just between these two companies, with about fifty kilometers, or about thirty-five miles of in-line exploration, that there could possibly be close to over one hundred million ounces of gold. If his estimate was close to accurate, then the areas being explored at two locations, by two different companies, could be as rich, or far richer, than the Carlin Trend. If that assumption was to become reality, then Mining Engineers, Inc., would want to claim as much of the land as they could for themselves. Given current low share prices in the industry, such companies could be bought out for pennies on the dollar.

Further, Larry told Dalton about his field work findings at various locations. He surmised that his findings could preliminarily support the theory of the possible northward direction of the Carlin Trend gold-bearing fault line.

Lastly, Larry revealed that in just one small area of the north central Clearwater Mountain range vicinity, it had been estimated by the US Bureau of Land Management, the US

Forest Service, and the USGS that several million ounces of gold had been "hand" mined between the late 1800s and the mid 1900s using only hand-wielded tools and water-powered dredgers. It was assumed that only perhaps, at most, 5 to 10 percent of the gold that was present could have been found. That means that perhaps as much as fifty or sixty million ounces of gold could have been undetected because of the technology used at the time. If so, just this central mountain region of Idaho alone could hold as much gold as was found, so far, in the northeast Nevada Carlin Trend. Larry riddled his explanation with constant caveats and conditions such as "if drilling proves it so…if it is of sufficient grade, quality, and quantity to be economical to mine," among other cautionary points that would have qualified as footnotes in his submitted written reports.

Larry was excited as he described how the early miners had essentially literally only scratched the surface with their hand digging and their inefficient washing of the soil looking for "visible" gold. He went on to say that there had to be ten times as much, or more, invisible gold, likely in addition to an untold amount of gold veins and gold-saturated shears that could be found. All it would take would be to mine the land using today's more efficient and effective modern technology.

"The place was merely occasionally tunneled in relatively few places," Larry said. "The tunnels were not long or deep. In the gravel beds, along streams, the early miners had only dredged the streams and washed the soils to extract whatever gold they could visibly see with their eyes, and they would have even missed most of what was visible. Ninety-nine percent of the surrounding land, in length, width, and depth, has never been mined. Yet my work indicates that it's all still there, untouched by man for an eternity. Of course, a lot more work would need to be done, and a company has already been doing it. And, they are proving my, and their own, theory.

"With their soil samples, their geomagnetic work, and their near 100 percent successful drilling results, they are well on their way to proving that they could have a piece of the Carlin, a piece much further to the north. The same holds true with another large exploration effort sixty miles further to the south where they continue to explore, and they are preparing to open a new mine that will have enough gold ore to provide a lifetime of work for all those who go there to work."

Larry paused for a moment to let all this sink in while Dalton tried to compute the magnitude of what he had just been told.

"And Wayde Ramsley knows all this?" asked Dalton.

"Yes, and so does the board. I urged them to consider buying out these two companies and any claims that other people or companies may have. But there is also plenty of land unspoken for. The question is, do they want to start fresh on unproven ground, on the basis of only soil sample assay results and prior hand mining results? Or do they want to claim the ground where both soil samples and the other tests indicate that the gold is also present. They could acquire all of the claims where the gold deposits have already been proven. Some are in the process of being drilled, in addition to what has already been deemed mineable for profit. It's all there and it's ripe for the picking," McGray said.

"I should add that the gold at those elevations has always been there. It wasn't moved there by ancient glaciers. That means that the gold isn't just at the surface nor was it deposited there by ice moving south from northern regions. The elevations of the deposits were higher than the glaciers. The gold at the surface is only the beginning. It goes deep to its origins, from where some was pushed up out of the ground and the mother lode, literally speaking, lies untouched just below the surface, just like in the Carlin Trend. It's there, all of it. We just need to drill down to see what the richness of it is and how deep the deposits are."

Larry McGray grinned. His facial expression showed his exuberance, excitement, energy, enthusiasm, and pride in what he had found out for the company.

Dalton added, "Yet, it is all inconclusive until the land is drilled, as you say. Drill cores have to be pulled out of the ground, split open, assayed, and the results received back from the lab have to be evaluated. Soil or rock chip samples alone wouldn't be seen as proof. And the drilling has to be close enough together to identify the width and the depth of any continuous deposit. The results have to be carefully studied by the best qualified people, people who know what they are looking at."

"Of course. You know, I'm not new to this, Dalton. I know what needs to be done," Larry said, sounding slightly offended. "Given the drill assay results of these two exploration efforts going on in a large part of Idaho, I already know the answers, the results. It's a given. The gold is there. Period. No guessing involved. My review of all the information is unequivocal. The empirical evidence speaks for itself. The results, the locations of the prior little mom and pop mines, the soil samples, every-thing, they all support the hypothesis. I'd stake my reputation on it, even my life. That's how sure I am. It's more than just theory or an educated guess. It's fact.

"One area called the Oro Grande Shear Zone is but one large example of all that exists north of the Carlin Trend," McGray continued. "As I mentioned a moment ago, in that vicinity alone it's believed that perhaps six million ounces of gold was hand-mined decades ago. That would have been just on the surface. Using that number as a basis, don't you think that at that one location there could be ten times that amount of gold, both on the surface and under it as well? If it is economical, profitable to pull it out of the ground, that one area alone could rival the sixty million ounces already found on the sixty-mile long Carlin Trend in northeast Nevada. You've been poking around in an area I know a little bit about in southern Nevada. What do you think?"

Dalton took a deep breath, thought for a moment, and replied, "I sense that your theory may be right, that my theory, from my days at Continental Mining may be right, and that Wayde is impatiently waiting for more data from us to make his decisions. Not just from you and me, but from the others as well.

"I've not sent in any conclusions but I've opined that it appeared that the north-south trend may stretch from the southern part of the Carlin between the Cortez Mountains and the Sulphur Range area below Elko, to the west of the Diamond Mountains, on a southwesterly direction on into Tonopah. Then south from there through the southern part of Esmeralda County right into Death Valley itself, and perhaps further south all the way to the Mexican border," Dalton related.

After pausing briefly to gather his thoughts, Dalton summarized by saying, "The exploration endeavors in Mexico have shown that deposits do indeed exist in a general north to south direction. It's as if a massive, earth changing tectonic plate eruption took place millions, maybe a billion, years ago, one of a magnitude that caused a tremendous rip in the earth's crust. Geez, I've even wondered if this fault line could be a part of what's been found in Central and South America. But we are dreaming. We'll never know. Not in our lifetimes. It's all so speculative to think in such an unbridled, unscientific manner."

After they finished their meal, the two geologists made their way back to their motel, said their farewells, and turned in for the night.

Dalton found it hard to sleep and he opened his laptop and sent Wayde Ramsley an e-mail detailing his conversation with Larry McGray. In summing up his e-mail, he asked but one question, "Do you see what we see or are you waiting on more data?"

After sending the e-mail to his boss in Denver, Dalton sent a message to Stuart Bergman asking if he could continue with his research in the southern half of Nevada. He also asked if he could team up with one of their other dozen geologists for many good reasons which he spelled out. Most importantly, Dalton said, "Two minds are better than one and the coming winter will shut down our geos work further north."

Dalton slept poorly that night even though he was in an average motel, with air conditioning that worked, which had an average bed to sleep on and hot water with which to take a shower. The television worked, the shower did not leak, and there were no rowdy all-night parties down the hallway.

The next morning, before leaving the motel, Dalton checked his e-mails and found one from Wayde Ramsley that he found wanting, which merely, and perhaps cryptically said, "We shall see."

Then Dalton read a reply from Stuart Bergman saying he understood and agreed with the reasoning for an added geo in southern Nevada and that perhaps the suggestion could be arranged in the not too distant future "when winter made it impossible to do further exploration further north." He'd consider reassigning one or more of their geologists to the south. Bergman's e-mail went on to say, "We are down to ten geologists and we have a few of them researching tons of mining records, claims files, and dozens of other corporate public drilling results in order to help fill in the blanks on what we don't yet know." Bergman ended his e-mail with the instruction for Dalton to focus on the area between the town of Goldfield and the village of Silver Creek, twenty miles south of Tonopah.

He decided to not take the week off as had been offered. He thought it best to show Bergman and Ramsley that he was committed, and that he was the kind of former geology manager who would have wanted the same of any of his own subordinates, especially under the circumstances. He wondered if the effort he was personally making was worth it. He had enough savings to last two lifetimes. The work he was doing intrigued him. It always had. He had been a believer in invisible gold and helped to prove its value. He had also been a believer in the north-south extension of the Carlin Trend and he was being given a chance to prove whether or not it really existed.

Dalton e-mailed a message to the company vice president for administration, Alice Harrison, saying that he could be reached on his cell phone instead of his home phone while again in the vicinity of Tonopah, Nevada.

He then headed southeast on Interstate 84 in the direction that would take him back towards Elko, Nevada. A few hours later, he stopped and filled up his gas tank, parked in a tractor trailer truck stop parking lot, and entered a restaurant for a late breakfast. Such places, he knew, served breakfast meals twenty four hours a day, every day, for truckers whose meal times varied depending on their driving schedules.

Upon returning to his pickup truck, Dalton froze in alarm when he saw that his truck door had been somehow unlocked, his truck had been entered, and his suitcase, camera, and his laptop had all been stolen. He was incensed with outrage as he called the local police to report the theft. He was told by the dispatcher to come into the police department to file a report. Dalton asked if they could check for fingerprints. He was told that they seldom checked for prints in small theft cases but that when he arrived at the department's sub-station, near his location, an officer could take a look.

After making the call to the police, and while still at the truck stop, Dalton walked around the general area looking for anyone, or any vehicle, that looked suspicious. His mind was racing and cluttered with a variety of thoughts and concerns. One such concern was the company-related information in his computer, including the e-mail he had sent to Ramsley and Bergman the night before. The information in his computer's hard drive was mostly sensitive and partly personal. He shuddered at the thought that the information could be extracted and used by someone who knew how to access it.

Dalton hoped that the thief only wanted the stolen items so that he could sell them for money. In any event, he surmised, the contents of the data on his laptop's hard drive was protected unless someone could decipher, or had possession of, his encrypted password. As an extra precaution, in case of a computer crash or a loss of data for whatever the reason, his computer automatically sent a copy of all data immediately upon sending and receiving to something called a "cloud" data storage service. The information could be retrieved and downloaded into a new computer if and when the need arose.

After filing a report with the local police, he called his auto insurance company and reported the theft, giving the insurance representative the police department's theft incident report identification number.

His last sequential phone call was to his private investigator, Sharon Bivens. Instead of getting to talk to Bivens, he heard a recording telling callers to leave a message with their name and phone number and she would get back to whoever was calling when she could. Dalton hastily explained what had just happened to his laptop, camera, and suitcase and said that the laptop contained sensitive information, some of which he could not tell her without clearing it first through his office in Denver. He knew there was nothing she could do about the theft, but felt that she should know that there had been yet another incident, perhaps only one more coincidence to be added to those that had already taken place.

After hanging up, Dalton thought to himself, *How ironic. I can't explain what Project X is all about to Bivens but some piece of shit has all of the information, in his dirty little hands, inside my laptop.*

Dalton knew Elko well and he found a shopping center with a clothing store, a supermarket, and an electronics retail store right where he remembered them to be. He spent a couple of hours buying new clothes, personal hygiene items, and a new laptop.

After making the final purchase, he got back into his truck and placed the new laptop on the front seat, right next to him, so he would not forget to take it with him wherever he stopped. Although the new computer did not contain any important information, he just didn't want to risk having it stolen like the last one.

Dalton seethed in disgust at himself for his own mistake at leaving his computer unattended, as he had always done, no matter where he had been, a computer that contained certain critical and sensitive information about Project X.

———∽∿∾⌒◌⌒∿∾∿∿———

Moments later, the Indian Plight charity chairwoman, Tiponi Isaw was notified by phone by her charity's vice chairman that their guy who had been shadowing Dalton Trindall had just obtained the "keys to the corporate palace."

Not quite, she thought to herself. *Our guy merely acquired the padlock and I have the possible keys.* She had received, among other notes, via their representative in Tonopah and his teenage meth-head minion, the one who had rummaged through Dalton Trindall's camper near Tonopah, a notation that said, "Passwords—E-mail is Au-4-me. Computer is jackpot42A17."

Tiponi thought that it would be unlikely that the computer's password, and Dalton's e-mail password, would have gone unchanged. Yet, lazy human nature, and the desire for convenience, often dictated that there was the possibility that either someone forgot to remind him to change his passwords, or that he thought it unnecessary if they had been encrypted. People often took the easier route.

Tiponi thought about what had been said and the notes she had received. She typed in "jackpot42A17" and the computer responded to life by opening to a home page. She was surprised, not really having expected the password to still be in use. Then, holding her breath, she typed in "Au-4-me." Dalton's e-mail account opened on command. Tiponi smiled and then said under her breath to herself, "Jackpot indeed."

CHAPTER 6

Port Ludlow, Washington

I look forward to coming back as soon as I'm gone.

When Sharon Bivens finally heard Dalton Trindall's phone message, she tried to call him back, but his own cell phone was out of range. She left him a message in return, saying that she had received his call. She asked him to try calling her again when he could.

During the past several hours, Bivens had met with her firm's electronics counter surveillance expert at Dalton Trindall's home where she retrieved a key from under the rock in the backyard where Dalton had told her to look. Finding the key was no easy task. Dalton Trindall had deposited hundreds of rocks in the vicinity he had said the key could be found. Geologists hoard rocks. They just can't part with them. Dumping the less desirable specimens around their yards was a common solution for thinning out their collections.

The electronics sweep revealed nothing out of the ordinary and Bivens then sent the expert on to Denver to conduct a sweep of the offices and homes of Mining Engineers, Inc., and its leadership.

At Dalton's invitation, Sharon Bivens stayed over that night in his house, in a guest room, so as to save on expenses that would later be billed to his employer. The next day, she was to let the security alarm system installers into the house to do their work before returning to Seattle.

While in the house, being curious, she opened a few of Dalton's home office desk drawers and thought it odd that there were no files one would routinely keep handy. She wondered if Dalton had removed them to some other part of the house and, if so, a burglar would have come to the same conclusion causing him to extend his search, if that was what he was looking for. Placing dummy or innocuous "red herring" files where files would normally be found would have been preferable. Bivens decided to not mention her observation to Dalton because it would reveal that she had been snooping around in places she had no need to be looking.

Bivens had been running various record checks on what little information she had to go on. She still didn't know who the man and woman were who had been in the car she tailed to and from Kingston a few days earlier. The car, she knew, was registered to The Indian Plight Charity Organization and there was another car, in the charity's name, both with the same Las Vegas address.

While the security alarm system was being installed at Dalton's home, rather than wasting the day, she busied herself doing research on her computer and by making phone calls to find out more about the charity in Las Vegas.

Sharon Bivens found out that the charity had been formed several years earlier and that the organization was headed by a Tiponi Isaw, an apparent Indian name. Bivens wondered if the initials of the first name was a play on the abbreviation or acronym for the charity "TIP" from which the charity name "The Indian Plight" was originally thought of. Usually, Indian names had meanings, like many other languages. Bivens didn't want to waste time trying to find out something likely inconsequential, given the dozens of Native American languages. There were too many variations in both terminology and interpretations used to refer to indigenous people's names.

Bivens read that the charity had a governing board of directors from the charity's website. The information on the charity's only web page was of a routine nature containing information about the work they performed to help the special needs of Native American people at various reservations—helping with diabetes issues due to a poor, high-flour diet that had been encouraged by the US government for decades, the repair of Indian homes, the purchase of hot water heaters, and the like. There was contact information listing the charity's addresses in Las Vegas along with one telephone number with a Las Vegas area code. There was a tab a viewer could click on to donate by credit card. The web page mentioned that the charity had cooperated with, and had close ties to, various reservation tribal councils to help identify the needs and also the needy.

Sharon Bivens was still unsure if perhaps the two people she followed to the local casino had only been there to conduct some sort of charity-related business. She was suspicious, after serving many years in law enforcement. She felt that there was much she didn't know but digging deeply into the charity and its people would take a lot of time and money, both of which she had not been authorized to expend.

Next, Bivens made contact with someone she knew who could do a criminal record check using a government computer and was told that there was no state or federal criminal record for a Tiponi Isaw.

Bivens called her husband to see if he had been able to learn anything about the charity from his former colleagues in the US Bureau of Indian Affairs. A couple of people told him that they had heard of the charity and that it seemed legitimate, from what they knew. Yet there was also the standing rumor that the charity might be involved in some kind of prostitution ring, but her husband had not been able to confirm it. One tribal police officer had said that he heard that the charity tried to help prostitutes leave their profession and had hired one or two former prostitutes who helped with the charity's various works.

Bivens had a friend in the IRS who would only reveal, unofficially, that the charity had filed the required annual reports and that its donations had steadily risen over a few years to just shy of two million dollars in the past year.

Dalton finally called Sharon Bivens back and she gave him a rundown of what she had learned. Dalton reminded her to send an e-mail to Wayde Ramsley containing the same information. He also told her that, in his view, maybe the two people she had followed were only engaging in charity-related work and that maybe they had not actually been following him.

Toward the end of the day, Bivens decided to take a short drive to visit a nearby resort community she had seen advertised on the ferry on her way over from Seattle to Kingston. It was billed as "The Village in the Woods by the Bay," a village called Port Ludlow. She also wanted to visit another town she had never been to before, to the north on the Olympic Peninsula, called Port Townsend, if she had the time. Port Townsend, she had heard, was a wonderful Victorian-era seaport town complete with a huge transient sailor's boatyard, marinas, and a waterfront main street that had many businesses, restaurants, street musicians, an old movie theater preserved in its 1940s original charm, and a playhouse. In certain locations, just off of the main street, there were stairways that led underground to seeming secret places, wine cellars, and restaurants. She had been told that one could walk the waterfront and envision stepping back in time to a century ago. If there was a fog present, the ambiance would feel pronounced.

She drove around Port Ludlow which she noted consisted of lovely homes. The village was well-kept and seemed serene, yet active. As a resort it had two community activity centers for its residents. One was on the water with a view of the towering and majestic Olympic mountain range to the west and the Cascade mountain range to the east on the other side of Puget Sound. The other community center was on a small body of water connecting to the larger bay that seemed to dissect the village into a north side and a south side. A golf course was prominent among other amenities such as a large marina containing private boats and yachts of various sizes.

On the north side of the village, she found a charming waterside inn, a large three-story facility, that had the same views as the nearby north side community center. At the water's edge, she saw a tall, colorful Native American totem pole with a place for visitors to sit and enjoy the scenery.

She decided to park her car at the inn and to go inside, see the facility, and to consider whether it was a place she and her husband might one day want to visit for a weekend getaway. The inn had a small parking lot to accommodate their select thirty-seven rooms, each with an unbelievable view and many with its own private fireplace and seating area. As she pulled into the inn's parking lot, she noticed a white Lexus parked nearby with a Nevada license plate. She checked her notes and was stunned at her luck. The car was the one that was registered to The Indian Plight Charity Organization.

She sat for a while wondering if she should try to find a way to meet the driver of the car. Upon deciding on a course of action, she walked from her car into the inn, went to the front registration desk and said to the clerk, "I was trying to park my car and I tapped another car by mistake and I'd like to let the owner know in case they want my name and insurance information."

The clerk showed a look of concern and asked, "Oh no, which car did you hit?"

"It's a white Lexus out there, off to the left," Bivens said, pointing in the direction where the Lexus was parked. "I have the license plate number if you need it to see if the people are here as guests. Or perhaps they are only here for dinner in your restaurant," she added.

The clerk wrote down the number and told her to feel free to have a seat in one of the lobby's easy chairs while she tried to find out if the car's license plate number was shown on any of their overnight guest's registration cards. If not, she would go to the restaurant and have the staff check with their customers.

Bivens picked up a brochure from the front desk counter-top and slowly walked around the lobby looking at the various gift shop items for sale, including items made by artists who, according to the signage, belonged to the local Port Ludlow Art League.

The desk clerk then said, "I think I found out who the car belongs to. Let me check her room to see if she's there."

Bivens walked back over to the front desk waiting while the clerk dialed a room number. After a moment, the clerk hung up her phone and said that there was no answer. She thanked the clerk for her trouble and said that she would stay for a while and have a drink in their lounge. She tried to compose herself. This was unexpected. An unforeseen opportunity. She mentally noted that the desk clerk had said "Let me check 'her' room," implying that whoever had registered to stay at the inn was a female.

She skipped the idea of having a drink and instead walked around the expansive first floor that had tall windows along two sides from which guests could enjoy the scenery. Off toward the totem pole, near the water's edge, she observed what appeared to be a female walking slowly towards the inn.

As she got closer, Bivens thought that maybe this was the person she had hoped to meet.

Bivens quickly walked back to the main lobby and sat back down on a bench by a fireplace. From her vantage point, she knew she would be partially obscured. The lobby door opened and someone walked in. She heard the desk clerk say, "Excuse me, but do you own a white Lexus?" Bivens craned her neck for a better view of the person in the lobby.

"Yes," said the same lady that Bivens had seen walking towards the inn just a couple of moments earlier.

The desk clerk then said, "I'm sorry, but another lady was just here who said she had an accident with your car and she was—"

Bivens interrupted the desk clerk, as she came away from the fireplace saying, "Yes, that was me." She walked towards the woman, saying, "I'm afraid I tapped your bumper while trying to park my car. I thought I should try to find the owner in case we needed to exchange names for insurance purposes."

The owner of the Lexus quickly asked, "Is it bad? Let's go out and see."

Bivens took the lead by opening the lobby door to the parking lot while escorting the other lady to her car.

The owner of the Lexus was perhaps fifty years old. She was five feet, three or four inches tall, slender, with a pleasing olive-skinned complexion, brown eyes, and a hint of gray in her long black hair which had been pulled back into a pony-tail. She was dressed in dark blue jeans, a long-sleeved white button-down collar shirt with a pendant on a silver necklace around her neck. On her wrists were a silver bangle and a delicate looking, feminine-sized wristwatch.

"I couldn't find any damage but I may have missed some-thing," said Bivens as the two of them got to the car. "I thought

I tapped your bumper, but it could have been the side, I just don't know."

"I don't see any damage," said the Lexus owner.

"I'm terribly sorry. This has never happened to me before," said Bevins.

"Everything looks okay to me," said the car's owner.

"I'm sorry, my name is Sharon Bivens," she said as she stuck out her hand to shake hands with the other woman. "I'm here on business from Seattle," she said, followed by the thought to try to continue to talk about something that is true so as to not slip up and say something that would raise suspicion.

"My name is Tiponi," said the other lady, while shaking Sharon Bivens' hand, apparently not wanting to say her last name.

Bivens quickly replied with a smile, "That's a pretty name."

"Thank you," said Tiponi, returning the smile.

"Do you feel we need to exchange any information? If so, I can write down my name and phone number in case you feel more comfortable having it," said Bivens, hoping that she could get Tiponi to do the same for her thereby providing more personal information, such as a private address or phone number.

"No, it's okay. There isn't any damage. But thank you for wanting to check with me first instead of just driving off," she replied.

Bivens wanted to try to engage Tiponi in more conversation to try learn anything else she could about the woman. "I see you are from Nevada. It's too hot down there this time of the year. I love the summer weather here. It's so much cooler. Where in Nevada?" she skillfully tried to probe.

"Las Vegas," Tiponi replied, then asking "What kind of business are you here for, or is it a vacation?"

"I'm a real estate agent from Seattle where I have clients who want me to line up some homes for them to visit and see sometime in the next week. They don't want me to take up their time by taking them from house to house that hasn't been previewed, trying to sell them something that doesn't fit their criteria. Anyway, for now they prefer to remain anonymous. I've known them for a long time. I know what they want. I can filter out the houses that don't fit their criteria. How about you?" Sharon Bivens asked.

"I work with a charity and come here maybe once every month or two. Sometimes I stay here in Port Ludlow. I love it here," Tiponi said. "I hate leaving every time I do. I look forward to coming back as soon as I'm gone."

"Is there a mister ah, how should I say it...are you alone? Can I offer you a drink inside? I don't want to take you away from whatever you were doing."

"No, no, I usually come up here by myself. Thank you for the offer but I need to get to my room to do a little work." Tiponi reached out to shake Bivens hand, thanked her for her concern and courtesy, then turned away and walked back towards the inn's lobby doors.

Tiponi Isaw wanted to get back to her room and to the stolen laptop computer that had been relayed to her, the one for which she hoped she held the password keys, so long as the passwords remained unchanged.

PART 2

CHAPTER 7

Denver, Colorado

Damage control.

Wayde Ramsley had been sitting at his desk when Alice Harrison barged into his office with a look of urgency on her face. She didn't display the usual professional calm she was known for and Wayde focused on her, threw himself back further into his leather swivel desk chair, and prepared himself for something that intuitively told him that she had bad news.

"Dalton Trindall's laptop computer was stolen from his vehicle, at a truck stop, I think, in Elko," she blurted out. Alice paused for an inordinately long moment. It was one of those "pregnant pauses," a moment of silence while she waited for her words to sink in, while she prepared to continue speaking.

"His laptop has Project X information in it, in his e-mails, his geo notes to himself, and God knows what else," she continued.

Wayde's expression slowly turned from one of preparing himself for some sort of unwanted news to one of slowly rising disbelief, followed by a look of questions forming in his mind as his eyes strayed from Alice towards anything else in his office, then by the look of anger as he refocused his eyes on Alice.

"And did they find it? I mean, does he know who took it? Did the cops catch the guy?" he hurriedly asked, searching for the right way of expressing his hope that this travesty might have a happy ending.

"No," was all she said.

"And if some person who took it then keeps it or sells it to someone else, can they get access to the information," he asked, now sitting on the edge of his chair, leaning forward, his head almost halfway over the top of his desk.

Alice explained, "The password is encrypted. Some specialist could break the code but those kinds of people are rare. Someone would have to have a reason to want to find an expert who could discover the password so that they could gain access to the information. The laptop is worth maybe fifty dollars to whoever would want to sell it. It wouldn't be worth the cost to have someone skilled break the code. They could buy a new laptop for that kind of money."

"Do we know who has the password?" he asked, now a bit less alarmed.

"No, I mean, I'm not sure. Dalton's not married. He doesn't have a need to share his computer with someone else. He probably is the only one who knows it," Alice said. "He bought a new one and I helped him install the needed software programs. He's up and running again but he no longer has all the data he had stored about his findings, a lot of data about soil sample locations, GPS locations for perhaps thousands of samples. Stuff like that. I got Stu to download all the data he had regarding this information from our backup data storage service. We can send it all to Dalton on a disc so he can reinstall the records and files that had been automatically captured and sent to our service in case it was ever needed."

"Do you have any reason to think that Project X will be compromised?" Wayde asked, thinking out loud.

"You have this private investigation and security outfit looking at some issues that you and Dalton have been talking about. They came here and searched for any bugging equipment. They didn't find anything. You would know more about all the reasons for concern than any of us. Is there something I don't know? Maybe a connection? Could the laptop have been stolen by someone who wants to learn what we are doing? Maybe some corporate espionage?"

Wayde wondered about Alice's questions. It had to be weighed, considered, and couldn't be dismissed, even if only a remote possibility. "Let me think about this for a while," he said while rubbing his temples with both hands as if a headache was setting in. "Is there anything else you can tell me?" he asked in finalizing the conversation.

"No, that's it," she responded. "I can't think of anything else."

Alice turned and walked back out of Wayde Ramsley's office. Wayde turned himself around in his leather swivel desk chair to face the window behind him. He slumped back into the chair and gazed somewhere out beyond at nothing in particular as he pondered the news and its much greater significance. Could Project X be discovered and compromised? Could a competitor have hired people to try to find out what his company was up to? What were the options? What should he do, if anything? Should they continue as they had been, as if nothing would change their strategy? What if the data was accessed? What would be the consequences... The endless questions came one after the other as he rubbed his temples once again, deep in thought. By now his head was throbbing.

A while later, he stepped outside his office door and asked his secretary-receptionist to call each of his company's board members in whatever order she could get them on the phone. "Tell them, or whoever you get a hold of, that it is urgent that I talk to them as soon as possible."

Wayde described to each board member the incident that had happened along with the various incidents, which he still choose to call "coincidences" when describing the sequence of suspicious events. He explained that it was possible that some kind of corporate spying was going on and asked each member for their opinion on what their Mining Engineers Company should do, if anything. The plethora of options he provided them ranged from doing nothing on the one end of possibilities to the extreme and more complicated option of moving the company to another location and changing its name, web page, phone number, and a host of other matters. He asked whether they felt that "damage control" was in order or not.

One board member had added to the range of options offered by Ramsley, the option of shutting down everything, and for good, as if nothing had existed. Another felt that nothing could be done if Project X was fully exposed, that it was "game over," as he said. The others opted for putting a brand new face on the initiative, like a submarine hiding under "deep cover," to dive down, so to speak, to go "silent," and hide everything they were attempting to do better than they had done previously. The submarine metaphor was characteristic for the board member mentioning it. He had been a naval officer in his younger years and seemed to enjoy bringing up his military experience in justifying one position or another.

He decided to dispense with the usual corporate protocol of holding a formal board meeting to make a decision. Instead, he felt circumstances compelled him to proceed with a command performance, one which required quick and decisive action. After pondering each member's suggestions, he thought that the string of small coincidences coupled with the theft of a computer containing detailed information about their operation could jeopardize their project. He couldn't take the chance that nothing further would occur. He had to assume that jeopardy was already in motion and that evasive defensive action was the safer approach to take, even though the decision would require a huge effort by all who were employed by Mining Engineers.

Wayde Ramsley was a man who would only take chances, and assume risk, if it seemed reasonable and necessary to do so. He knew that nothing concrete about a corporate espionage effort, or any other scenario, had been presented to him, and nor by him, in turn, to the board. Yet, he had to maintain secrecy, at almost, but not all, cost. He would risk losing the majority of the board's support if Project X was fully discovered and if he had done nothing about it when he had the chance. Secondly, he risked the board voting to terminate the project in its entirety.

His position was one that was not unusual in his industry in that he got paid by other mining companies to oversee an exploration effort in what is referred to as a joint venture or a JV. If the joint venture was dissolved by those who ultimately paid the bills for Mining Engineers, Inc., his income would come to an end. Then again, he knew, the project could be voted to be terminated anyway if sufficient and convincing data failed to support the existence of what they had set out to prove.

As CEOs of individual publicly held mining companies, the board members would be assuming a significant burden one day for themselves and for their shareholders by committing huge sums of money to implementing Project X's phase two. It could cost hundreds of millions of dollars to take control over major segments of a land mass stretching from Mexico to Canada.

The model for the execution of the plan, it had been agreed by the board, would be to then proceed with a massive drilling program. It would be done at select locations in a concentrated fashion to sufficiently prove the value of the gold in the ground. Then, for each zone drilled, they hoped to sell off a percentage of each zone created. They hoped to keep a smaller percentage for their own company and to receive royalties for each ounce of gold recovered by their joint venture partners. This phase, the board had decided, would be privately referred to in-house as Operation Tera. It was a reference to the prefix in the international system of units denoting "one trillion." The number one trillion was thought to be a minimum possible dollar value of their new intercontinental, record-breaking, gold-bearing Mega Trend. The name "Mega Trend" would become their brand name for their discovery. One for the history books, if everything they were working on came to pass.

Wayde Ramsley's headache had subsided but the day's unfolding drama, coupled with the migraine he had endured, left him worn out. The implementation of a significant change in their corporate profile would have to wait for the next day. The added time for decision making and developing a list of things that would have to be accomplished would allow for some creative thinking time. In the interim, board members could stew over what he had discussed with them. He would send them an e-mail early the next morning with his decision to give Mining Engineers a makeover, a change of appearance, making it unrecognizable from what it was to something new.

The next day, after board members had been informed, Ramsley called a meeting with his staff who were appalled at the undertaking they were presented with. He never wavered as protests were raised, road blocks were erected, and seemingly intractable issues were discussed. A list of things that would need to be accomplished was lengthy and the staff was sent off to the boardroom to work with each other in completing the list of required tasks, all of which were to be accomplished within thirty days.

saw gold specs and flakes ranging in size from microscopic to being large enough to see with the naked eye.

Of added benefit, a string of sequential assays for one particular mile-long area indicated a very high concentration of silver. Although not as profitable as gold per ounce, silver could, and in this case did, exceed the value of the gold that seemed to be present. The silver concentration was of such quantity that the silver's mineable value could be superior to the gold that had been also found present in the very same samples.

There was a huge bonus waiting for a company that would one day mine the area. Bergman felt that the general five mile-long stretch of land containing the rich silver and gold samples could possibly support the operation of a medium-sized mine for at least two or three decades. He circled the area on a map with his pen. He intended to take the map to show to Ramsley. If his company filed claims in all promising locations, then this area in particular should be singled out as a place to concentrate drilling operations.

Bergman knew that the most promising claim areas needed to be proven to such an extent that the areas would be desirable for negotiating either a joint venture arrangement with, or an outright sale to, some other mining company. Aside from cash up front, there would be royalties going to Bergman's employer and the companies that were putting up the money for the ongoing border-to-border preliminary exploration effort. It wouldn't take long for the investing companies, represented by members of his board, to recoup their original investments. Indeed, perhaps they would bid on some of the land for their own companies. If so, they would have to resign from their Denver-based exploration company's board so as to not engage in a conflict of interest. There was always one other possibility, and that would be for the board to set up its own mining operations which, if done, would take a very significant commitment by those companies represented by the board's members. They could not move slowly in either case because of the requirement for an annual payment fee for each and every claim. The ongoing costs of holding all of the possible claims indefinitely would likely eventually prove cost prohibitive.

The best approach, Bergman and Ramsley knew, would be to drill, identify major deposits in the most promising locations, and sell or lease a portion or all of that land. They would want to also create a stream of income for the exploration company. Any such joint venture or sale would require the new partner or purchaser of an area to pay an annual fee for each delayed year the explorer did not receive their royalty income from production. It was a fail-safe method, one used by a few other successful discoverers. Find the metal, sell or lease out the claims. Require the buyer to pay a fair price up front, and also require them to pay an annual fee until they could pay a royalty for each ounce of refined precious metal they produced.

Bergman had tried to calculate the potential for this entire project if everything fell into place for them. He, along with others, had surmised that it was possible that the metal in the ground to the north and the south of the Carlin Trend could one day be valued in the trillions of dollars.

Wayde Ramsley had wondered if the Chinese government's sovereign investment corporation would be interested in buying out Mining Engineers, Inc., soon to be known as Consultants International. He intended to try for the easier route of dealing with but one possible partner or buyer. The news of his company's discovery, when made public, would rocket around the world in less than an hour of it being announced. Wayde thought it worth a try to sell Consultants

International and its border-to-border string of claims, before any drilling, and attendant expense, was initiated.

It was unlikely that any individual existing mining company could afford to buy the company and its claims in its entirety. They could do so if many of them formed their own consortium, pooled their resources, and incorporated as if one.

Perhaps the Chinese would sell a lot of their US bond holdings and instead invest in the new Mega Trend Wayde Ramsley was leading the discovery of. They could sign a non-disclosure agreement, be thoroughly briefed, and then be given time to consider their interest. The price would be steep but much less than the sum that could be accumulated from selling off parcels to multiple buyers over a period of several years.

Surely the Chinese government knew that the two trillion dollars of US bonds they held would decline in value once interest rates began to rise again. Their bond investment could perhaps decline in value to only one trillion dollars over the next decade or two. There was already talk of the Chinese government beginning to unload some of their bonds in favor of more wisely using the money to buy up various commodities, metals, chemicals, coal, and precious metals, all of which would increase in value quite significantly as opposed to the US bonds they held, which would lose value. Conversely, any amount they invested in the Mega Trend discovery could increase in value in multiple ways. Gold alone was expected to triple in value over the next few years. Their return on investment could turn out to be one of the wisest investments made by a government in over a century. Simultaneously, Consultants International could secure an unimaginable return on their own expenses up to this point. Then there was also the lip smacking fees and royalties they could receive for decades. The notion of dealing with the Chinese government was worth pursuing.

It was a long shot, but then again so was everything being attempted by explorers and miners everywhere. Chances were taken and failures or successes were the result. The newly named Consultants International was getting closer with each passing week to eventually becoming well-known, especially in the worldwide investment, precious metals, mining, and commodity communities. Wayde's company would be the envy of governments everywhere. The revenue in profits and taxes they could derive from within a "safe geographical location" would have only been exceeded perhaps by all the oil in the usually violent, hostile, and unpredictable Middle East.

As was the usual case in the mining industry, chances had to be taken from time to time, sometimes significant ones. It was always a roll of the dice. In order to try to interest possible buyers or very significant potential partners, sometimes a mining company had to take the chance of exposing some of what they were working on in order to sell or acquire a partner, if the profit margin at stake was worth the risk. The board of directors had considered and approved Wayde Ramsley's suggestion that they make contact with the Chinese government to see if there might be any genuine interest in buying out Consultant's International. Ramsley had made a request to meet with China's ambassador and his economic development liaison, briefly describing the significant reason why. He had yet to hear back from the Chinese embassy.

CHAPTER 8

Las Vegas, Nevada

So live your life so the fear of death
can never enter your heart.

New e-mail instructions pertaining to the new corporate "cover" were sent from the Denver headquarters to the eleven field geologists. The one who had taken sick was back at work and a new highly-acclaimed geologist had been hired from Alaska who would be reporting to Denver for a complete briefing of his duties and then on to his geographical area of focus within a month. Simultaneously, Tiponi Isaw, from her Las Vegas condominium, smiled at how the ongoing flow of information, which she was reading from Dalton Trindall's stolen laptop computer, could be used by her. She had an insider's vantage point from which she could monitor the new Consultants International inner workings.

Although vague at this early juncture, she was beginning to formulate possibilities for how she and her staff could capitalize on the Consultants International goal, if ever achieved. It was a long-range possibility which she knew could falter and fail, as many exploration endeavors often do. She knew that whatever plan she decided upon might require the involvement and assistance of her wide ranging contacts in Native American reservations and communities within some of the western states.

Isaw's condo doorbell rang and she knew that it would be her charity's vice chairman, Tony Rappaport, who was expected for the purpose of briefing her with updates on the various activities their people were working on or had completed. Rappaport was the only person who worked for her who had ever been allowed to visit Isaw at her home. He was her most trusted subordinate. On occasion he had accompanied her on her visits to meet with various Native Americans and tribal leaders when personally delivering checks to them for charitable needs that she had said she would try to fulfill. Tiponi Isaw was seen as caring and reliable, a woman of her word, who almost always was able to deliver on her promises to help with one need or another. Some of her recipients' needs were small and easy to satisfy, while others required larger sums of money and a longer period of time before the required funds could be obtained and disbursed by their benefactor.

Tony Rappaport gave Tiponi a brief hug and sat down in a chair across from her in her living room. He retrieved from his pocket a list of matters he wanted to inform her of, a list which would be destroyed once the briefing was finished. The list simply had key words to help jog Tony's memory about the matters he wanted to address. This was done so that there would be no paper or electronic record of the operations the charity was working on.

"Tell me first an update on the number of casinos in our areas of interest," Tiponi asked. She had wanted to learn which reservations were financially doing very well as a result of their growing businesses. Revenue from certain casinos would allow those well-off reservations to be able to take care of their own people's needs. Those that were not doing as well were the ones she needed to direct her charity's funds to.

"The number has grown since I last checked for you. There are now one hundred and fifty-eight of them. Five are in Nevada, sixty-eight in California, only seven for Idaho, Arizona's added a couple for twenty-five, Oregon has ten, Washington thirty-two, and there are still only eleven in New Mexico. That's one hundred and fifty-eight, or about 33 percent of them out of a total of four hundred and seventy in the US," Tony recited from his notes. "I was also able to find out that in the US, the total gross income for the Native American casinos was about thirty billion dollars last year but the profit was far less because of expenses and payouts to lucky visitors. There are some small casino operations that are unable to meet their expenses. And then there are those that are so profitable they are talking about extending their Native American-owned holdings to as far east as India itself. They want the Taj Mahal," Tony said, making a small joke.

Tiponi showed her unamusement when she replied, "And the Europeans thought they had discovered India when they landed here in North America. They named us Indians because of it. And the name stuck."

"Even we use it," Tony said.

"Yes, we both know how tragic that acceptance is. I think the joke's on us. They have our people calling themselves Indians instead of Native Americans who were from western Asia before that," she said as she got up from her sofa to pour two cups of coffee in her kitchen.

"As you know better than anyone, we have contacts on many of our reservations in the states we are in," Tiponi continued. "And we have had dealings in many of those Native American and local communities. But we can't expand anymore then we have. We lose control if we get too big. We could draw attention to ourselves if we spread ourselves too thin and start making mistakes. Our board members have to keep a close watch on their people. No one should cross the line we set for them. No one!" she reiterated with emphasis.

"Our field lieutenants know our instructions. They are reminded, every chance I get, to tell their people what is allowed and what isn't," Tony replied.

"Sometimes I feel as though we don't have enough control and that we don't know what we should know. We can't cover all the bases. The costs have gone up some and the gift giving we do doesn't stretch as far as I wish it would. Maybe we need to do more corporate stuff," she thought out loud.

"Like the one we are working on with those Denver people?" Tony Rappaport asked.

"That's different. Really different. I call it 'Operation Jackpot,' if it works out. But that may be a long ways off, if we get to work it at all. But, yes, like that one but on a smaller scale. Like the one I think you plan to tell me more about this morning," Tiponi Isaw instructed.

"The one in Bakersfield?" he asked.

"Yes, like that one. We need to do more. My contacts on reservations need to keep their eyes and ears open to any possibility to get businesses to contribute to the fund."

The two continued to talk about shake-down opportunities, extortions for money, the legal kind that are done routinely by certain African American civil rights leaders involving businesses. Their discussion went on for several minutes. Then Tiponi said, "Okay, let's get to some of the specific incidents."

Tiponi Isaw at one time had to rely on sex for her livelihood. She had been young, unmarried, uneducated, and with no decent source of income. She learned the brothel business from the ground up, both literally and figuratively. Her current operation was no less than a multistate mobile enterprise and her field people were the equivalent of pimps with a grudge. They enjoyed catching people wanting to pay for sex, and pay they did. But there was a limit to which the chairwoman would go. The female, and the occasional male prostitutes, had to be ones who had been looking for "pleasure" without the expectation for a stated specific compensation. They were found by way of the personal ads they had placed expressing their own desire for friendship, love, romance, encounters, and casual sex, of which there were many. The people who placed such ads were approached by the charity's people. Some were found willing to make money for their pleasures. But once a particular location yielded the right person who they could employ, then the organization often placed their own advertisements looking to entice customers who, depending on their stature in life, they would target. Some ads, they learned, yielded potential customers who turned out to be undesirables, losers, even penniless perverts. Other advertisements, if worded right, resulted in encounters with gentlemen or gentlewomen, ones who often had money, a private business or home life they wanted to protect, yet were eager for a no-strings-attached rendezvous with someone who they could "join up with" with from time to time.

"As you know, some of the ads don't get us the right kind of customer," Tony Rappaport said as he went on giving examples. "'Married, thirtyish, looking for evening fun.' 'Insomniac seeks nighttime pal, your place or mine. Must be clean. No drugs, please. A little pot is okay.' 'Single and twenty-seven, looking for occasional partner. No fatties please. Weekend fun guaranteed.' 'New to SF, horny and no boyfriend—yet, send pic and I'll do the same. I'm sexy and looking for Mr. Stud.' 'Looking for a workout and party buddy, anything goes once I get to know you. Well-shaved and ready to romp only,' and 'Slender, sexy lady to love another, male or female, any age possible.'"

Tony went on to say, "And then there are the ads that seem to draw the better clients, the ones who might be Mr. or Ms. Success, or Moneybags. The ads used words that might eliminate some of the less well-off responding possibilities in favor of those who might be able to better fund the charity. 'Looking for someone willing to take me to special places, away from here, romance possible. Gentlemen over fifty only, please.' 'Occasional love partner wanted. I'm very married, looking for same. No commitments. Hope you are the same.'

"Here are some that seem to draw in the best customers, it paints the picture that our lady is seemingly harmless, not a threat, and yet titillating,

'In my thirties, love-starved, marriage not working, will meet only at the best of hotels. I have my favorites I'd like to visit here or elsewhere. You pick. Anything goes. Weekend retreat if you are Mr. Right. Can meet somewhere you and I both like for champagne.' 'Busy student, for one-time vacation in Hawaii or Cabo, share bed and breakfast literally, I want to be treated like royalty,' and 'Transgender, twenties, male or female, one on one only, rendezvous in style a must, no public appearances, please be intellectual, successful, and must be discreet.'"

Tony added, "I'll make sure that our board members thoroughly understand what works and what doesn't. We waste too much time and effort on the sleazes who want something for nothing, can't pay up, and have nothing to hide. I stress again and again that our marks have to have a reason to want to keep their liaisons secret, ones that would have something to lose if their tryst is ever discovered by friends, coworkers, or family members."

Next, Tony Rappaport went into detailed descriptions of some of their recent success stories as they unfolded.

In Portland, Gene Clayborne saw an advertisement in one of the many publications he liked to review. It was under the personal ads section and it said, "If you like big-time cards at the casino, so do I. I'm youngish, pretty, and available for a weekend stay while hubby is away." Clayborne answered the AD. He enjoyed occasionally visiting a blackjack table and he would more often than not lose a thousand in an evening as opposed to winning. He wasn't what the casinos would call a high roller, but his presence often resulted in a notice being mailed to his residence inviting him for a free weekend for two at the casino's motel, complete with a fifty-dollar credit for the gaming table of his choice.

Clayborne was anxious to use the offer that would expire in the next few weeks. He was a manager of a large bank in Portland and he had money to spare. The lady who had placed the advertisement answered Gene Clayborne back saying she could meet him for a drink at a local well-known upscale lounge. They met and the discussion that ensued convinced the girl, only known to him as Ellen, that Clayborne would make a good target. On his part, Gene Clayborne saw only a very pretty lady close to his age, in her late thirties, who was a delight to talk to and who had a sense of humor he seldom experienced from anyone who worked in the humorless suite of offices that surrounded him. He was balding, chubby looking, but engaging. He had a kind of self-assurance about himself, but one with vulnerabilities.

A date was set for the following Friday, when Clayborne could make excuses for being away on a fishing trip. Ellen had said that her husband would be away on business. Ellen met her man at a casino in eastern Oregon, one with a large motel complex attached to it. They checked in, went to their room and Clayborne immediately suggested a nap before they went down to the casino. Ellen, being wise enough to know better, suggested that they have a couple of drinks, a steak dinner, and try their luck at blackjack before calling it a night. She asked him to stake her for a thousand dollars for her to play with at the table next to the one he would play at.

Clayborne hesitated and said, "How about five hundred?" to which she agreed with a big smile.

"Come on," she expertly said. "Let's go have some fun before we have some real fun."

Ellen bet very small amounts and was able to pocket close to four hundred dollars when she left her table and joined Gene Clayborne at his. She put her arm around him and simply said, "I lost."

Clayborne replied, "I'm ahead here. Do you want to play some more while I finish?"

"Sure," she beamed as she made a few dance-like moves with her feet, indicating her excitement and that she was having fun.

Clayborne handed her five hundred more dollars, this time in "chips" from in front of him. "Go play," he said with a smile as the blackjack dealer asked him if he wanted another card or if he wanted to stay, the term used for not wanting another card.

Ellen managed to pocket another three hundred and fifty dollars in chips into her purse. They were hers, for sure. They had been given to her to play cards with. But she wasn't playing cards with all of the money. Nor did she win anything, other than the cash she had not lost at the gaming table. She reported back to Claiborne that she didn't want to waste anymore of his money. "I never learned to play well. I lose more than I win. I think I'll quit," wanting Clayborne to think that she wasn't just out to fleece him for money to support a gambling habit in exchange for sex.

Later that evening, they crawled into bed and after a brief interlude, they both fell asleep exhausted. The next morning while Clayborne was taking a shower, Ellen called her local overseer, who had been nearby all evening, listening to Ellen's conversations through a listening device she had worn for the occasion. The electronic device served two purposes. One was to keep track of any financial matter he needed to make note of as well as to protect his employee, Ellen. He had driven back to his own home after Ellen and her mark had called it a night. He was on his way back to the casino the next morning for the final act, the grand performance he knew was coming, when Ellen called him on his cell phone. She hurriedly told him that they'd be going down to the restaurant in about an hour. She reminded him that her love buddy was named Gene Clayborne and where he worked and what he did for a living.

About an hour later, Ellen and her mark entered the hotel restaurant. Seated at a table inside was Ellen's controller, sitting with another man. Ellen froze in place with horror on her face.

"What's wrong?" Clayborne asked.

"My husband is over there. Oh, no, he just saw me. He's getting up. Let's leave, quick," she exclaimed in a terrifying whisper. Ellen and Clayborne headed towards an exterior exit to the restaurant. She gasped "Oh, God," as she led him out the side door onto the casino parking lot a hundred yards away from the front doors and other people.

"Ellen," her purported husband said angrily, as if in shock, from behind them.

Ellen turned, and as her husband approached, he said, "Caught you a second time. No more. It's finished. You're out on your own."

"And what were *you* doing here?" she asked. "With another man no less," she added, hoping to shift the accusatory stage of the incident away from her to her supposed husband.

"Don't bother coming home," he hissed between his teeth. He quickly added, "Who's this piece of shit?"

Ellen turned in the opposite direction, grabbing and cling-
ing to Clayborne's arm while quickly walking further out into
the casino parking lot.

"Don't worry," she said while looking straight ahead, "I
won't ever tell him who you are."

Clayborne looked as if someone was about to shout from
the rooftops who he was and, worse, where he worked.

"What should we do?" he asked in a breathless manner, as
if as worried about himself as much or more than he was worried about his new paramour.

"You just go home. Stay out of this. This is my problem.
Not yours. I don't want you to have to get involved. Here's my
business card," she said as she reached into her purse, containing the previous night's casino chips. "I want to see you again,
if you feel the same," Ellen added.

"I mean, what will you do?" Clayborne asked as he turned
towards her after reaching her car, while she rummaged
through her purse looking for her car keys.

"I can't go home. Not now anyways. He has our checkbook and I accidentally left my credit cards in my wallet in
my other purse. He won't let me in the house, I know. He has
a violent temper. I don't know what to do," she said, looking
lost, scared, and exasperated. "I don't want to tell any of our
friends so I can't stay with any of them."

"Do you want some money to hold you over for a while?"
he asked, hoping to win over her silence and weak loyalty, for
whatever it was worth. Maybe they could meet up again, he
wondered, as she said, "How much can you spare? I might
have to stay in a motel and get some clothes and stuff until
I work this out with my husband or get a lawyer to help me
access our money and my things."

Clayborne hesitated for a second, thought about the
amount of money he had in his wallet, wondered how much it

might cost him to ensure Ellen's silence and a possible future meeting, maybe at the motel she would go to. Before he could answer her question, she said, "I'm not staying in a flea bag motel. I'll pay you back once I get my checkbook, my money. I don't know how long that'll take. Can you spare a couple of thousand for motel and food?" she asked pleadingly, looking him in his eyes while stepping closer to him.

Clayborne stuttered for a moment, thinking quickly about all he had at stake if this incident ever became known.

"I–I don't know," he replied while opening his wallet. "Let me see…"

Ellen knew that her mark could begin to have second thoughts so she quickly added, "If I need to get a hold of you, should I call you at the bank or maybe at some other number?"

That one comment sealed his decision. He didn't want to have Ellen call him at the bank. Not ever. "Yes, I have it. Here's a couple thousand."

Ellen took the cash and affectionately hugged him, briefly kissed him on the lips, and said thank you.

The crisis seemed to be over. Both Gene Clayborne and what he thought was his newly acquired mistress parted, each by way of their own cars, he in his Mercedes and she in her less expensive Nissan Altima, a car that spoke good taste but not luxury.

Ellen circled the parking lot while Clayborne drove off. He might be good for some more money in a few days, she thought. For now she had to get back to her controller who had acted out his role, as her shattered husband, like a Broadway star.

"Well?" he asked. "Good job, Ellen," he said with a smile. "Let's divvy up the money. I calculate seven hundred and fifty dollars in cash and chips from inside the casino last night, and two thousand this morning. You take your 10 percent and

I'll take mine." Her pimp would later report the details of the scam and funnel the remaining couple of thousand dollars back through his channels to The Indian Plight Charity. There were bills to be paid by the charity before dispersing what remained to Native American causes. The recipients of dispersed donations never knew anything other than there had been donations made to the charity from which they, to varying degrees, benefited.

"Then there was that operation in San Diego," Tony Rappaport continued, as the chairwoman poured them each another cup of coffee…

Wealthy retired entrepreneur George Vitterson, a strong looking, physically fit man in his fifties, had sailed his forty-eight-foot sailboat from his Hawaiian oceanfront condominium and docked it at a marina in San Diego. He was a bit of a recluse, preferring no social life or a steady partner with whom he could share his significant fortune and life. He made the mistake of wanting some male companionship while staying in southern California. He preferred younger, effeminate looking men for hookups of short duration.

Vitterson placed an AD in a local periodical advertising, "Wanted, twenty-something, hang out, watch movie, maybe more, sail my yacht, and rub downs."

The charity's local contact had just the right person respond to the AD with his picture and an offer to meet at a restaurant or park. Vitterson took his time in replying, apparently reviewing his options after having received eager responses from other young men of the same persuasion. Their guy, known as Jerome, won the selection process, met with Vitterson and was invited for a brief tour of Vitterson's yacht. Jerome was a cautious, but at times flamboyant, submissive-acting, athletic-looking man, well-dressed, effervescent in demeanor, with an easy personality, one that made establishing such a liaison less stressful.

Jerome had noted the name painted on the stern of Vitterson's yacht and reported it, and other information he had learned from Vitterson, to his handler.

The yacht's name, *Rapture*, was possibly indicative of a religious connotation or perhaps a deeper, more personal infatuation with unspoken desires. Jerome's handler had done an internet check on the boat and on George Vitterson and found that his name had appeared in a published article as a board member of a nationally recognized church organization. Board members of churches serve on governing bodies and are held to a higher standard than the people of the church's congregation. They are the people who help to ensure the final and ultimate accountability of a church and its intended ministry. The charity's pimp reported to the charity's hierarchy the developing operation and asked if they should merely focus on the seedy side of the upcoming expected sexual encounter or to hit the mark up for money for the charity.

The charity's board member for the southern California region had replied with "both," so the operation was to take the form of obtaining money from George Vitterson for whatever sexual liaison that ensued. However, it was possible he would not succumb to personal embarrassment or fear because the man was wealthy, independent, unmarried, and a loner for the most part. His sexual preferences were not so unusual, given the changing times so much so as to cause the usual case of conscience that accompanied such episodes. But he did have something to hide or lose. And that was his reputation with the church, its leaders, and pastor, and the congregation. The Catholic Church had experienced similar issues as a result of the many reported sexual incidents committed by its priests. The church, on the other hand, had been slow to remedy its embarrassing nightmares. It was commonplace for them to try to hide such affairs with skill and foot dragging, fearing their own reputation and legal consequences. Malicious whispers would reduce Sunday service attendance and commensurately lighten the weekly collection plates.

The sting was carefully planned and initiated. George Vitterson had his romp with Jerome and he paid Jerome for the intimate encounter.

After Jerome had left Vitterson's yacht for the last time, a man approached Vitterson while he was lounging under an umbrella at the marina's water side beach.

"I'm Jerome's father," lied the pimp. "My son told me about what you did to him. I won't bore you with the salacious details. You already know them. We have two choices. We can either go to the authorities or go to the church that you are a board member of. If you get up and walk away, or sail away, thinking that will end this, you'll be wrong. I'll take this to the highest levels of whoever will listen to me. We either settle this here and now or I will take revenge in every manner possible. Leave, and I will bring you down. Stay, and let's talk about what you can do to resurrect yourself.

Vitterson, being seasoned at negotiating business deals, ever poker faced while doing so, quickly calculated the situation he now found himself in and said, "What do you want?"

"My son wants to finish college. I can't afford to pay for it. You pay for it and I'll walk away. You'll never see me or Jerome again."

Vitterson recognized what was at stake. He could easily just resign from the church's board and the sexual liaison might not be exploitable. Yet, there was the country club he belonged to in Hawaii and the board he also belonged to for a corporation that paid him one hundred thousand dollars a year essentially for the use of his name and reputation.

Vitterson thought about his two daughters and his son from a prior long-ended marriage. They had grandchildren. What if this guy standing before him went so far as to try to tell as many people as he could?

Jerome's pimp, acting as his father, added for insurance, "You have family and income elsewhere, I know."

Vitterson winced. The poker face had shown that the pimp had hit a raw nerve, that there was family he did not want to embarrass or alienate. They were members of the church of which he was a board member.

Vitterson loosened up his tough stance and asked with a smile, "So what are you thinking of? How much will this college education cost me, if I pay it?

"You can give Jerome cash or a check for fifteen thousand dollars. Or you can go to hell. And I will help you get there."

Vitterson didn't know if it was being suggested that violence was being insinuated at or if Jerome's father was merely saying that he would move heaven and earth to ruin him.

"And," Jerome's fake father continued, "if you want to make me happy, you can add a little bit more. You can afford it. You'll never miss it. You're worth millions. You know it and I know it. Save yourself a whole lot of trouble. I can become your worst nightmare or I can go away with your cash or check in hand. Nightmare over. Finished. And I never want you to ever try to contact my son again."

Tony Rappaport told Tiponi Isaw that Vitterson had written a check for seventeen thousand dollars instead of the suggested fifteen. After paying for their people's work, to the tune of a total of 20 percent, ten for Jerome and ten for his pimp, the charity would be receiving the balance in cash.

"What's more," Tony said with a sly smile on his face, "our guy had also demanded that Vitterson send a check to *our* favorite charity, The Indian Plight Charity Organization. We suggested a tax deductible gift of a couple of thousand, to pay penitence and to assuage his conscience, for seducing an innocent young man on the boat he had the gall to call *Rapture*."

"Good, good. We need more like that one. How many more do you have for me?" asked Tiponi Isaw.

"A couple of others this week, but I'll keep it short and tell you about the one in Bakersfield," Tony Rappaport replied.

"Go ahead," Tiponi said, looking tired and distracted by something else that was on her mind.

Tony said, "In Bakersfield, a company that had just built an office complex for about four hundred new employees had not hired any native Americans that anyone knew of. Our representative was instructed to visit the senior manager, if she could get in to see him, and to bring with her several Native American-looking supporters."

"How did we know for sure that they had not hired any Native Americans?" Tiponi asked. "Seems hard to know for sure."

"We got a list of nearby Native Americans who had applied from a local reservation. Fourteen had applied. Fourteen did not get hired," Tony answered. "They had been referred from the reservation's unemployment office."The business oversees an interstate transportation fleet of trucks for transporting shipments. They also coordinate train car shipments and some air cargo transports from places as far away as the east coast. It took only one visit to see the regional manager. He was told that his company had ignored the employment applications of dozens of Native Americans. He was gently told that, although he might not have been aware of it, Native Americans had been discriminated against because of their race and culture. The regional director vowed an internal inquiry to try to identify if the allegation was accurate and, if so, he would personally remedy it.

"Our rep told him that she had three requests of the company. One was that at least 20 percent of their truck drivers were to be Native Americans and that was to be accomplished within three years. Second, that he would agree to hire a discrimination sensitivity training firm to put on a seminar for all of his supervisors and managers to be done in ninety days. Lastly, he was asked to donate one hundred thousand dollars to a certain Native American charity. Failure to agree would result in the swooping in of busloads of Native American demonstrators who would stay in front of their building until the remedies had been agreed to in writing. Television cameras would arrive and a press release would go out on the internet and to news organizations in the US, Russia, China, Canada, Mexico, and elsewhere announcing the demonstration and the reasons for it.

"The company regional manager thought about it for a moment and asked our representative if she could wait out in the conference room. He then called his company's vice-president who asked him to tell the representative that the training would be done, through her charity, the number of eventual replacement truck drivers could only be 10 percent of their total truck driver personnel, but over a period of five years, and the contribution would have to be limited to the amount he had the authority to sign off on, being twenty five thousand dollars. The representative was to sign an agreement stipulating to all of the terms. Lastly, their legal counsel would have to have the signature of the nearest local tribal official who could also agree to the conditions."

Tony finished by saying that the sensitivity training to be provided would be worth about an additional twelve thousand five hundred dollars minus expenses.

"It never ceases to amaze me the lengths people will go to get themselves out of the trouble they got themselves into," Tiponi said.

Tony folded up his note papers and put them into his pocket as he said goodbye to Tiponi.

She sat on her sofa for a while thinking about how the sums of money that were accumulated were quickly dispersed almost as quickly as they had been received. It was an insufficient amount, she knew, for the much greater needs of the Paiute, the Navajo, the Shoshone in Idaho, the Winnemucca, Snohomish, the Apache, and so many others who could use a helping hand for those who were poor and destitute on their reservations. Her thoughts turned to Project X that was now called Our Clients, and the former company in Denver that had been called Mining Engineers, Inc., but was now being reestablished as Consultants International, LLC.

How much gold might they find on the lands that had been taken from Native Americans who had been driven onto reservations? Any future demand or claim to government agencies or the courts on what was under the ground would fall on deaf ears. And, importantly, how could she play a role? Was there even a role for her to play? If so, how could she do it with something so big? Something potentially of this magnitude. Tiponi weighed all that she had learned in her own past. But was it enough to deal with something as big as what she had been contemplating?

Her thoughts then moved to her upcoming trip to disperse money to a few reservation people and to one tribal council. They were people who knew nothing about the methods she had resorted to in order to acquire the funds they needed. As word of her work and generosity grew, so did the requests for financial aid. At times it all seemed overwhelming, while her stamina and zeal had been waning.

The trip she would make would take her northward again, up through Nevada, through parts of Oregon and on into Washington state, making it a three-day drive to the midway point of her planned itinerary.

Along the way, she would stop at one reservation to participate in an Innovation Day event where select reservation people and one of the tribal leaders planned to discuss possible new initiatives for their reservation. She had been invited to sit in and participate in a part of their discussions. Then there was another event she had to arrive at promptly, a ribbon cutting ceremony at a different reservation, for the opening of a new convenience store and gas station which had been partly funded by her charity.

Tiponi leaned forward and picked up a piece of paper she had placed on her coffee table long ago. She had left it there so she could easily retrieve it when she felt the need to read it or to just be reminded of what it said, of what was important in life. It was a kind of prayer from a Native American chief from long ago. It said:

> So live your life so the fear of death can never enter your heart.
> Trouble no one about their religion.
> Respect others in their views, and demand that they respect yours.
> Love your life, perfect your life, beautify all things in your life.
> Seek to make your life long and of service to your people.
> Prepare a noble death song for the day when you go over the great divide. Always give a word or sign of salute when meeting or passing a stranger if in a lonely place.
> Show respect to all people, but grovel to none.
> When you arise in the morning, give thanks for the light, for your life and strength. Give thanks for your food

and for the joy of living. If you see no reason for giving thanks, the fault lies in yourself.

When your time comes to die, be not like those whose hearts are filled with fear of death, so that when their time comes they weep and pray for a little more time to live their lives over again in a different way. Sing your death song, and die like a hero going home.

Tiponi felt the tension from her morning briefing leave her body as she read the piece of paper she had read many times before. Then, she visualized in her mind her most recent trip to the Pacific Northwest, a mother raccoon urging her kits from tree to tree as they headed to wherever it was that the mother wanted to go; the golden eagles that flew overhead and perched from places where they could see the fish they hunted; the sea otters playfully playing a kind of game of tag on a marina dock; and the kayak she longed to paddle once again. In her mind's eye, she strolled along a snowmelt-fed stream and felt deeply the peace and tranquility that drew her, that rejuvenated her, that made her feel so much more at home, than she did in Las Vegas.

Tiponi Isaw was weary of the scams, the illicit rendezvous her people arranged, the staging of confrontations with businesses in an attempt to solicit donations. Her income had been more than sufficient and she had put her days as a "woman of the night" and a Madam behind her long ago.

The sordid variety of activities she and her people were engaging in for the charity she had built were weighing heavily on her and her conscience.

She was approaching fifty, but had turned to legal Nevada prostitution while still very young, beautiful, and, as she had come to learn, desirable. Those youthful days were gone forever and couldn't be restored for a second chance at trying to do it right. Tiponi thought to herself that she had spent thirty years supporting herself while working for others, and now for her charity.

She sat on her sofa, seemingly gazing nowhere, deep in her own very personal thoughts. Tony Rappaport's briefings seldom brought her joy or excitement. They were necessary but not occasions to rejoice in. The only part of it all that made her efforts seem worthwhile were those when she could hand money to people who genuinely needed it, people who thanked her profusely, people who, like her, were descendants of the first Native Americans.

Tiponi slowly read the prayer a second time. She let the words, sentence by sentence, and their meaning, seep into her consciousness, her soul. They gave her strength and helped her to remember the importance she gave the words, the respect she had for them, and how she intended them to be a road map, a model for how she should live what remained of her life.

Then Tiponi opened the laptop that had belonged to Dalton Trindall. There was one new e-mail to both him, a Larry McGray in Boise, Idaho, and about ten other people, presumably also geologists. It was from the newly-named Consultants International, LLC, lead geologist Stuart Bergman, which read:

> From: Stu Bergman
> To: All field geologists
> Subject: Designation of two regional supervisory appointments.
>
> Geos in Idaho, effective immediately, Larry McGray is designated as our Idaho exploration overseer and Dalton Trindall is designated as our Nevada and California exploration overseer. When sending me messages, please send a copy to whichever one of the above-named individuals represents your geographical area of focus.

Interesting, thought Tiponi, as she assumed that she would soon be seeing other e-mails from others working on Dalton Trindall's part of this project and whatever it was they would have to say.

Next, she clicked on Saved E-mails and read a few of the ones unrelated to his employment. There were a few from a person she took to be his son. The e-mails Dalton had written to him seemed well thought out advice and at times encouragement for one matter or another. There were some e-mails he had saved from people who were likely friends. A couple of the e-mails often had some indirect religious aspect to them. One was titled "Words of Wisdom," which she read:

> On occasion we become complacent during our life and we forget the good things in our lives. The sad part about such complacency is that with time a dark gray cloud can fall all around us, smothering our heart, our joy, our desires, our appreciation, and gradually our joy in living will fade almost imperceptively.

Then, Tiponi found a poem. It was titled "The Chesapeake Skipjack Skipper's Dream." She read it carefully and felt that Trindall had been writing about a man who worked hard every day as a fisherman but had no one to share his success and life with.

Last, she read a religious saying, one that someone had sent to Trindall. It was titled "Cross in My Pocket." Whatever Dalton Trindall was or wasn't, Tiponi sensed that he was a person with values, one who respected life and nature, a person who believed in something, and likely had reverence for the Creator.

Tiponi closed the laptop and began packing for her trip the next day. Along the route she planned to take she hoped she would have time to stop at the Nez Perce reservation in northern Idaho. She had nothing to deliver to the tribe or its people this time around but she liked to visit those she had come to know and who had come to know, respect, and appreciate her in return.

Further in the trip, if she could visit the Kitsap Peninsula of Washington, she wanted to visit the friends she had made years ago at the S'Klallam tribe in Port Gamble. They had stayed in touch with her, often asking her to visit any time she was in their area. Tiponi had provided some help to the tribe on various occasions. One significant fact that stood out in her mind was the beauty of the people and their surrounding environment.

Tiponi's Native American prayer had given her sustenance, and had revived her both physically and emotionally. And Dalton Trindall's poem had piqued her interest. She was curious about him. The poem seemed vague, as if intended to leave a reader caught in an enigma, an unfinished piece of poetry begging an answer to the questions it raised. Perhaps that was the reaction the writer had intended to create, one which left the reader wanting to know more.

CHAPTER 9

Boise, Idaho

Be on the lookout for wolves.

"I'll be back up in the mountains tomorrow," Larry McGray said to his Denver lead geologist. "I'll check the news releases of both companies and compare their published charts to the ones I got for the other company's mining operations up near Coeur d'Alene."

Stu Bergman replied, "The existing claims seem to be somewhat in a straight pattern running from southern Idaho north to the top of the state. It speaks volumes, yet we need to finish working on all the land in between those claims to see what we find. Further north, our other geos' work indicates that the matrix rock material in many places has decayed, it crumbles. The more of that we find the better. It would save on mining expense for crushing all of the rock material. If there is gold and silver in those soil samples then we'd want to possibly include that land in any claims we might want to file some day. What do you think?"

"I believe the Carlin Trend does run north from Nevada," Larry McGray said emphatically. "You know that already. Thanks to you we have more of our geos up here than we have in Nevada. We're ahead of schedule and the snow will be falling up in the mountains in about another month, in October. Let me put our geos on the land up above the twenty-five miles of claims already owned by that exploration company that's planning to set up a mine. The land to the north of Elk City."

"You mean in the Clearwater mountain range?" asked Stu Bergman.

"Yes," McGray said, "and further north a ways. Then we can work our way back down into the lower valleys and hills on the north side of the range, if we can get that far before winter. That way we can get the high ground sampled where we need to and then maybe squeeze a few more weeks of work at lower elevations."

"There are a string of mines further north that indicates this gold fault line may have already been discovered. But no company has claimed all the land in between them."

"They are all busy enough as it is. They can't get to all of their existing claims. Taking on more would be costly for them. They'd have to pay the annual claims fees for each twenty-acre parcel. They don't have the time or inclination. It would eat into their current profits. Their shareholders want to see corporate gains from production as opposed to more costly idle claims."

"Shortsighted of them. They could use their profits to tie up more claims for themselves for the out years. That's okay. Means more for us, if we move on it all."

"I agree. The existing mines and their exploration results seem to make our theory unequivocal. The Carlin stretches north, period! It's just that no one company has tried to do what we're doing. The cost would be too high for just one small- or medium-sized company to pull off," McGray said.

"Well, you got six geos including yourself," answered Bergman. "With each geo moving quickly, maybe not taking quite as many soil samples so close together, maybe we can cover two or three miles a day, five days a week. That would mean that possibly they could finish this leg of the state in less than a month. They could cover maybe thirty or forty miles north of Elk City before the snow gets too deep."

"That's possibly doable," McGray replied. "But those woods are hard to get through, it's steep in places. I'd rather think a mile a day at most. It's not like a flat open field. We are going to have one hell of a lot of samples to send to the assay lab. I'll try to shuttle them to our delivery service's pickup location whenever we have enough to send out. You're going to be inundated with the results. I hope you can keep up with it all."

"I'm getting a couple of new kids from the Denver College of Mining to help. They're new grads looking to do an internship. Our warehouse we use for our samples is plenty big enough to hold the new stuff. Just keep it coming. We'll get the assay results, do the analysis and math work."

"Oh, before you go, I had asked if I could work in southern Nevada with Dalton when winter gets bad up here. I mean, when we get to the point when we can't work north of here when the snow gets too deep to walk through and we can't see what we may want to take samples from. I know you'll be sending the Idaho geos home for a while till spring—"

Stu Bergman interrupted, saying, "Wayde wants us to expedite. He wants to speed up the schedule. Sooner, quicker. So we'll be assigning you and the other guys in Idaho to southern California and southern Nevada. I wish I could join you all. Sunny, warm, not like here in Denver."

"Great. Maybe by early December?" asked McGray.

"Maybe."

The two men ended their conversation and Larry McGray opened up his map of the region he and his people were to focus on.

They had already sampled many miles of the soils thirty miles south of Elk City, in places where a prior forest fire had burnt off a lot of the vegetation. The fire had made walking the charred land much easier to navigate which put them ahead of their schedule. Plus the extra help he now had would make the next leg of their work north of Elk City through heavily forested US Forest Service land go about as quickly as what lay behind them.

In contrast, to their detriment, the length of daylight each day was gradually growing shorter, the days were noticeably cooler and soon, perhaps very soon, cold winds would blow from the north and the west making their work uncomfortable. Yet, it might make his people move more quickly so as to try to finish before winter set in and to also help keep them warmer by maintaining a quicker pace.

McGray called a motel he knew in Grangeville, about a forty-five-minute drive west of Elk City. He negotiated a reduced long-term room rate for himself and his five geologists and then contacted his team and asked them to check into the motel the next evening and to meet him at six in the motel lobby. He reminded them to not discuss any of their work within listening distance of anyone else. If anyone asked what they were there for, they were to say that they were just retired friends who got together for a month-long hunting get-together and that they first wanted to scout out places to hunt deer and elk in the coming weeks.

The next evening, the team met in the lobby and then went to Larry McGray's room for a briefing on their change of assignments. He advised them that after this assignment was completed, they would be assigned to southern Nevada and parts of southern California for a few months. The team seemed pleased and McGray gave each man the needed maps and the places he felt would be best for grabbing their soil and rock chip samples. Each man was a seasoned professional, each knowing instinctively what needed to be done without having to be told. The meeting ended and the next morning they were to caravan their four-wheel drive pickup trucks behind Larry McGray's from Grangeville to Elk City. From there, they were to follow certain known and mapped old logging trails northward to specific locations identified by GPS coordinates, one for each member of the team. McGray, for his part, said he would try to locate some bright orange hunting vests for each member to wear and try to learn any information that might prove helpful to know about.

The plan was for the geologists to try to cover the ground assigned to each. They would line up, five abreast, each a considerable distance apart from the other. It was arranged to be a grid search in which samples would eventually be taken over a wide width of the land as they slowly moved further northwards toward State Highway 12 about thirty miles north. Upon completing that assignment, phase two was to continue in a northerly direction for as long as the fall weather would hold out for them. It was an impossibility to cover the eighty miles of terrain that Stuart Bergman had mentioned, McGray realized. But they would push themselves as far and as fast as possible over the coming weeks before the weather turned on them, making further progress too difficult and costly.

There were mapped out sections from their previous samplings that showed them the likely direction of precious metal-bearing soil. Experience had taught each member of the team that only assay results would tell them if they had continued on the proper path. It would take a lot of luck and the experienced eye of each and every one of them to make sure that they had not strayed away from what they were looking for.

There were many different geographical signs that would help to guide them, such as the color of the soils, rust-colored rock from iron in the soil, swales in the ground, known prior assay results from previous explorers, and other geographical indications that might give a hint as to whether they might be in the right place or not. They all were to meet at the end of the day to discuss what they detected so that adjustments in their direction could be made, as necessary, as best as they could determine.

Larry McGray drove back into the small village called Elk City. As he entered it, he saw a herd of elk grazing, with some bedded down, on a ten-acre treeless pasture on the north side of the village. Come elk hunting season, the elk wouldn't be seen for miles around. Somehow, they knew when it was time to leave. It seemed almost instinctive to the animals. The day before hunting season, they were there for everyone to see. The next day, they were gone.

Every year, hunters would always try staking out the elk before they disappeared back into the forest and mountains. The village had been named after the elk, in their honor. They had returned to the pasture on the north side of the little quaint village year after year, to graze on the sweet field grass during the summer months, only to disappear the day before hunting season opened. But the honor of naming the village after the elk did the hunters little good. The hunters had to try to follow the elk far back into the isolated and uninhabited forests knowing that the further away they got from civilization, the further they would have to ferry back, by hand, pieces of the elk's carcass should they be lucky enough to kill one with their hunting rifles.

Apparently, the village of Elk City's forefathers either thought the place would one day blossom into a larger city, one bolstered by a vibrant economy created by logging, minerals, camping, outdoor recreation, or because of the beauty of the surrounding mountains. Or, was naming the quaint village a city meant as a joke, a kind of tongue-in-cheek amusement that took hold, became entrenched in everyday discussion, and later was incorporated in the more formal creation of the village's existence? Elk City was larger than a hamlet but certainly smaller than a town. Regardless, the village never took off, except during periods of mining in the general area when an open pit mine had been producing gold in the 1980s. Then there was the logging profession. For those who could not work at the mine, there were plenty of massive trees to cut and be transported to a local mill. In addition, there were modern-day mountain men and women who retired to Elk City, to be as far back away from other civilization as a road could take them.

There didn't appear to have been enough money flowing from job wages to support a local economy. More people and jobs would have meant a better village, something more spectacular than the existing poor community comprised of people who didn't have sufficient funds. Not only were there insufficient funds to build additional and better structures, it appeared there were little funds to paint and maintain what they had already erected. The folks of Elk City seemed, on par, content with what they had created and lived in. It seemed many preferred what they had, and what existed, compared to something better. There was but one small county road into and out of Elk City with its termination point just to the east of the village.

Driving around the village took only a few minutes. There wasn't much to see. There was no real commercial district to speak of. The only small family-owned grocery store didn't carry all of what the village's people needed. All were compelled to drive for forty-five minutes west on a curving slow going state road to Grangeville where there were medical facilities, dentists, a pharmacy, a theater, and a variety of businesses that could fill one's gas tank, fix a flat tire, provide a lawyer or an accountant's services, and the other routine needs of the people of Elk City. One had to plan to be away from home for a half day, perhaps once every week or two to go to Grangeville for what they could not have, or find, in Elk City.

Larry McGray knew that his arrival in Elk City would awaken people's curiosity. He would be quickly noticed by some people who lived there. Phones would ring from one house to another informing others of a stranger's arrival. Conspiracy theories or reasons for the new person's presence would be hatched within moments. McGray thought they might say things such as, "I know he's the tax assessor," "It's a game warden undercover," "The guy must be scouting out a place to open a new logging yard," "They are snooping around to set up a new mine," "Someone campaigning, looking for our vote," or "I wonder if he's gonna buy a house," of which many were for sale. There would be no end to the gossip until he had long departed. So, he knew he needed to settle the village arguments about why he was there. He parked his car, walked into the grocery store, gossip central, and announced he was looking for bright red hunting jackets. That would explain everything. He was scouting out the area for hunting season. "Why didn't anyone think of it?" he could almost hear one say. To his surprise, the elderly woman behind the counter pointed towards a shelf at the end of the store, saying, "Over there."

McGray was amused. They didn't have baby powder. Didn't need it. They didn't have aspirin. They didn't have steak probably because most people provided their own meat during hunting season. Red hunting jackets? Yes. A baseball cap? No. Not unless you wanted a red one for hunting season. It seemed to Larry McGray that two of the four older men sitting at the counter having coffee were wearing red hunting caps. Perhaps it was because they were in such local demand

and were the only ones that could be found for sale within a thirty-five-mile radius.

One of the old men sitting at the counter said, "Did you hear about the two city men who came up into the mountains to go bear huntin'? Well, when they got to a fork in the road they saw a sign that said 'Bear left,' so they both went home."

The other men at the counter chuckled.

Larry had been an old hand at wiggling into such communities. He knew they would be nosy and suspicious, but approachable. His days as a junior and a senior field geologist for mining companies had taught him a lot about what to say and what not to say. He just had to have a reasonable reason for being there. He would buy the six red vests on his way out. He saw a vacant seat at the counter and sat down asking for a cup of coffee. He smiled and nodded to the older man to his left and asked the man to his right for the sugar and cream container. That was the ice breaker.

The one on the left asked, "You planning on huntin'?"

"Thinking about it," Larry replied, knowing that the old-timer was just warming up.

"You've been here before?" he asked.

"Nope," Larry said. "We're just looking over the surrounding area for a possible place to come back to."

"Oh, there's more than one of ya?" the old guy asked.

"Yup," Larry simply said, knowing what the next question would be.

"You all need a huntin' guide, maybe? I can help you get one here in town."

"No, thank you," Larry replied. "But maybe you can tell me where all those elk out there on the hill go once they leave."

The men at the counter all broke out in laughter, as one said, "That's what we always want to know. We try to figure it out every year but they seem to take different directions and they can travel miles in just a few hours. When season opens they're long gone," followed by a little more laughter from the men at the counter.

"I hear there are wolves around," Larry asked, looking serious.

"You're right. We've had some problems with them. For a while we had to watch ourselves. They'd sneak into town at night, tip over garbage cans. One snarled at someone who went and got a gun and shot at it. Scared it and the others off back into the woods. It's not safe in the forest. But if you're huntin', you'll have a rifle with you. You should be okay."

Another man at the counter jumped into the conversation. They had a one-man captive audience and seemed glad to have someone new to tell their stories to. "Had a drill rig operator to the south of us get surrounded by three of them. He said they were larger than he had expected. He'd never seen one before. He was drillin' the night shift when they appeared. They fanned out around him not but twenty yards away. They were pacing back and forth, never takin' their eyes off him. Yellow eyes that glared in the light on the rig."

"What did he do?" Larry asked, thinking the coffee drinkers wanted him to ask the obvious next question.

"Why, the rig guy said he jumped up and down waving his arms yellin' at 'em. It only seemed to aggravate them a bit more. He reached into the rig and got out his gun and fired a round into the air. Then they ran off."

"That was it?" Larry asked, faking an incredulous look on his face.

"Yea," said the guy next to Larry. "Them's the ones they set loose in Wyoming and Montana a few years ago. The stupid do-gooders thought the wolves would stay put, happy to be free in some national park like some kind of tourists." This was followed by more laughter from the other men. "Them people have 'bout as much sense as a two-year-old. Now the wolves multiplied and moved to where there is less competition. They see us and the elk here. The elk, they know are hard to bring down, big as they are. People are easy prey to them. Had to get the game warden up here. He said there was a federal law that even he couldn't shoot 'em. But finally, after a woman was killed ten miles from here while camping, they changed their law. We've picked off a few of 'em and they took off. But there are plenty of 'em still out there."

"Do you have a mine operation goin' on here?" Larry asked, knowing better.

"Nope, not yet, at least," the guy to his right said casually. "Them's was drillers. They been finding plenty of gold, we hear. We been hearing about it from a couple of them drillers when they come in here for something."

Another man at the counter chimed in, saying, "And from some guy who reads their news releases in Grangeville, a stock seller guy."

"Why'd they quit drilling?" Larry asked, hoping for a good answer.

"Gold price went down a couple years ago. They done some drillin' since then, but not as much as before. But they're fixin' to start up again soon when gold goes back up. We hear that they are planning a mine over that way," he said, pointing towards a wall inside the store.

"They also bought up the old lumber and logging property near town. They've made a camp out of it for the men to sleep at when they come back."

"Sounds serious. Would that help you all here in town? More people, jobs," Larry asked.

"We could use the jobs but we don't want more people. We like it as it is," said the man to Larry's left.

"Wrong," said the guy to Larry's right. "I'm tryin' to sell my house. When the drillers come back for good, I hope they stay and buy my place," he added.

There was a little more lighter laughter as another quipped, "You're gonna die here, Charlie. You'll never sell, even if they offer you your askin' price."

"Do you think there really is enough gold here to justify a mine?" asked Larry.

"No doubt about it. We all know how much was picked up off the ground over a hundred years. That was easy pickings. Most of it is still underground. It ain't goin' nowheres till they come and get it. All they gotta do is dig."

Another of the men added, "We seen them come and go for decades with their rigs. We know what they been findin'. When they feel the time is right, they'll show up with dozens of people and their equipment and Elk City will be on its way to being on the map again," said one of the men.

"We don't all look forward to all that commotion. Some of us like 'er the way it is."

McGray drained what was left in his coffee cup and said his thanks to the men for their discussion and their warning about the wolves. He walked to the back of the store where he found a pile of red hunting vests and a stack of red caps. He sorted through them and saw that everything was marked as either small or large. He selected six large vests and caps, and a handful of bright red plastic whistles. Then he went to the cash register, paid for his coffee and the gear, and left a tip on the counter. After saying thanks again to the men at the counter, he waved and went out the grocery store door.

McGray got into his truck and drove off in the direction of where he last saw his crew. When he got to where they had parked their trucks, he proceeded further along the old logging trail, hoping to see one of them along the way. He wanted to relieve them all of the soil sample bags they had been filling and carrying. The weight would only slow them down and tire them out before the day was over. He beeped his horn, as he had said he would do, and gradually over about a twenty minute-period each found their way to Larry's truck. Each dropped off what they had gathered and had been carrying and then disappeared back into the woods to where they had been working. Larry doubted that they would finish even one of the miles he and Stuart Bergman had hoped they could complete on average each day. The geos had reported that it had been tough going all morning.

Larry McGray had given each man a bright red hunting vest, cap, and a whistle, and told them he would park his truck a few hundred yards further north on the trail. He had also warned them to be on the lookout for wolves, and that if they saw one to blow the whistle to try to scare them away and to alert the other team members as well.

After moving his truck, he got out his GPS and grabbed his backpack and dozens of small cloth bags. He then walked back into the woods to start filling and marking each bag. This was but the first day at this new location and he wondered if all this work would pay off. They had to know where the gold was. They couldn't be off in their calculations. They were either on top of it or they weren't. They had studied the ground and maps and were making their best decision as to where to focus their efforts. If they were off, they could waste an entire month of time and expense. McGray knew that time was running out and that the pressure would be on very soon to ramp up their exploring success. He was anxious to help make one more discovery in his career. One big one. The one he had always believed existed. One like the world had never seen before.

CHAPTER 10

Washington, DC

He is leaving tomorrow morning for Beijing.

Wayde Ramsley and the man he had brought with him from his company's retained law firm stood outside their downtown Washington, DC, hotel attempting to hail a taxi.

The lawyer, Arthur Mercer, was experienced in matters pertaining to the corporate exploration and mining industry. He had graduated from the University of Colorado, obtained his law degree, and eventually became the chief legal counsel for one of the largest mining companies in the US. He then went on to work for one of the well-known law firms in the country that specialized in mining and related environmental issues, strategically headquartered in Denver.

It was raining and each of the two men held their umbrellas while standing on a curb fronting Pennsylvania Avenue. The last of the fall foliage's colorful leaves were dropping from the weight of the rain. Traffic was heavy in spite of the morning rush hour having ended. Their appointment at the Chinese embassy was for an hour later but Wayde Ramsley preferred arriving early.

A taxi pulled over to the curb and both men got into the back seat. Ramsley gave the driver the address he was to take them to and asked that he keep the cab's meter running and wait for them outside the embassy until they returned.

Along the short distance, Ramsley thought about the new snow that had fallen on the Rocky Mountains to the west of Denver. It had even snowed some in Denver, as was normal, but the little that fell melted by the next day. Denver's weather, he thought, could vacillate quickly between mere sweater weather and subfreezing temperatures from day to day. He wondered if it had also snowed up in the Idaho mountains north of Boise. If so, he knew that their geologist team would have to shut down their continuing work in that region, perhaps for the upcoming winter. The team had made significant progress, more than either Stuart Bergman or he had thought possible. If the decent weather up there could hold until mid-December as it sometimes did, then they would finish sampling the area they had feared would have to wait until spring.

The taxi pulled up to the embassy gates that provided a walkway which led to the entrance to a large, impressive building. On the rail fence to the side of the gates was a gold-lettered sign on a black metal plate, saying "Embassy of the People's Republic Of China." The gold lettering caught Ramsley's eye as he very briefly thought of the irony of its gold color and the reason for his visit.

The two men entered the building and announced to one of the receptionists their names and the reason for their visit. After sitting for almost a half hour, a man came over to them and asked Ramsley and his legal adviser to follow him. The men were required to place their briefcases on an x-ray machine's conveyor belt while they walked through a magnetometer and then posed briefly in front of an x-ray machine which doubled for explosives and chemical detection. They were then led down a hallway to an elevator which took them to the second floor, and the lobby to the Chinese ambassador's office complex.

Ramsley noted that he had previously thought that the office he would enter would be quiet, sedate, with people wanting to be unseen, whispering to each other as they came and went, trying to maintain the decorum he visualized the ambassador's office would require of them. Instead, people hurried in and out, dropping off and picking up documents, engaging in brief normal-toned conversations in Mandarin, with phones ringing and a television mounted on a wall which was tuned to the mostly English-speaking version of China's national cable television station, CCTV.

The two men had to wait only a moment before they were asked by a secretary to follow her into the ambassador's office. They went through an interior office and came to another door which was open in expectation of their arrival.

The ambassador got up from behind his oversized desk, smiled, and said in perfect English, "Welcome, Mr. Ramsley and Mr. Mercer." He came around his desk and extended his hand to Ramsley and his lawyer and then motioned them toward chairs that ringed a coffee table.

"This is our attaché for our embassy's Office of Economic and Commercial Affairs, Mr. Quon Zhong. Given the nature of your request to meet with me, I thought Mr. Zhong might be of some assistance to us while we talk." Ramsley was to learn later from his lawyer's inquiries that Mr. Zhong was the son of one of the Chinese Communist Party leaders.

Wayde Ramsley had been told that the ambassador had set aside fifteen minutes for their brief meeting. He had hoped that the ambassador would not only develop an interest in what he came to propose but that he would also have someone else present with whom more in-depth discussion could be continued later.

"Thank you, Mr. Ambassador," Ramsley replied. He then proceeded to hand to the ambassador, Mr. Zhong, and Arthur

Mercer a map of the western states, only depicting pick and shovel symbols of all the known prior mining operations in the region. The symbols were all over the region but a heavier concentration of them seemed to be from north in Montana and Idaho southward through Nevada, Arizona, and California.

"The symbols you see, Mr. Ambassador, represent where mines had been established over the past one hundred and fifty years. We only selected the locations, represented by the symbols you see, that were precious metal-bearing ones that produced gold, silver, platinum, and palladium. Where you see the heaviest concentration of symbols, we believe prior miners merely scratched the surface and only found a couple or few percent of what still remains in the ground. Back then, they would mine for what precious metals they could see while using antiquated tools of the day. Their discoveries way back then were far larger than anyone could detect or imagine. The miners could not see the concentration of microscopic metals and so they left behind the vast majority of precious metals they had hoped to mine. Without getting into the specific locations, our geologists have been researching this area of interest."

"You mean where all these symbols are running from north to south?" Mr. Zhong asked.

"Yes," Ramsley replied. "We believe we have discovered the golden trail that runs from the United States' border with Canada all the way south to the Mexican border. If we are right with what we have been discovering, and we are convinced that we are, then the amount of gold that could eventually be mined and produced could be worth somewhere in the vicinity of a minimum of one trillion US dollars, or about six trillion yuan, in Chinese currency."

The ambassador showed no new expression on his face when Wayde Ramsley stated the numbers.

"We are aware that your government has had to accept payment in US dollars for the goods it has been shipping to the United Sates over recent years. Your government, and your nation's companies, can't just take those dollars back to China to spend. US dollars can be used in many places as a form of international payment, such as for oil. But the dollar will likely devalue. It always has for the past century. It will buy less as time goes by. Obviously, as you know, not only can't your companies and government spend US dollars on anything in China, those dollars can't be spent in many other places of the world. Other governments have their own currency. The dollar is sometimes a backup currency, a reserve currency, but it is losing its desirability and spendability. Yes, some places will accept US dollars but your nation's options are limited and will likely diminish as time goes on while the dollar becomes less and less of a pseudo internationally accepted form of payment.

"The problem has been what to do with all those dollars. Your government has had to invest those US dollars in US bonds, for both practical and political reasons. I know. We understand. But those bonds you are holding will be worth less and less in value as time goes on. Interest rates on new bonds are just beginning to rise. I estimate the bonds held by Chinese entities have already lost about 10 percent of their cash value. In other words, the two trillion dollars are now only worth about one trillion and eight hundred billion dollars. As I said, as new bonds are sold at higher interest rates, the older bonds with lower interest rates will devalue even more, perhaps by as much as a trillion dollars."

Both the ambassador and Mr. Zhong nodded as if they understood. A more serious look was now on the ambassador's face.

"The interest rates on your existing US bonds," Ramsley continued, "are locked in at low interest rates, so your bond owners will take an even greater loss. They will be paid interest well below the rate of inflation both here in the US, in China, and, I dare say, in most parts of the world. In other words, the bond holders lose on both ends and, with rising inflation coupled with the devaluation of the bonds and US dollars, I wouldn't be surprised if in a few years those two trillion dollars' worth of bonds wouldn't be worth only a fourth of what they are valued at today. In other words, your country and its bond holder's two trillion-dollar investment in US dollar-denominated bonds could lose as much as the equivalent of one trillion five hundred billion dollars, leaving a paltry five hundred billion dollars for your trouble."

Ramsley paused for a moment to allow the ambassador and Mr. Zhong a chance to absorb what he had just said, or to ask any questions.

"If, on the other hand," Ramsley said, "your bond holders were to cash in those bonds and buy gold or other commodities, they would have something they could sell in China or anywhere else in the world. No US dollars would be used, none exchanged, none would be needed. Gold, as your country well knows, is more of an international currency. It is accepted and exchanged everywhere in the world. And," Ramsley said with added emphasis, "it will likely increase in value over the coming few years. Instead of your country's bond values slipping from two trillion all the way down to five hundred billion dollars in value, the equivalent in gold could increase in value to six trillion dollars or more as the price of gold rises because of the inflation that has been with us for 99 percent of the time ever since currency was invented."

"Yes, Mr. Ramsley, I do very much understand. Our government has been discussing this coming problem with your government at the highest levels ever since we realized that your currency would eventually have to be devalued. We know what is coming. So what are you proposing?" the ambassador asked.

"This is very sensitive for us to say. I ask that what I am about to say not be discussed over telephones or by way of electronic communications. I don't know whether or not anything that you say or send electronically can be intercepted by anyone, but I have to assume that it can and has been done," Ramsley stated while expressing his overriding concern for secrecy about his company's information.

The ambassador interjected, "If we communicate at all, about whatever it is you are looking to protect, I will instruct Mr. Zhong to do so only by diplomatic pouch carried by staff who have diplomatic immunity. Our communications will only be read by those who we designate.

"We think we have perhaps as much as a trillion dollars, or possibly much more, worth of gold being discovered. We plan to possibly file legal claims for a very large part of this land in the coming months. In the US, such claims, once filed, entitle us to all of the mineral rights on that land. No one can take it from us," said Ramsley. "The low number of one trillion dollars is the possible value based on half of the claims yielding one million ounces of gold per mile at today's processed price. The figure would be closer to two to three to as much as five trillion dollars if the price of gold triples over the next few years, as many experts say it will. On the other hand, the price of gold still in the ground is worth far less because it hasn't been dug out and processed. I estimate that our claims may be worth at the moment about one hundred to two hundred billion dollars, including royalties, and could be worth about half a trillion dollars as gold's retail price increases."

"These are very large numbers," Mr Zhong said.

"But small compared to your nation's US bond holdings," Ramsley replied. "Here is a better way of saying it. If only two hundred billion dollars worth of US bonds were sold and those funds were used to buy our company, then the eventual profit would be in the trillions of US dollars and the gold could be shipped to China instead of having to be converted into US dollars which wouldn't help you at all. It is the gold that is the ultimate reward. Gold is money that can be used anywhere in the world to buy farms, chemicals, copper, coal, beef, lumber, or anything else.

"And the claims are transferable?" asked Mr. Zhong.

"It is both sellable and transferable," replied Ramsley. "Again, it would be ours to do with as we please. All we, or whoever owns the claims, would have to do is pay a fee every year for the claims that are in our, or some other company's, name. Some work would need to be done with each claim each year, but that is mostly a paperwork exercise—"

"Excuse me, Mr. Ramsley, a paperwork exercise?" asked Mr. Zhong.

"Something that can be easily certified to in writing by merely doing very little with each claim," Ramsley answered.

Ramsley knew he was understating the requirement as he continued, "A Chinese company could also file for those claims or we could transfer those claims to your sovereign corporation fund. There are many legal ways of doing it. If you became interested, I suggest my company work out a plan for some kind of arrangement before we file for possession of all of the claims. Once we file claims on such a huge expanse of the land in the US, it will become international news within minutes of it becoming realized and verified by someone," Ramsley said.

Ramsley wanted his next words to sink in., "A better way of saying this is that our claims could eventually be seen as a national treasure by citizens and politicians alike. If a deal is consummated before that realization, then my company would profit as would your Chinese sovereign fund company. Once our discovery is announced and becomes publicly understood for what it is, I doubt a foreign company could ever get the US government's approval to buy a portion, or all, of a US company that had control of potentially a trillion or a few trillion dollars' worth of gold. If someone in your country were interested in what I have explained, before our discovery becomes public, it would be relatively easy for the sale of our company, or our future assets, to get the necessary approvals from our US Department of Treasury before, rather than after, they, or the public, learns what we have found."

"How can all this be verified, Mr. Ramsley?" asked the ambassador. "The information you have shared seems it would need to be supported by many expert opinions."

Ramsley replied, "We have assembled many well-known experts in their field, people who are working with us in this endeavor as we speak. They are experts from the academic community and highly acclaimed geological managers, among others, who have been successful in their own right. People who have proven themselves beyond question within the international mining industry."

"And our representatives could meet with them, if interested?" asked Mr. Zhong,

"Yes, your geologists and others, who are also experts in geology and mining, could sign a nondisclosure agreement and we could show them all of our work, our maps, our assay results. They could meet with our chief geologist and our field members. The evidence we have been accumulating will speak for itself, especially to those who know what they are reading and seeing.

"Keep in mind," Ramsley said as an afterthought, "this is a stretch of land consisting of about one thousand miles, or over three thousand kilometers. It is more massive than anything ever discovered before, anywhere in the world. If a Chinese company were to own my company before this all leaks out, or has to be publicly announced, then all the claims are theirs. If your people decide they are interested *after* all this becomes known, then I'm afraid it will be too late."

The ambassador looked at his watch and said, "I, for one, am very interested in what you have shared with us. I wish I could involve myself in any discussions about this. All Mr. Zhong can do is travel back to China with this information, strictly under his control, and then discuss it with those who make such decisions. He is leaving tomorrow morning for Beijing and I am sure he will carry with him your generous good will and your offer for us to be considered first before all others."

The ambassador stood up, signaling that the meeting had come to a conclusion. He stepped toward Ramsley and Mercer to once again shake their hands, while Mr. Zhong asked Mr. Ramsley for his business card.

Wayde Ramsley apologized, saying that he was having new cards made for himself. He wrote down his contact numbers asking that no one from the embassy call to discuss the proposal with him via an embassy land line telephone. Mr. Zhong asked if Mr. Ramsley would feel comfortable receiving a call from one of their business representatives who routinely works on developing new opportunities for Chinese investors. Ramsley agreed and they departed the ambassador's office. Out in the reception area, Mr. Zhong said that if one of their representatives was interested, perhaps he would join the representative in meeting Ramsley in Denver or elsewhere.

Ramsley urged Mr. Zhong to tell whoever might be interested that his company's board of directors consisted of chief executive officers of a few of the large gold mining companies based in the United States. The companies they worked for were equal owners of Consultants International, which were indirectly publicly owned by retail and institutional shareholders.

"My board," Wayde Ramsley said, "might be interested in selling the company if the timing and the price is right."

Mr. Zhong replied, "It is too soon to be able to say if our people in Beijing will be interested in your proposal, Mr. Ramsley. First, let me convey what was said in our meeting here to those who make such decisions."

Outside the embassy, Ramsley's and Mercer's ride was still waiting for them as they approached the street. Without them realizing it, a routine photograph was taken of the two, from some distance away, as they entered their taxi. The photograph along with a brief report would be provided to certain US government agency representatives and placed into their computers, for whatever action they deemed appropriate.

Their taxi took them back to their hotel where the two men would have dinner and discuss their meeting before retiring for the night and their return back to Denver the following morning.

The rain had stopped but the sky still appeared threatening. At their hotel, Wayde Ramsley paid the taxi driver and the two men stepped out to the sidewalk where they were confronted by two young men. They had positioned themselves in a way that caused Ramsley and Mercer to have to acknowledge their presence and walk around them.

One of the men opened up a two panel, black leather credential folder containing an identification card on the top panel. On it were large, faded blue, printed letters which said

"FBI," overprinted by black identification information and a photograph. On the bottom portion of the credential was a small gold FBI badge. The man displaying the credential folder then said, "We are with the FBI, gentlemen, and we are wondering if we can have a moment with you either out here or inside your hotel?"

PART 3

CHAPTER 11

Las Vegas, Nevada

The pictures are on this USB drive device.

Wayde Ramsley received a request from a Chinese investment executive in Beijing, China, to meet with him and three others including a precious metals resource expert, a geologist, and a mineral exploration expert. They would be accompanied by the Chinese embassy's attaché, Mr. Zhong. The request asked for the opportunity to meet sometime in mid-December.

Ramsley responded, suggesting that they meet in Denver at his corporate office location for a day followed by a visit to Las Vegas where he would assemble his team of field geologists for a one-day briefing session.

After the dates had been agreed to, Ramsley had his staff make all of the arrangements and sent a message to their people who were now working an area that was about a two-hour drive northwest of Las Vegas. The message was sufficient in detail to alert the geologists of the reason for the briefing and what they should prepare to say and present to their Chinese guests.

Unknown to anyone else, the e-mail message containing the Chinese guests' names, an outline of what would be presented, and the itinerary was also read by Tiponi Isaw from Dalton Trindall's stolen laptop computer.

Ramsley contacted their legal representative, Arthur Mercer, asking for him to attend the upcoming meeting in

Denver and Las Vegas. Mercer took the opportunity to briefly explain to Ramsley that he had learned, since their visit to Washington, DC, that the two FBI agents had only been performing a routine followup inquiry into the reasons for Ramsley's and Mercer's visit to the Chinese embassy. They used such occasions for further information gathering and to try to learn anything that could be of value from a national security perspective. Mercer said that his explanation to the two agents, that he and Ramsley represented a mineral exploration company looking to raise funds through investments from the Chinese or any other entity, should have sufficed. Mercer reminded Ramsley that he had given the two FBI agents his phone number and offered to speak with them should they have any further questions. They had not called since the first encounter.

Ramsley knew that the Chinese culture included a strong recreational interest in gambling. He thought the Las Vegas venue to be an ideal place to brief the delegation while allowing them time to enjoy the famous city's gambling opportunities.

The day prior to the arrival of the Chinese delegation, Ramsley contacted his board of directors by e-mail informing them of the upcoming show-and-tell event. He explained, "As you know, the Chinese are very methodical, purposeful, thorough, and I do not expect the meetings with them to result in any kind of serious offer any time soon, if ever. However, they have purchased some mining businesses both here in the US and elsewhere around the world. Those purchases had been for ongoing businesses that were already operating and producing. I don't know if they have yet purchased a "pig in a poke" where there was only the promise of possible future mineral production." Ramsley knew that it would be a stretch for the Chinese to buy something they could not see, that was still purported to be under the ground, as compared to something already being extracted from the ground, processed, and sold on the open markets.

Ramsley continued in his e-mail, "It's possible that I might be asked what dollar amount we were looking for. I propose to tell them one suggested price applicable for the duration of phase one, prior to initiating any surveying and claim filing activities, and then a higher price, subject to revision, once that phase of our possible operation is initiated. Please sharpen your pencils and let me know what you think is reasonable. I will add my own thoughts on the matter to those of yours and come up with an average for suggested numbers."

Ramsley knew that the board members, being leaders of their individual companies, likely had incentive contracts that would boost their incomes based on each individual's job performance as it related to company profitability and increased share price. The board members would be thinking about the potential to make a fortune as a result of any sale of Consultants International. Wayde Ramsley knew that he and all of his staff would also be richly rewarded in the process by receiving a small percentage of any sale proceeds, which would be significant in dollars, if the sale price was high enough.

Ramsley had Alice Harrison ensure that all of Consultants International's staff had reservations at one of the Las Vegas Strip's casino hotels. Then she checked to be sure that their guests had made reservations at a hotel next door and then sent an e-mail to Stu Bergman and his field geologists advising of the final arrangements.

Again, Tiponi Isaw was able to read the e-mail, a copy of which had been sent to Dalton Trindall. She knew who the Chinese and the American attendees would be and where they would be staying. She contacted her charity's vice chairman, Tony Rappaport, and asked him to meet her for a discussion. Upon his arrival, Tiponi instructed him to have one of his people try to identify the geologists and one or more of the Chinese delegation so that one or more could be approached by their ladies, given the opportunity.

Rappaport had dinner with Tiponi. She had prepared for him his favorite Mexican food. During the course of the meal, Rappaport mentioned to Tiponi in passing that they had received, what had become the usual inquiries to some of their people's ads. One AD that had been responded to had been listed under the classification of "males seeking males." The AD said "Twink, young, submissive looking for an evening of fun in Vegas."

"In two other new cases," Rappaport continued, "we have a couple of men replying to ads for 'women seeking male companionship at your place or mine.' The three new prospects' rendezvous had been assigned to three of our people, one male and two females."

—————⁓⌁⊶⊙⊷⊶⊙⊷⌁⁓—————

The next day was a busy one for Wayde Ramsley, Stu Bergman, and Alice Harrison, with Arthur Mercer in attendance should any legal question require an answer. They greeted their Chinese guests, at Consultants International's office complex, and put on their "dog and pony show" using a slide projector to display documents maps and photographs. The reason for using a projector was so as to not have to provide paper handouts which could fall into unintended hands. The attendees had been asked to turn off their cell phones, to make no recordings, take no pictures, and to sign a legally binding agreement to not disclose the information they would receive to anyone else without Ramsley's approval.

As the day progressed, dozens of questions were asked and answered. Ramsley and his own staff did not receive any impression that the delegation was overtly interested in moving on the opportunity to buy out Consultants International, LLC. However, during breaks for coffee, using the rest room, and snacks, the Chinese delegation often huddled to discuss what they were learning. To Ramsley, such discussions might be a hint of a more "covert" interest, one which they preferred to not show in front of their American counterparts. Interestingly, Ramsley noticed that after such breaks, the Chinese men would return to their seats and have no immediate questions. To Ramsley, this was further proof that the Chinese men were trying not to show too much interest.

Upon the conclusion of the day's briefing, Ramsley informed the Chinese delegation that he would have a van pick them up the next morning at their motel to take them to the airport. He handed each person a piece of paper showing the time and the location for their next meeting in a conference room they had rented, at the hotel where they would be staying in Las Vegas.

Ramsley was disappointed that no one had raised the matter of possible sale price. He had been prepared to tell them one hundred and fifty billion dollars if a sale was finalized prior to the initiation of phase two's surveyor activity and land claim filing operation. The other figure he had planned to mention was more fluid, within a range of two hundred billion dollars or more. The costs would increase commensurate with surveyor and claim filing costs, as well as the more expensive drilling campaigns that would need to be initiated. He had thought one hundred fifty billion dollars, but it was based on the approximate supposed value of unmined gold still in the ground, but potentially worth several trillion dollars in the years ahead.

In Las Vegas, the Chinese delegation was met and transported to their hotel. They were told that they would need to make their own arrangements in getting back to the airport whenever they concluded their visit. They were handed maps of the city and advertisement brochures for various entertainment opportunities that would be ongoing during their stay. Additionally, they had been provided with the name and location of sightseeing tours in and around the vicinity. With no apparent interest being expressed about any of the other opportunities, it was assumed their visit would be mostly for business and maybe a visit to one of the hotel's neighboring magnificent casinos, the ones the Las Vegas Strip was world famous for.

The delegation was left to check into their rooms on their own. They were reminded that the meeting would be held the next morning in a conference room on the first floor and told that the room would have a sign outside the door that said "Gold Rush." Alice Harrison had selected the room when she was making reservations for the event. Harrison chose the conference room to be rented for the day on the basis of its size and also its name, thinking it would add a little primer for the purpose of the meeting.

Later that day, the twelve field geologists checked into their rooms in the hotel next door to the one where the Chinese delegation was staying. They had met with Stu Bergman briefly outside the hotel and were told to try to avoid visiting the casinos and local restaurants so as to avoid running into the Chinese delegation. They did not want any of the Chinese guests to get the impression that they were being shadowed or watched by company employees. Discussions outside of the conference room were to be avoided and if the delegation was encountered at a restaurant, they were merely to smile and look friendly, but nothing more.

The next morning the delegation received their briefing from the assembled geologists. Questions were asked pertaining to the number of grams per ton of gold, on average, for various areas; the kind of "host" rock or matrix found from place to place; the vicinity where visible gold had been discovered; the anticipated environmental resistance that could be expected in certain places; how nearby residents would react to drilling or mining operations near their communities; whether one state or another was considered "mining friendly;" and the like.

The day went by quickly as the discussions picked up in pace. Stu Bergman inserted questions into the conversations from time to time to try to draw out the Chinese delegates. One particular question he asked seemed to generate some conversation between the Chinese geologist and mining expert and his team members. Bergman's team consisted of a few men who had been geologist explorers and mining engineers who had advanced in their careers to do economic feasibility studies, to prepare mining operation reports, and to managing both exploration and mining operations. The question Bergman asked was whether or not they preferred the new less expensive method of using mobile crusher machines which could be moved, as needed, to where the ore was being extracted. The method significantly reduced the number of very expensive trucks and heavy equipment needed, which in turn reduced fuel costs and the need for about 30 percent of personnel that would otherwise need to be employed. A lively discussion ensued and the Chinese men began to show some excitement as they described other methods and technology that would make mining less expensive and increase the profits for those who adapted to new thinking.

Not having the required expertise, Embassy attaché, Mr. Zhong, listened intently but made no comments nor asked any questions.

Towards the end of the day, the Chinese delegation leader from Beijing asked, "Can you tell me when you plan to start surveys and filing your claims?"

Bergman replied that his geologists had a few more areas to test along the north and south ends of the Carlin Trend. He said, "We haven't decided whether to just survey and claim the land to the north first or to the south. But, once word gets out as to what we are doing, other exploration and mining companies would likely swoop down on wherever our people had been, try to figure out what's left for them to claim, and then try to figure out if we were done filing claims or if we were continuing to work areas and file new claims elsewhere."

Bergman pulled out a map and showed them their prioritized areas of interest. He intentionally gave them a false description of the locations. He did not want to risk having the Chinese delegation knowing too much about their precise plan. Pointing to the map, he continued, "Both of us know that, just like any other discovery, there are areas void of the gold and silver. Conversely, in some places the ore is richer in quantity and grade. We are at the stage where we are deciding which areas will be surveyed and claimed first. The best areas we have found. Then once those are in our possession, we will survey and claim land in between, if we feel it is worth the time and effort."

"And you will start when?" asked the delegation leader once again.

"We are starting to make our plans now. We are directing our team of geologists to the most promising areas of interest. Once that is completed, we will reassign them to lesser places of interest while we bring in surveyors and our legal people to file all the claims as the surveys are completed and the claims are marked with corner posts. I can't tell for sure when that decision will be made. Our company's board of directors will be meeting with Mr. Ramsley in a couple of weeks for an update and for discussion about the very question you asked," said Bergman, wanting to remain somewhat vague so as to draw out more interest on the same subject.

"Do you have some kind of time schedule?" asked one of the delegate members. "I ask because we do not know how much time we have to review your project before you begin your phase two."

"My guess is that we will likely be in a position to ask our board of directors for their opinions perhaps between this coming March and June. Wayde Ramsley is pushing for an early decision," said Bergman.

"And," Wayde Ramsley said, "our decision could depend on whether we think we have to move fast on most of the areas we have identified. If we feel that our exploration effort's intentions and our substantial success begins to be found out, we may have to start sooner rather than later. If you decide that you have an interest in pursuing ownership of our company, you would need to sign a letter of intent, and to initiate the acquisition process before this March or April. We could agree to keep all the staff working while pushing the plan forward, and while the new owners take control, make the decisions, and run the company.

"A new owner would want to have some continuity," Ramsley continued. "We would ensure that by way of a purchase agreement. We would continue working as we had been before. We have identified all the survey companies we would hire. We know the logistics we would need and we know how to get it all done quickly. Once the buyer, or we, have the claims, we can deploy drilling companies over many locations of the new Mega Trend. The Carlin will become but a small and less important piece of the new discovery. Instead of talking about the Carlin, they will substitute the Carlin's name with the new Mega Trend's name. With gold already beginning to rise in price, and given its predicted price in a few years, this land will become the biggest hot bed for drilling and mining the world has ever seen."

"Do you envision mostly open pit mining or tunneling? Have you determined which areas would require one method or the other?" asked Mr. Zhong.

"Not until drilling results pinpoint the width, the length, and the depth of the gold ore, location by location, place by place. I'm guessing that it will be mostly open pit, but it would be a huge benefit if an open pit still could not find the bottom of the gold deposit. In such a case, an underground method could be employed if the miner wanted to chase the gold down deeper. Then I suppose one mine could be both open pit as well as underground. We all know of gold discoveries that have ended up going down thousands of feet. The gold came up out of the earth from way down somewhere," Ramsley finished saying.

"If we were interested in your company," asked the delegation's leader, "would you give us advance notice before you begin phase two, so that we could make a final decision before it was too late, before the cost would be far greater to buy your company?"

"Unfortunately, no," said Ramsley.

"How many others have you provided this briefing to? Are you asking us to compete with several others? You mentioned at the embassy something like one hundred and fifty billion dollars. Is that the figure you used in briefing others?" asked Mr. Zhong, looking to try to get Ramsley to divulge additional information.

"I can't say Mr. Zhong," Ramsley answered. "All I can say is that there is some interest, although it is minimal because what we are doing has not yet been made public. But others will learn about us and I expect we will do more of these kinds of briefings."

"Have you received any offers yet?" asked Mr. Zhong. "Or is that something else you can not discuss?"

"We can't say. You're right in your assumption," Ramsley said. "As to your earlier question about whether we would give you advance notice before we begin our phase two, let me try to answer better than I did. We couldn't, not unless we already had executed a letter of intent for a purchase and the process for such a purchase was already underway. In that case, we would coordinate with a buyer and the buyer would already have locked in the lower purchase price for the company. The finalizing of such an arrangement could not be delayed. A date would have to be agreed to so that the buyer did not delay going through with a purchase indefinitely."

"We understand, Mr. Ramsley," said the delegation's leader.

Mr. Zhong provided, on behalf of the delegation, a gift to Wayde Ramsley. It was a cut jadestone stamp with his name carved in both Mandarin and English. Along with it was a pretty bowl containing red ink. Mr. Zhong thanked Wayde Ramsley and his people for taking time to meet with the Chinese delegation.

When the meeting was concluded, it appeared that the Chinese delegation members had relaxed their prior stiff approach to one of a friendlier tone. Wayde Ramsley and his team of people and the delegation were smiling, shaking hands, and exchanging well wishes. Talk had turned to questions about each other's credentials, how long they would be staying in Las Vegas, and well wishes for getting lucky while visiting the casinos.

After the Chinese delegation had departed the meeting room, Wayde Ramsley complimented everyone present on their skilled performance. He then announced that in a couple of weeks it would be Christmas and that everyone would be receiving an end-of-the-year bonus of a week's paid vacation between Christmas and New Year. Many broke out into smiles and a few expressed their thanks at the welcomed news. Ramsley then asked a question. "The Chinese love to celebrate their Lunar New Year. I have heard that it often brings things to a crawl over there. I'm wondering if the date for the celebration will interfere with any of the decision making their people may want to make regarding our company?"

Arthur Mercer knew the answer and offered, "It is usually some time between the end of January and mid-February. But the country's new economic drive has made the holiday less of a priority, especially when it comes to pending opportunities and money."

——————

Quon Zhong accompanied the Chinese delegation back to Beijing where together they were debriefed by a Chinese intelligence agent who was looking for any information that might prove useful. From there they briefed the officials of their Economic Development Office in their equivalent of the US Department of Commerce and a representative of the country's Sovereign Investment Fund who expressed serious interest in what had been proposed. Zhong, suffering from severe jet lag, stayed for the night with his mother and father. He was their only child and while his mother doted on him, his father always encouraged Quon Zhong with news about his possible career opportunities. On this evening, his father told him that it was expected that he would be appointed to an ambassadorship within the coming year. After discussing the many location possibilities, the conversation turned to the upcoming Chinese New Year and their asking their son

if he would be able to come back home for the highly anticipated celebration.

While the Consultants International people were meeting
with the Chinese delegation, Tiponi Isaw was paid a visit by
Tony Rappaport. He had brought her an itinerary, and envelopes containing checks from the charity, for her upcoming
trip to Arizona and southern California. As was her custom,
she preferred to hand deliver the checks in person whenever
possible so that she could see the joy her efforts brought to
others and maintain ties with those she helped. "One more
thing. You remember the matter I mentioned to you last evening about a possible person responding to our ad under the
heading of 'males seeking males?'" Rappaport asked.

"Yes."

"Our guy completed his mission and got paid. The charity
will get its share. Our guy said just in case of violence, he took
a pinhole camera with him. It looks like a pen. He attached it
to a bag he carried with him. He placed the bag on a chair that
would have the right vantage point. The camera took digital
pictures every thirty seconds for over an hour. The pictures are
on this USB drive," Rappaport said, as he handed it to Tiponi.
"You just plug it into your computer and the pictures come
up. It turns out the guy in the hotel room was a foreigner but
he spoke English well enough. While this guy went into the
bathroom, our guy took a peek at a hotel room receipt that
had been slipped under the door. It had the guy's name on it.
I don't know if the name will mean anything to you but you
had asked me last night to try to identify who the people were
with that Chinese group you are interested in. In the pictures
the guy looks Chinese. His name is Quon Zhong."

CHAPTER 12

Washington, DC

Compliments of the casino.

"There are dozens of environmental groups backing your next campaign, Senator. They've been loyal supporters of yours and they'll appreciate the press release you are about to make," California Senator Henry Maxwell's press assistant said as she escorted the senator to the outdoor microphone set up in front of the Capitol building.

"We have been inundated with inquires from both within the state and others. Congressman Al Serento from Colorado will be joining you at the microphone. He'll be spearheading a variety of the legislative initiatives needed to get legislation introduced in the House. His office will coordinate with yours for whatever legislation is eventually introduced. Hearings will have to be held in the Senate and the House. The lobbyists have been increasingly applying pressure, as you know. I suspect you could get a couple million dollars for next year's campaign out of this initiative," she explained.

Senator Maxwell reviewed his brief press announcement as he neared the makeshift podium. Then he put his speech in his suit coat's breast pocket and began shaking hands with the few news media people who were present. He then moved toward the lobbyists, and various curious onlookers who had stopped for a moment to see why the news media was there. Maxwell saw Congressman Serento approaching and he took a moment to speak privately with him before the two stepped up to the microphone.

Also present was Consultants International's legal representative, Arthur Mercer, who had learned of the upcoming announcement. He had flown to Washington, DC, and asked certain members of the media to attend who he knew would be sympathetic to the commercial industries that would be impacted.

"Good morning, everyone. I'm Senator Henry Maxwell and I am joined here today by Congressman Al Serento from Colorado to announce our intentions to hold hearings and to introduce legislation on matters which we consider to be of great importance to the nation, to the environment, and to our citizens for generations to come.

"Congressman Serento and I intend to work closely with our colleagues, both in the House and the Senate, to discover the legislative needs in order to designate a significant portion of the American West as regions to be protected from any kind of development whatsoever. It is our hope that steps can be taken that will result in mutually agreed legislation from both Houses of the Congress which can then be signed into law by the President.

"We believe the environment needs to be protected and preserved to promote tourism and outdoor recreation across the regions affected. Among our area of focus will be to limit or eliminate any further prospecting, timbering, real estate development, and anything else that would be done on both private and federal lands. We hope to start the ball rolling in certain locations and then to gradually expand those areas to envelop regions we believe to be in need of our attention. I'd now like to turn the microphone over to Congressman Serento for any questions you may have."

Congressman Serento gave an equally brief speech, essentially mirroring the same subjects. One reporter asked him, "Can you elaborate what kinds of changes could be made at the federal level?"

"As you know, there are several parts of the US government that play a hand in preserving and protecting federal land. I envision, among many other possibilities, possible restrictions on the commercial cutting of trees and the digging up of land for monetary gain."

"What about the jobs these industries create? Why not just introduce legislation to preserve wildlife?" asked one reporter.

Serento continued, "We have many constituency groups who have been demanding that all levels of government protect our lands—"

Another reporter interrupted, "Cutting down trees? They grow back."

"Yes, but the damage done by soil erosion—"

"Are you getting campaign contributions from these environmental groups?" yet another reporter interrupted.

Senator Maxwell leaned over and whispered to Serento, "Looks like the right wing media outnumbers our friends. Maybe we should wrap it up."

Congressman Serento answered the question, saying that all members of Congress receive contributions from many opposing constituencies, but that does not sway those who are elected from doing what's in the best interests of the voters and the nation.

A last question asked of him by a reporter was, "Can't you extend your areas of focus to include all of the United States?"

Serento replied that their focus would be on certain areas at first but that eventually any subsequent legislation could be applied elsewhere. There was the political reality they had to accept. Other members of the House and Senate might vote for legislation that did not affect their own states as readily as they would for legislation for other places. Voting for something elsewhere could earn them a reciprocal favor one day from some other member of Congress who had not wanted such legislation to be applied to his own congressional district or state.

With the press announcement concluded, Arthur Mercer next went to a meeting he had scheduled with a major lobbying firm on K Street. *This is going to cost Consultants International big bucks*, he thought to himself. The timing for all this attention on matters that could affect his client's Mega Trend initiative from Congress was lousy. But he couldn't divulge the ongoing initiative. It had to be handled as merely an ongoing concern of the logging and mining industries, one that would affect many significant companies who employed hundreds of thousands of people across the country. Consultants International's board members would each chip in the needed funds directly from their own company's check books. They would be seen as the lobbyist's clients. Wayde Ramsley would only be seen as a kind of behind-the-scenes coordinator for the other companies. He arranged for the lobbying firm to get into contact with Wayde Ramsley in Denver to work out the details for an effort that could counter Senator Maxwell's intentions.

Mercer sat and listened to the options the lobby firm's manager laid out to him. They could launch a multipronged approach soliciting campaign contributions from mining and timber industry associations, all of which represented hundreds of individual and corporate interests favorable to countering the Senator's planned initiative. There were also individual corporations that would want to participate in a counterattack. Their corporate executives would be scheduled to visit their congressional representatives to protest any legislation that could harm their business interests. An additional approach would be to contact labor unions for the mining sector to ask for their support and efforts to convince their local congressional representatives that such legislation would hurt their current and future union members. There were local- and state-elected officials who would weigh in, ones who wanted to grow their economies, increase tax revenues, and provide an increasing tax base from wages and profits earned through industry-related businesses.

As the meeting progressed, Mercer got the picture that the lobbying firm could have a meaningful role to play provided they did what they said they could do. The amount of pressure they could raise could be substantial. Choosing one of the most successful and expensive lobbying firms was like choosing a top-notch law firm comprised of highly successful and talented people. Success depended on the knowledge, skills, and abilities of those they employed.

The discussion moved forward to organizations that would favor such legislation. They discussed the pros and cons of trying to dissuade them from outright support for the possible coming proposed legislation. There were methods they could use but they would add to the costs of killing Senator Maxwell and Congressman Serento's proposal. They could be bought off by the industry with contributions to their organizations.

One such possible concern, for example, was how the many dozens of Indian reservations would react to such sweeping legislation. They would be caught in the middle. Many mining operations were located in remote locations where the labor pool consisted, to a significant degree, of Indians. Those that were employed by mining companies earned excellent wages. It allowed many to benefit their families and their reservations with the added extra income. They bought or built new homes or renovated existing ones. They employed reservation-

based contractors and many other reservation-based businesses with the wages they earned. Most Native American
seasoned mining employees who were also members of unions
had moved their lifestyle affordability into the upper middle
income range.

Some reservations had already established considerable
commercial developments including shopping centers and
other types of businesses previously only found off of reservations. Many reservations had established very profitable
casinos, some more than one casino, both on and off reservation on land they purchased and which became "tribal" land.
The proceeds of the casinos often went towards acquiring
new businesses such as remarkably well-run commercial golf
courses, resorts, marinas, restaurants, commercial real estate to
be rented out, and nurseries. The list was endless.

On the other hand, there were continuing sentiments and
grievances among many Native Americans and their tribal
governments, one that contradicted the employment and
business benefits of supporting the mining and lumber industries. They still saw all land as having previously been theirs.
They felt that the land contained riches that rightfully histori-
cally belonged to them. It had been a tug of war of sentiments
that had existed ever since reservations had been created. On
many reservations where mining companies wanted to set up
operations, tribes had negotiated contracts to hire a percentage of the needed personnel from the reservation and to pay a
percentage of the proceeds to the reservation for the minerals
extracted from their reservation land. But they also held some
sentiment that the land outside of their reservations belonged
to them. It had been taken from them and some believed they
should benefit in some way from those lands as well.

It was the lobby firm's manager's opinion that the Native American community could become a factor in their effort to defeat Senator Maxwell's plans.

It would be costly to visit all of the possible impacted reservations to try to convince them of which side they should be on. Perhaps they could employ Native American organizations, associations, and charitable entities for a fee, a contribution to win them over to not resist the mining industry's counterpunch to Maxwell's new initiatives. Through such contacts, inroads could be made with those who counted on the reservations.

"Importantly," the lobbyist said, "the last thing you and I need to do is to alienate these people. They are a powerful lobby in their own right. There are many sympathetic ears on the Hill who would listen to them and support their concerns. Better to get as many of the Native American reservation leaders on our side and to keep them there. The alternative is to alienate them and to cause them to make your job and ours to kill Maxwell's plans all that much more difficult."

After the meeting with the lobbyists, Mercer returned to his hotel room and prepared an e-mail that he would send directly to Wayde Ramsley. In it he included all that had been said at that morning's press announcement by Maxwell and Serento, and the ideas presented by their new lobbying firm. Soon after sending the e-mail, he got a phone call from Ramsley who wanted to discuss some of the issues that Mercer had raised in conjunction with some concerns that were partly related.

"Art," Ramsley began, "some of the ideas the lobbyists expressed intrigues me. I see some potential."

"I think I know what you're going to say," replied Mercer.

"The part about winning over the Indian people from all the western states, how could we go about it?" Ramsley asked.

"I suspect there are over a hundred reservations that could be affected. I just don't know how to approach it."

"We could hire a public relations firm. One with experience in Native American concerns and issues."

"Such as helping them get approvals, agreements, contracts with local and state governments for new casinos?" asked Ramsley.

"Yes," Mercer continued. "There are a few such organizations that the various reservation tribal councils employed very successfully. In many locations, they were able to get local and state governments to support their desires to be able to extend previously confined reservation lands to new commercial properties for tourist initiatives, hotels, casinos, commercial buildings, etc."

Ramsley countered, "Do you know who these public relations people are? I mean, do they work alone? Do they visit politicians and tribal leaders? Do they gain the support of local people, towns?"

"I'm aware of one such effort and the plan was similar to what you said. The lobbyist thought that there were many organizations that supported Indian causes. Sympathetic legal services, church groups, charities," Mercer responded.

"So," Ramsley continued, "a local hodgepodge of people working to help their reservation neighbors get what they wanted to help their own people."

"Yes," Mercer said. "The benefits for them to do so are obvious, such as reducing local crime rates and increasing the standard of living for both the Indians and those off the reservations. New businesses, offshoots, so to speak, and good will between local and state authorities with the tribes."

"And this senator and congressman will have to do battle with us and tribal, local, and state governments?"

"If we can enlist their support. Make them see reason for doing so. How it would hurt them on the one hand or help them on the other," Mercer replied.

"I have some other concerns, if you have a moment. I don't know if you, or we, are in a position to do much about it," said Ramsley.

"Go ahead, Wayde. My plane doesn't leave until tomorrow morning. I was just making some notes of ideas that we could pursue."

"I've been worrying a bit about some changes that the industry has experienced in the last few years. It has to do with the industry's, and perhaps soon with our, attempts to get routine processes accomplished. Federal agencies, almost to the exclusion of ones at the state level, seem to either be foot dragging by design, through no fault of their own, in processing claims filed by exploration and mining outfits. Then they have trouble getting permits for one thing or another, such as drilling. Worse, they have to wait years to get approval to build a mine, sometimes as much as ten years. It's unconscionable. You'd think what used to take a matter of months a decade or two ago would only take as long to do today. What the hell are they doing? They're killing the industry and the economy."

"In some cases, they use such ploys to shake down companies and businesses for donations to their election campaigns," Mercer said.

"Shakedowns seem to be everywhere these days. It's always been their way. Maybe it's damn time to reverse the tables and shake them down. Why do we always have to buy our way into getting something done that should have been done in the first place? When things are broken, fix 'em. Just do it. Make it happen," said Wayde Ramsley.

"Do you think any of it is partially related to the budget cuts these agencies have been experiencing?" asked Mercer. "If so, maybe it was by design by certain members of Congress to try to slow down the agencies which would in turn slow down industry, to frustrate them, make them want to do their exploration in some other country," he said, seemingly thinking out loud.

"The people in these government field offices are always professional," Ramsley added. "Perhaps I shouldn't have used the words foot dragging. These people don't set policy. They just do what they can with what they have. The requirements placed on them to do studies, write reports, allow for public comment time frames, to hold public meetings, etc., I mean, the process is getting lengthier while their staffing levels and funding are getting reduced."

"Perhaps it is by design, as you mentioned," Ramsley explained. "I don't know whether this could be a part of our lobbyist's efforts or not, to try to influence favorable members of Congress to reduce the number of hoops we all have to jump through. Maybe they can go to others in Congress and build their own support for a bill, one that could get support for adding more money to these agencies' budgets. Require that the money be used to staff their field offices, and not their headquarters or regional offices. Require some sort of measurable improvement rate in processing their work like we have to do each and every day in order to stay ahead of the competition in processing ore, efficiency, and effectiveness, and all that."

"That's the trouble, Wayde. They have no competition. They don't have to compete. Only the elected officials have to compete when they run for election. That's the playing field," Mercer said, using a sports metaphor. "They compete for dollars so they can campaign, so they can win. Ironic, isn't it? Government agencies don't compete. They set the rules and call the shots. Only a court of law can reverse their decisions."

"Shameful," replied Ramsley.

Mercer continued, "I'll bring it up with our lobbyist. It wouldn't hurt to develop a broader offensive to include pushing certain members of Congress favorable to our concerns to plan their own in-house political offensive. They will naturally want to protect their constituents' interests back home. It's instinctive for them to want to do it. Their own reelections would benefit from it. But they'll expect campaign contributions. As you know, members of Congress usually prefer to only meet with constituents and others if they were campaign contributors. Everyone else is at the back of the line. Most people and business owners will never get to visit with their representatives. Not unless they pay for the privilege."

"That means us also," Ramsley thought out loud. "How much is that going to cost us?"

"We'll have to let the lobbyists figure that one out for you. Millions, I assume," Mercer stated. "There will likely be a lot of local- and state-elected officials with their hands out. This isn't going to be easy or cheap."

"It makes me feel that influencing government officials is as difficult a task as is finding the Mega Trend," Ramsley answered. "My God, Art. They stand right in front of us with their barricades preventing us from moving forward while they say we have to pay for the right to get past them."

"Yes, it's worse today than ever before," Art Mercer responded. "It's just another cost of doing business, Wayde. But then again, you know that it's far worse in most other countries. Bribes, shakedowns, payoffs."

"Yeah, we gotta play their game, I know. But I don't like playing defense. The more shit we throw back at them the better. Make it happen from every angle. Overwhelm them so that they end up playing defense. Not us." Ramsley paused for a moment and then said, before ending the phone call, "I plan to put some of this into an e-mail to all my staff here and in the field, and to include your e-mail to me. A kind of newsletter of things we have going on. Not a lot of detail but enough to keep my people here and my board of directors apprised."

———— ⁓◦◦◦◦◦◦◦⁓ ————

Later that day, each member of the company's board, Stuart Bergman, Alice Harrison, Larry McGray, and Dalton Trindall received a message from Wayde Ramsley. Attached to it was the e-mail Ramsley had received from Arthur Mercer outlining his day's activities. Although certainly not intended, distribution was also received by Tiponi Isaw on Dalton Trindall's stolen laptop.

Tiponi turned to look out her living room's sliding glass door to the balcony railing where she had placed a small bird feeder. She thought briefly about the small finch that was there feeding on the seeds. She enjoyed nurturing the one species. At the same time, she deplored the menacing birds of prey that occasionally used her balcony perch as a vantage point from which they could attack the ones that were comparatively weak and more vulnerable. There were the victimizers and there were the victims, the winners and the losers.

———— ⁓◦◦◦◦◦◦◦⁓ ————

Simultaneously, in Denver, Wayde Ramsley turned his leather, swivel, oversized executive chair to look out his window where he watched traffic out in the street. Cars that moved slowly were cut off by those whose drivers were more alert. It was a constant game, one that sorted out the meek from the aggressive. Ramsley knew that to make a business succeed, they had to employ every tool at their disposal to make the end objective a reality. He had to be aggressive and ahead of the competition if he wanted to win.

———∽∿∾⊙∾⊙∿∾———

In Washington, DC, Arthur Mercer turned on his television set and pressed its channel selector until he found a replay of a football game. He loved football and usually spent a part of his weekends watching his favorite teams out on the field defending their goal part of the time while taking the offense in an attempt to score a touchdown on the other.

While watching, he compared the two teams, each trying to have the advantage over the other, each trying to score points, doing battle up one side of the field and then down to the other. Battles in life were ever constant, even in the courtroom, he thought. Battles that had to be won by one side or the other. The winner, although sometimes unexpected, often successfully employed one particular play, the one that stood out as having made the difference. He wondered which one play would decide the outcome for Consultants International and the industry he was representing, in general. It was what was on "thinking people's" minds, how to get the upper hand and acquire an advantage that would spell the outcome of the game they played.

———∽∿∾⊙∾⊙∿∾———

Back in Senator Maxwell's office, he turned on his three televisions to tune in the evening news broadcasts for the channels whose reporters had attended his morning press announcement. The coverage was only carried by one.

After turning off the televisions, Maxwell looked out his Senate office window to see people scurrying out on the sidewalk quickly moving from one congressional office to another. Each person, he knew, was trying to curry political favor, or was trying to bolster their career. It was how they played their own game.

THE PROMISCUOUS PUPPETEER 183

Maxwell wondered whether his new environmental push would win him some new voters. The past election had been won by a large enough margin, but his possible upcoming contender was a battler, one who was smart, aggressive, and who wouldn't merely be on the defensive when on the ropes. Politics was all about winning, he knew, and taking one side or another meant there would be winners and losers. Some would lose something they believed strongly about and others, conversely, would eventually win what they were after. Maxwell was planning out a part of his next election's strategy. Whatever the issue, whether he believed in it or not, had to serve his re-electability. Just as it was for the people out on the sidewalk, it was always all about winning. To people like US Senator Henry Maxwell, it was how the game of politics was played.

———⁓⌒◦◦⌒⌒◦⌒⌒◦◦⌒⁓———

At the People's Republic of China Embassy, Quon Zhong had settled back into his chair looking out his window, wondering how he could benefit from the Consultants International matter. He contemplated what role he could play to take advantage of the situation, to take the offensive in a way that could benefit his career.

Zhong wanted to identify economic opportunities that his nation and its businesses could capitalize on. He thought about the slow down in work he had to address because of his host nation's traditional Christmas and New Year holiday season which was soon to also be interrupted with his own nation's fast approaching Chinese New Year celebrations. They would result in the temporary closure of the embassy to the public. Behind the closed doors, more urgent, non-public matters would continue to be addressed by a handful of their essential staff, including himself.

Mr. Zhong had given almost daily thought to his father's admonition to be very careful with whatever he did. Making any kind of serious mistake could come to the attention of his father's Party leadership cohorts. "That," his father had said, "could end your ambition for receiving an ambassadorial appointment."

Contrary to his own ambassador's assurances to Consultants International's two visitors, Zhong had resorted to using a different communications system with his contacts in Beijing for matters related to the opportunity that had been presented to them. Instead of using the very slow method of diplomatic pouch courier, which could take a week in sending and then another week before receiving back communications, he used the embassy's encryption system which usually expedited the process significantly.

In one communiqué, he had been asked if he knew which companies had ownership of Consultants International and who the company's board members were.

Zhong replied, "No. It is not discoverable. Mr. Wayde's company is a private company. It is in the form of a shell company. It is privately owned by a few publicly-owned companies with shareholders. In the United States, such companies can be created and kept secret if it is in the best interest of the companies. Shareholders are only entitled to know things that they legally call material information, things that public corporations would eventually need to make known to their shareholders and to the public."

Zhong's counterparts replied, "We urge you to try to discover the names of the parent companies or the names of the shell company's board members. Or do you think it should be done by our intelligence services? We can gain access to their computer system without their realizing it before it is too late.

But doing so will eventually be discovered, as we know from prior computer break-ins."

Zhong responded, "I advise to not enter their computer system. If we decide to take them up on their offer, we will need to have no questions in their minds about our trustworthiness. If they suspect we have broken into their computer system, they may withdraw the offer they have made to us. Allow me to try another way. We have a Chinese national who is a practicing lawyer and who we have used before for legal purposes. Let me see if he can find a way to find out what you are asking."

Zhong contacted the lawyer by cell phone. He gave the lawyer Consultants International's name and address and asked if he could find out who the owners were. After a period of time, the lawyer called Zhong back saying that the company had not been incorporated in Colorado or in the United States. The company had been incorporated in the Bahamas. The lawyer offered to help make contact with a Bahamian law firm where he knew an attorney. Zhong was told that there would likely be a price for obtaining the information, if Zhong wanted him to continue with his research.

Zhong reported to his contact in Beijing what he had been told. The reply he then received said, "Yes, pursue this for us. Tell our lawyer friend in the United States that we can have one of our people at the embassy send him payment, if it is not unreasonable. Do not tell him how we can make such a payment. Protect our methods. All he needs to know is that we can pay a small reasonable amount for the information."

Quon Zhong relayed the request to his friendly lawyer contact and asked to first agree on what the cost would be. A couple of days later, Zhong was told the price for the information would be five thousand dollars payable only if the Bahamian attorney could ascertain the information that was wanted.

Zhong then instructed the lawyer to tell his Bahamian lawyer that he agreed to the cost.

A week later, Quon Zhong's US-based lawyer reported back. The names were for other companies but not for individuals. Zhong wrote down the list of corporate names and then looked up the corporations on the internet. They consisted of a few of the largest mining companies with huge assets in multiple locations in the US and elsewhere around the world. One had an ongoing mining operation in China itself. Zhong looked up the names of the CEOs of the companies and wrote them into a communiqué back to his Beijing contacts along with the other information that had been relayed.

Shortly later, he received a reply authorizing him to arrange the five thousand-dollar payment to the lawyer in the Bahamas. It also said, "We have had occasion to learn of the company's CEO whose company has a 50 percent control over a mining operation in China. We are aware of some information he would not want known. We will let you know further when necessary."

What Zhong was not told was that China's internal intelligence service had arranged for the CEO of Becklen Mining, Robert Mendelson, to lose a very large sum of money. He had been served a beverage that contained a substance that made him incapable of using good judgment. He had already lost what money he could obtain through his credit card. He was offered a very large advance on credit while at a casino in Hong Kong. Having lost all the money, as had also been arranged, a very young looking female model had been sent to his room, "compliments of the casino." After they spent some time together in the room satisfying drug-induced erotic desires he had not previously possessed, he was intentionally lied to by the woman who told Mendelson that she was a fifteen-year-old school girl, when in fact she was of legal age.

She told him that the casino employed her and that she had been told to very specifically tell him "my visit with you is on the house and to not forget to pay the eight hundred thousand dollars you owe the casino."

CHAPTER 13

Vancouver, British Columbia

Someone…had slipped him a Mickey.

Gordon Bessert finished a phone call with his subordinate David Ritter who was the CEO of Bessert Resources. The company was a privately-held enterprise consisting of a large investment brokerage business with offices spanning the width of Canada. Included in Bessert Resources were major stakes in various exploration and mining companies and a chain of hotels in both the US and Canada. His net worth was assumed to be well in excess of several billion dollars.

He had used his wealth to become the largest shareholder of Becklen Mining, one of the largest precious metals mining companies in North America. As a result, he had asked for and received the opportunity to place his executive vice president of Bessert Resources, Les Grundall, on the board of directors for Becklen Mining.

The call from David Ritter had been to inform Bessert of information Grundall had passed on to Ritter. It was information that Grundall was prohibited from disclosing, scant as it was. Gordon Bessert had wanted to place one of his people on the board of Becklen Mining so that he could, on occasion, learn of anything that would cause him to want to sell his shares or conversely perhaps increase his stake in the company.

Grundall had mentioned to Ritter that a consortium of companies had joined together to form a new exploration and mining initiative to include Becklen Mining itself. The purpose of the new company was to investigate the potential for identifying the long-speculated gold-bearing fault line that was believed by some to run from somewhere in Canada southward into Mexico, and possibly Central America.

Gordon Bessert had been around the mining industry long enough to have heard the gold fault line hypothesis from a great many well-known industry people. It was the kind of lore that many believed possible but likely impossible to ever prove. The costs would be too high and the risks too great. Yet here it was. There was a group of major mining visionaries attempting to establish at least a part of what had always been assumed as unachievable. There would seemingly be insurmountable obstacles, he knew, and such a project had previously been written off by industry experts as a fanciful delusion.

The major mining companies, pooling their resources, could afford the exploration effort, but what about the next stage and the stage after that? At some point, they would have to go public with what they were doing and how much it was costing. Those companies' share prices could plummet unless the answers to shareholders' questions were sufficient to convince them that the effort was viable and would be profitable. The quandary Gordon Bessert found himself in was whether to sell all of his stock, slowly over a period of time so as to not be noticed, or to wait a while so he could learn more about the project.

Gordon Bessert thought about the information he had been given. He knew better than to try to directly obtain any other specific information about it either through David Ritter or Les Grundall.

One question that kept coming back to him as he paced back and forth in his massive home was whether or not this new company, owned by a few others, would ever be "spun off" as a public offering with shares for sale to the general public. If so, it would need to be done before any announcement about what the company had been working on. It would also need to be done before the new company took any steps that would prematurely make its secret known by way of any significant action that would draw attention to itself. He knew that the other mining companies that were backing the effort would want it no other way. They would want a pro rata share of the new company while everything was seemingly quiet. Then, after a period of time, they would announce the plan once it was safe to do so. If everything was timed right, an initial offering for the purchase of shares, say at thirty cents a share, could skyrocket ten times higher, twenty times higher, maybe even more over time, becoming a stock worth maybe two, four, six, or even eight dollars a share almost overnight.

It was the way Gordon Bessert had originally made his fortune back in the late 1970s and early 1980s by buying so-called exploration company penny stocks, ones that had gold in the ground, ones who timed their news releases of what they discovered for when the price of gold was constantly rising, making new highs, ones that had made him extraordinarily rich at a very early age.

The gold market had been going through a correction and the time was approaching when it was expected that the price of gold would double or triple and silver would increase more than gold over the not-too-distant future. Bessert felt the adrenalin flow through his veins and the quickened pace of his heart beat as he relished the thoughts going through his mind. *One last chance for another bite of the apple*, he thought. It didn't matter whether this new company actually found as much as what they had hoped. It didn't matter whether any drill bits ever dug into the earth. The opportunity for a quick fortune would be in the early days of any announcement about the finding of a new gold trend that stretched from the icy cold regions of the north all the way to the hot sun-drenched lands to the south.

It wasn't the money he wanted as much as the "score," the big win, the thrill he experienced many times before that he wanted to feel once again. His quest had become a driving force that made him what he was today. It had become addicting and his successive successes since nearly thirty-five years earlier proved that his talents had been a match for searching out, finding, and capitalizing on certain opportunities. If this new company was to become one of them, he needed to find out more, a lot more, before he could better judge the risks involved and whether it would be the kind of investment he would try to participate in.

Gordon Bessert picked up his phone and placed a call to the head of his investment company. He directed that one or two of their best researchers be devoted to monitoring any and all activity that smelled like new initial public offerings, or IPOs, as they were called. Next, he called one of his confidants, an attorney who also moonlighted as an investigator. Bessert explained to him what little he knew and suggested a good starting place to dig for information would be with Becklen Mining, headquartered in Vancouver, B.C., where most new venture companies began their start in life and where many remained as they became industry powerhouses.

"Find me what you can," he instructed his long-time friend, "but don't make any contact with our guy on Becklen's board. I don't want to be accused of trying to find out insider information through one of my employees. It's okay if I find out information through research and the like, but not through any quid pro quo, something in exchange for something."

Bessert's investigator assured him that he knew where the bright line was and when not to cross it. He would see what he could find out.

Bessert's investigator called him back two days later to report what he had learned. The investigator had called someone with the North American Miners Association to try to learn the names of companies exploring land in Idaho and Nevada. He received an e-mail back from his contact saying that there were several thousand exploration companies in existence and a couple of dozen of them were known to have done some work in Nevada and Idaho. His contact said that the list was surely incomplete but he provided the names of a couple dozen possibilities. Next, the investigator had checked with various US Bureau of Land Management offices in the region and he was provided a public website he could access which showed claims filed, the names of those who filed them, the locations, and the dates of when they had been filed. The investigator checked with contacts in the mining industry and learned the names of possible prior CEOs who had left their old jobs and moved on to new ones as CEOs. He had acquired a list of new corporations established in Nevada, Idaho, and the usual location for new exploration and mining companies, in Vancouver, B.C. The list was extensive.

Having nothing new that was revealing and still wanting to know more, he took the chance of calling Les Grundall. After exchanging the usual casual greetings to each other, Bessert invited Grundall to his home for lunch. He asked Grundall to bring information with him pertaining to how Bessert's investment business was doing and what the quarterly report figures might look like if the economy continued to slowly improve. Bessert said that he and many others were beginning to believe that the stock markets could double in value over the upcoming few years for a variety of plausible reasons. Bessert intended to slip into their luncheon briefing a question or two that might reveal more about what he really wanted to know.

That noon, Les Grundall sat at Gorden Bessert's kitchen table. It was large enough and of the quality that most would have thought it to be the kind that is usually found in the average well-furnished formal dining room. Bessert's wife had prepared sandwiches and soup for the two men and then went to another part of the home.

After discussing his investment business, Bessert asked Grundall how CEO Bob Mendelson was doing at Becklen Mining. Grundall was mindful that Bessert had arranged for him to be a board member of Becklen, something that would help on his resume should he want to be considered for a higher position someday with Bessert Resources, or anywhere else.

Gordon Bessert asked, "Does Bob Mendelson have any blind spots, flaws that could jeopardize our investment?"

"Well, I guess the usual, like all of us," Les Grundall replied, trying to dodge the question with an innocuous reply.

"Nothing you have seen or heard about?" Bessert pressed.

Les Grundall thought for a few seconds and wondered if Bessert could have learned the same information he had been recently told. "I got a call from one of Mendelson's VPs who had been on a trip with Mendelson last week to visit their Chinese mine. On the way back, they laid over in Hong Kong for a night. The hotel had a large casino on the first floor. This VP said that Mendelson got blind drunk, and ran up a debt he didn't pay for while in the casino," Grundall said.

Gordon Bessert interrupted, asking, "What do you think was this VP's motive for telling you this?"

"Stuff happens," Grundall said and then continued, "maybe the VP has a grudge or he wants to get Mendelson removed, maybe so that the VP could be considered for the CEO position, I don't know for sure. But this VP has occasionally told me some things to try to get me to rely on him, to trust him for whatever reason."

"What else?" Bessert asked.

"There's more," said Grundall. "The VP said that while Mendelson was at the craps table he noticed Mendelson seemingly unsteady on his feet. There was an American couple talking to others in their group, maybe a tour group. He heard one say that the guy at the craps table had been advanced eight hundred thousand dollars' worth of chips to play with, and that in the course of less than a half hour, he had lost it all. The gambler, the tourist said, seemed unfazed by it."

"This just doesn't sound right. It makes me feel that there must be more to it. Things like that just don't happen as a matter of course," Bessert thought out loud.

"Perhaps we'll never know," said Grundall. "I can think of a couple reasons why someone could have arranged all this. Maybe to compromise him. Make him vulnerable. Something more than what it appears to be."

Gordon Bessert thought briefly that Mendelson probably had not paid back the debt. "And that's it?" he asked.

"No, not exactly. The VP said Mendelson left the casino and he saw him get on an elevator to go back up to his room. About a half hour later, the VP went up to his own room and as he was preparing to insert his room's key card, he heard a door open further down the hallway. He saw a very young looking girl come out and walk past him. The VP fiddled with his key card as if having trouble getting it to unlock his door. After the girl was gone, the VP walked down the hallway to the door the girl had come out of. He noted the room number posted on the door, went back to his own room and dialed the room number to see who would answer. The voice that answered was Mendelson's. The VP disguised his voice and said 'Sorry I have the wrong number,' and hung up."

Bessert sat transfixed, surprised, while he thought about what had just been said. "This girl thing. Do you believe what the VP told you? Might it have been made up to spice up the story to try to create a situation that might eventually bring Mendelson down?" asked Bessert. "It seems surreal, concocted for some reason."

"I have no way of knowing," Grundall simply said.

The two men discussed other things while they finished their meal together. Bessert thanked Grundall for the briefing, they shook hands, and Les Grundall headed back to his office.

Bessert knew the Becklen Mining CEO, Bob Mendelson, from the many work-related and social functions they had both attended during recent years in Vancouver. Bessert wasted no time in wanting to try to learn more. He placed a call to Mendelson, who took the call. The opening words they exchanged between each other were friendly and Bessert then asked, "Can you meet me this evening at five for dinner at Rowe's Surf and Turf down on Howe street? I have something for you."

Later that afternoon, Bessert and Mendelson were escorted to a table with a window, and ordered drinks and placed their food order. The conversation at first ranged from the economy, to the price of various precious metals, followed by the problems small explorers and miners were expected to continue to experience in acquiring needed funding until the mining sector recovered after a nearly two year-long slump. Prices had solidified in related stocks and precious metals prices and significant increases had been predicted in the coming few years.

Then, at just the right moment, Gorden Bessert softened his voice and said, "I've learned that you have a debt to pay in Asia. I know you won't want to talk about it so I won't ask you to tell me all about it. I just want to know if it is true and that the amount is somewhere close to a million dollars."

Bob Mendelson's face turned red. After a few seconds of each man staring at each other, Mendelson asked, "Where did you hear this?"

"It doesn't matter. You have a friend who wants to help you. In fact, more than just one. Was I close to right in what I have heard?" asked Bessert.

"I don't know," Mendelson began to say in denial, not wanting to have to discuss what happened in Hong Kong.

"Look, Bob. You and I have been friends for many years. I helped you with your selection as Becklen's CEO. I have been one of your largest shareholders, if not the largest. I'm worried that maybe you have a problem. If so, I can help to fix it. I have a lot at stake. You don't need any kind of scandal. Nor does Becklen Mining. Here's a check that should help pay half or more of what you owe. You pay the balance. You can pay me back later, over time. For now, I want to help you get this debt behind you. We both have too much to lose."

Gordon Bessert reached across the table and handed Bob Mendelson a folded check. Mendelson opened it and saw that it was made out to him for five hundred thousand Canadian dollars. He folded the check back up and put it into his shirt pocket. Then he said, unsmiling, "A short-term loan," as if a statement and not a question.

"Yes," replied Bessert, "just for a while until you can arrange your finances to pay me back. I wrote on the bottom of the check in the memo section 'Loan.' I don't want to know about the details. I just want to know that you won't owe those people anything."

"Thank you, Gordon," was all Mendelson could find words to say. He was embarrassed and at the same time his guard went up. Something told him that there could be more to this check, some kind of unspoken strings attached to it.

Both men continued with their meals and Bessert asked Mendelson if he would be interested in going salmon fishing sometime in the future when the season was right. Bessert explained that he had a beach home with a guest cottage over in Victoria, on the island of Vancouver, and a fishing boat they could use.

Then Gordon Bessert asked, "Is Becklen Mining involved in expanding their exploration division?"

"Not directly, but we are always having our geos checking out areas of interest for us in South and North America, Africa, places like that."

Gordon Bessert noticed how Mendelson had skillfully tried to avoid the question by using the words "not directly." He then asked with equal skill, and uncharacteristic bluntness, "How about indirectly?"

"Well, you know I can't talk about it, insider stuff and all that, but we are a part of something we and others put together to explore something we have all been interested in doing for years. We pooled our company's funds to check out something that may or may not pay off. It's too early to tell," explained Bob Mendelson.

"Do you have someone who can handle it, someone you trust?"

"Wayde—I mean, our guy has what it takes. If there is a stone unturned in their search, he will make sure it gets looked under."

"Could this help Becklen Mining? Is there good reason to believe it will help our share price?" asked Bessert.

"Could be. Maybe we'll know soon, in a few months. I can't tell you anything about it, Gordon. You understand, don't you? I really appreciate your wanting to make a loan to me but let me return this check to you," Mendelson said, as his hand went towards his shirt pocket.

"No, no," Bessert quickly said as he held up his hand in protest, not wanting the check back. "There's no quid pro quo here. I'm not looking for information in exchange for loaning you some money."

"Thank you anyway, Gordon," Mendelson said with genuine warmth as he handed the folded check back to Gordon Bessert. "I can solve my little problem, and I will."

After their meal together, Gordon Bessert drove towards his home on the outskirts of Vancouver. Along the way he recalled that Bob Mendelson had begun saying something that sounded like he had used the first name of someone heading up the new company, someone named Wayde. Bessert made a mental note to have his investigator research all industry-related names, with similar spellings.

———⁓⌇⊙⟨⊙⟩⊙⌇⁓———

While Bob Mendelson drove towards his home, he thought about how he had been set up at the Hong Kong casino. He wondered if there was more to it. He planned to pay the sum he owed. He would have to make a significant shift in his investments, sell a lot of his assets, and then pay the debt.

Someone, Mendelson believed, had slipped him a Mickey, and they got him where they wanted him and did what they did for some reason. There had to be more to this than to just take what money he had already lost and to obligate him for the amount they said he still owed. It was likely a setup.

Maybe it had something to do with his company's 50 percent ownership in their Chinese mining operation. *Or*, it suddenly dawned on him, *could it be related to the Chinese interest in the Mega Trend initiative?* They had been invited to consider buying it from Consultants International and the companies that owned it. All of Consultants' board members had been informed of Wayde Ramsley's meeting with the Chinese both in Washington, DC, and in Las Vegas. Robert Mendelson quickly discounted that notion as quickly as he had thought of it. It was absurd. *But,* he then thought, *if there was such a connection, and if the Chinese made an offer to buy Consultants International, that would be the time when they would somehow try to sway my vote to be in favor of a low offer. They could try to blackmail me by saying that I should vote in favor of their offer. Failing to vote for such an offer could result in having my debt and young girl problem, which they may have created, become public information.* His career would be finished. And he wondered what else might happen as a result?

Mendelson feared that if Gordon Bessert was already aware of the debt issue, he also might know about the setup with the girl. If so, how could Bessert try to use the information? Or had had Bessert already tried? If not, what else could he do? Could Bessert try to blackmail him for whatever reason that financially motivated him? He had been willing to risk loaning five hundred thousand dollars for some much bigger reason.

Then, as Mendelson pulled into his garage, he wondered who tipped off Gordon Bessert. How did he learn about the gambling debt issue? Who else knew about his Hong Kong problem? Who else would have leverage over him if they chose to try to use it? There were a lot of unscrupulous people always watching and waiting to learn of something they could use to their advantage. Blackmail, extortion, and the shakedown racket, he knew, was unfortunately alive and well in every walk of life.

CHAPTER 14

Denver, Colorado

Time to fish or cut bait.

An e-mail had been sent by Stuart Bergman to his two field supervisors, Dalton Trindall and Larry McGray, asking them to come to Denver. They had been working an area that stretched from the village of Goldfield and Silver Peak, Nevada, southward to the almost imperceptible village of Gold Point, all of which were about thirty to fifty miles south of Tonopah. The names of the villages had been a clear indication that prior mining done in those areas had resulted in visible precious metal discoveries and recoveries, sufficient to have been worthy of the names given to the villages.

Dalton Trindall and Larry McGray had decided to ride together so that each could get cleaned up and gather what they would need for the two-day trip. Stu Bergman planned to meet with them to discuss their progress in the field and to review maps and newly received assay results from the laboratory. The information would help the field teams adjust their areas of exploration so as to keep working along the clearly developing gold-bearing fault line.

They would spend a night south of Tonopah and then proceed on to Las Vegas the next day for a flight to Denver. Dalton had placed a call to Rodrigo Black Coyote to see if he would be available to join him for a beer at a local restaurant. Rodrigo's wife, Susan, answered and said that it was good to hear from him after so long. She thanked him for the dinner gift certificate he had sent them a few months back and said that her husband and his mother were at a jewelry show and wouldn't be home until the coming weekend. Her husband, she had said, would be disappointed.

Trindall and McGray landed at Denver's Stapleton Airport, rented a car, checked into a motel, and then went to Consultants International to meet with Stu Bergman.

"We are approaching nut crunching time," Bergman said as the three sat around the conference room table. "We received back the assays from your people's work in northern Idaho and the results are better then we had expected. Gold and silver was indicated almost everywhere your team went. They were on the right trajectory as they moved further north. We can see from this map that there's a clear path delineated by the results we inputted into our database. The other test results for the area were overlaid on top of the results from your soil sampling and we have a match. I don't know if we'll have time to proceed further north from where we stopped when winter set in. We could send Larry and his team back up there, now that spring is approaching and the snow is melting, and they would be able to better see the ground for what to pick up as samples, or we can all stay on our path headed towards the Nevada and California border."

"Do you have any of the assays back for the samples we gathered so far this winter in Nevada?" asked Larry McGray, hoping to not have to return to the still cold and snow-covered ground south of Coeur d'Alene, Idaho.

"Yes," said Bergman. "Here are the results." He handed a packet of papers showing the numbers. "You both have been right on the money, on the right path heading south. Then again, maybe gold is everywhere down that way. The location of the villages named after gold and the mining results from decades ago seem to indicate that you can't help not finding it. There could be more than one gold ore-bearing fault line. Conversely, gold could have been sprayed out of the ground in all directions for miles to the east and to the west, from many places back when the dinosaurs ruled."

Dalton interjected, "Then we know that the gold is widespread. We just don't know how wide. The dilemma is in deciding how wide we may eventually want to go in staking out claims. As for the length, we know it likely continues south to Death Valley just across the border to California. Maybe we should try to split up the two teams and widen our search so we can determine which acreage in between would be best for filing claims."

"Right," Bergman said. "But this time, do a grid search further apart. Maybe the assays will tell us where the gold in the ground would likely begin to thin out, where the edge of the gold is to the east and to the west moving in a southerly direction."

All three discussed at length that afternoon the areas remaining to be sampled. Then their attention was refocused on discussing having Larry McGray's team getting back up north to Idaho within several weeks for one more push further north. They also discussed the possibility of sending Dalton Trindall's team to the south side of Death Valley to see if the gold fault line could be identified and followed the rest of the way towards the Mexican border. After much discussion, it was decided to leave the decision up to Wayde Ramsley. It was already early March and, Bergman knew, Ramsley would soon feel the need to make a decision about setting up arrangements to meet with his board of directors to discuss whether the information they had literally unearthed was sufficient to make a decision to proceed in implementing their phase two. The board members would need sufficient time to prepare the necessary funding for staking out all the land they had an interest in and the significant costs associated with the filing of all the necessary claims, an effort that would, at the very least, take them well into late summer or early fall for the areas of greatest interest.

Dalton and McGray returned to Las Vegas from Denver and Dalton again made a quick call to Emelina Black Coyote. Susan answered the phone and explained that her husband and Emelina would be back from a jewelry show trip at any moment. Dalton told her that he was on his way to a favored Tonopah restaurant and he invited the family to join him as his guests at six that evening should they wish to meet him.

———————

That evening, Rodrigo and his mother walked into the restaurant. Dalton had somehow not expected them to accept his invitation after having just returned from an arts festival in San Diego. The meal was better than Dalton had expected. The conversation partly evolved to the turquoise and silversmith work Rodrigo had to do to replenish his inventory for an upcoming outdoor retail event.

As they were leaving the restaurant, Dalton turned to Emelina and asked her if she might want to join him some time in the near future for a movie and a meal. Emelina hesitated for a moment while looking up at Dalton's face, seemingly searching for any sign that would tell her more about him, and then gave a brief smile saying she would enjoy that. "But," she had said, "I'm often away a lot with Rodrigo so please give me plenty of advance notice."

Dalton simply replied that he would be working south of Tonopah for a few weeks.

———————

In Denver, Stu Bergman laid out all the maps and the assay results for Wayde Ramsley to see while he explained what they all indicated.

Ramsley quickly absorbed all of the newly updated information. He was not a novice in his field and he knew well that they were on the right track. He called in Alice Harrison, who also served as Consultants International's official corporate secretary and asked her to set up a board meeting at their Denver office for as early in April that the board members' schedules would allow.

"Do you have a meeting agenda of what you plan to cover, something that you want to me to convey to them?" she asked.

"Yes," Ramsley said. "Merely tell them that it's for an update on our progress and that it's time for a preliminary discussion about our possible time schedule if we are to proceed with phase two."

Ramsley turned toward Stu Bergman and with a chuckle he quipped, "Maybe we should tell them to bring their check books."

"How about bringing their golf clubs?" asked Bergman. "I can set up a day for you all to play together."

Ramsley quickly replied, "I need to get our work with them done. We can't spare an extra day."

———

There was a noticeable excitement in the air when Wayde Ramsley received a phone call from Beijing. They knew it was time, or getting close to the time, when they would have to "shit or get off the pot," as Ramsley was fond of saying.

The caller, Tai Shi Xin, had been the leader of the delegation that they had briefed and entertained. He wanted to know if he could visit with Wayde Ramsley within the next few days to talk about their interest in what had been proposed to them. Ramsley told him that he had no travel plans and would be available for whichever date he wanted. A day was chosen and agreed to. In the Mandarin language, Ramsley had learned, the first one or two words, if there happened to be three, were actually the last name, just the reverse of what it was for names in the English language.

Three days later, Wayde Ramsley met his guest, Mr. Tai Shi. He had practiced the phonetic pronunciation in his mind as Mr. "Tie She." He had wanted to have him wait a couple of minutes upon his arrival. Then, at the right moment, Wayde Ramsley opened his office door and briskly walked over to his guest and greeted him warmly.

In the conference room, with Stu Bergman present, the three engaged in brief conversation before settling down to the subject at hand. Mr. Tai Shi said, "I would like to ask if we can have more time to consider your proposal Mr. Ramsley."

"As you may recall, sir, we've been planning to make a decision on our phase two work this spring, in March or April," Ramsley replied. "We extended our field work by perhaps another two or three months because we've been having great success with our continuing assay results in the places where we want to continue to work. The map I had showed to you has been updated. Up here on this screen are two maps. As you can see, the one on the left is the one we showed you and your delegation when you last were here. The map on the right is the updated version showing the new results."

"That is very impressive Mr. Ramsley. You do move quickly. More quickly than we had thought you could. But we know that there is more to be done. We would like you to allow us to wait for our decision until you have completed more portions of your soil sampling work. We would like to see the results for new locations and compare them with the other tests that have been done," Mr. Tai Shi said.

Wayde Ramsley was familiar with the delaying tactic often used by companies, regardless of their home locations. They often wanted to preserve some sort of "first come, first served" status but always wanted to know more before deciding their interest, making a commitment, followed by making an offer.

"This was a very long trip for you to make," Ramsley prodded. "You must be very tired. If at any point you want to return to your hotel room to get some sleep, please don't hesitate to say so. I imagine you must have some questions you'd like to ask of me.

"First, as I said. Can you tell me if you plan to start your phase two and if so, when?" Mr. Tai Shi asked, not mincing words.

"We've not decided yet on when we will implement phase two. I have scheduled a meeting with my company's board of directors to discuss that very question. They may decide to implement the next phase quickly or, like you, they may want to see more field work done which could delay implementing phase two by two or three months. In either case, once our board gives us their decision, we will immediately be sending a large number of people to start securing new claims. Money will be committed, and the price we mentioned will increase for our company," Ramsley said.

"And will your company become a public one, with shares for sale at that point?" Tai Shi intuitively asked.

"That is always a possibility," replied Ramsley.

"And, then if you did that, and also announced your project, what you have discovered, the share prices would rise, I think," Tai Shi said. "Unless something interfered with your news, something that was not good for investors to hear," Tai Shi added, seeming to be hinting at some tactic they could employ to their advantage, something that could keep the expected significant rise in a share price from happening.

"Such as what?" asked Ramsley

"Bad news can come in all forms," Tai Shi said. "If we were to become the owner of your company, we would have to weigh all possibilities that could hurt our investment. Do you know of any news that I should be aware of? Is there anything we should know that could affect such a decision? I think you call it full disclosure?"

"No, Mr. Tai Shi. Are you aware of any bad news that I should be aware of?"

"We heard rumors but it is only rumor. We have to ask, as you know."

"What kind of rumor?" Ramsley asked.

Mr. Tai Shi demurred in providing any specifics by merely shaking his head from left to right, indicating his preference in not pursuing the matter further. Ramsley's interest was heightened. Was this a ploy, a fabrication, a negotiating tactic, or was there something that Ramsley didn't know, something that the Chinese delegation was aware of that could impact Consultants International?

The meeting continued with discussions about the details of what had been discovered. Ramsley was in awe of Mr. Tai Shi's grasp of the many nuances found in his industry and its many facets. At certain points in their talk, Stu Bergman detected what he perceived to be questions that were being asked that were meant to merely try to "punch holes" in the project, to raise unfounded doubts about the project's viability and its eventual potential, ones that the Chinese could use to negotiate a lower price point for further discussion. His intuitions were proven correct when Mr. Tai Shi said, "We have no guarantees what the price for gold will be in the years ahead. It is a risk to assume the kinds of numbers you mentioned. Circumstances might dictate a much lower gold market price."

Ramsley retorted, "If you are aware of what the price of precious metals has been and where it has always gone, over the decades, even centuries, you know that the general trend is for new highs, not the other way around. I mentioned to you, Mr. Tai Shi, that your country's US dollar-denominated bonds would go down. I assert that the price of gold will go up, in the next five years, the next fifty years, the next five hundred years, and beyond."

Ramsley continued, "There will be gold and silver price corrections along the way for sure, but this huge project couldn't be mined in fifty years. The Carlin Trend in northeast Nevada has been mined for decades now and there still is no end in sight. The reason for that is because we believe there is no end immediately to the north or to the south of the Carlin Trend. We believe this gold-bearing fault line extends so far north and south that those who own the claims could continue to mine the gold for a century or longer while gold prices go up higher and higher from time to time. Those who own the claims and buy them at today's 'gold in the ground' values lock in that price forever. The cost of acquiring the land does not go up while the price of the gold, which the land contains, does. The owner of this project could control the gold market, control how much gold is released into the market from year to year. The profits should be so great that the owner could afford to continue to produce the gold when gold prices are in a correction mode. They could hold that gold in storage for the duration and then release it when gold prices rise once again, again, and again throughout our children's, our grandchildren's, and even our great-grandchildren's lifetimes."

Wayde Ramsley paused for a moment to let what he had just heard sink in. "I suspect that your people don't think that our company is worth one hundred and fifty billion dollars right now. I understand the caution. But if we do publicly market our company and its project, the share price could make our company worth far more than even two hundred billion dollars. It's possible we could see much higher values being applied to our company. No one knows for sure, but it is possible. You asked if we would sell off our company to public investors through stock issuances. Yes, we know that's one of our options. You wanted a part of what we are finding. The cost to you and any other investor will likely be much higher as the share price rises both immediately and in the future. If your people are interested they need to say so very soon, so we can all start the process leading to you being the new owners. Failing that, you may one day regret having passed up the opportunity we've presented to you. If you think we're in need of money to continue, and that we're desperate to sell a portion or all of our company, you would be mistaken. We are backed by a consortium of major very successful mining companies who can easily afford to bring this project to the next phase followed by the mining phase after that. In fact, I don't even have their permission to sell our company to you or anyone else. They will entertain all offers, as they should. I mention one hundred fifty billion dollars as an approximate minimum price. That does not mean that our board will accept such an offer. I hope my explanations and answers to your questions have been helpful to you, Mr. Tai Shi.

"On another subject," Ramsley continued. "I've never been to your country and my wife and I very much look forward to visiting it one day, perhaps soon, if we need to help you with the new ownership of our company. I don't think any of our board members have been to China. Perhaps we should think about having a final board meeting in China before we hand control of the company over to you if you decide to buy us out."

"All but one," Mr. Tai Shi quietly said.

"Pardon," said Ramsley.

"Maybe all but one have not yet been to China," he softly said.

"Then have you learned who our board members are, who they represent?" Ramsley asked, trying to suppress his rising anxiety that more of their company's secrets may have been discovered.

"All but one," was all he would say.

Mr. Tai Shi thanked Wayde Ramsley and Stu Bergman for taking time to allow him to visit. He was on his way to Washington, DC, to visit with one of their people before returning home.

"To see Mr. Quon Zhong?" asked Ramsley.

"Yes," said Mr. Tai Shi as they shook hands and ended the meeting. "As you know, he is our country's representative for economic development at our embassy. We have this and other opportunities to discuss with him. It is his job to help people like me when considering business opportunities in your country.

After his guest's departure, Wayde Ramsley wondered what his guest had been hinting at, if anything at all, about one of their board members having been to China.

On Ramsley's calendar for the next day, he was to meet with a well known multibillionaire from Vancouver, a sort of legend in their industry, Gordon Bessert. When the request for the meeting had been made, Ramsley wondered what it could be about. Ramsley had never met Bessert before, although they did know of each other. Ramsley wondered if there was yet another "leak in the dam" and whether Bessert had learned what Consultants International was doing.

Before leaving his office for the day, Ramsley sent a brief e-mail to his two field supervisors and Alice Harrison, outlining his take on how the meeting with his Chinese guest had gone. In it, he said that he had his doubts as to whether the Chinese people would make an offer for the company. It was a very high price to pay for a company that had essentially proven nothing. He added, "As you well know, gold in the ground will likely need to be proven with a hundred drill bits boring down, showing that what we have already said was backed further by assay results. They would likely hesitate wanting further validation. I sense that they might have a trick up their sleeve, something they might try at the final hour to make us feel pressure. They could want to put Consultants International in a position to feel compelled to consider a low offer. Something didn't sit right with me about a part of our conversation. Perhaps something about one of our board members. In any event," he finished, "I will be meeting with the board to present them with an update on your work. I hope to get a sense from them as to what their feelings are about further field work. Please let me know if you have anything new you would like me to consider presenting to them while they are here."

Ramsley then stopped in Stu Bergman's office while on his way out and asked, "Do you know if any of our board members have a connection to China? Some project going on there?"

Bergman replied, "Our members have dozens of projects going on all over the world. Let me check their company websites to see if I can find any who have a Chinese project already publicly disclosed. If not, it could be that perhaps one is in the making and we won't know until it reaches a news release stage where they need to disclose it. I'll check and let you know what I find tomorrow when you get in."

"Better yet," Ramsley replied, "call me right away if you find anything."

While driving to his home, Ramsley got a call from Stuart Bergman who told him that Becklen Mining had a 50 percent interest in a mine in China. Becklen Mining was the operator of the mine and that Consultants International's board member Robert Mendelson was the company's CEO.

The next day at nine in the morning, Gordon Bessert arrived at Consultants International and was immediately escorted into Wayde Ramsley's office. After greeting each other, the two sat in wingback chairs in the corner of Ramsley's office.

Bessert began saying, "I'll try to keep this short. I found out about your company through someone you don't know, at least someone I don't think you know."

"Anyone whose name you can share with me?" asked Ramsley.

"No, I'd prefer not to say who told me, Wayde," replied Bessert.

"I know you need to keep what you are working on secret and that you are not at liberty to tell me much if anything," Bessert continued. "But I'd like to know more. I'll understand your reluctance, but please know that I didn't come all the way down here from Vancouver to shake hands, do a song and dance for you, and then go back home."

"I don't know how I can help you," said Ramsley, waiting for the reason for Bessert's visit to reveal itself.

"I think you are conducting a major exploration effort and I'm wondering if you need any financing, maybe a 'private placement' financing, or a loan type of debenture, or perhaps a stock option type of arrangement," Bessert said, hoping he would see some eagerness in Ramsley's reaction.

"We have all the financing we need, as it stands today. Thank you for offering. It's hard to get exploration money from investors at the moment because of the declines in our market's sector. I can keep your offer to finance some of our costs in mind," Ramsley said, still wondering how much Bessert knew and from who.

"Do you need a partner or do you already have one?" Bessert asked, already knowing the answer.

"No, we don't, and I don't suppose we will be needing one, but we never can be sure. Maybe we will in the future. We have a few already working with us, funding us. They primarily own our company. If one decides to drop out, would you like for me to let you know?" Ramsley cautiously asked.

"Yes, but allow me to ask if you'd be interested in selling a part of the company, if not all of it."

"I know you could afford a good part of it and that you have extensive resources at your disposal," Ramsley countered, realizing that this conversation had become a cat and mouse game. He wondered which of them was the cat and which the mouse. Ramsley knew Bessert was far from a fool and certainly not gullible.

"I'd like to sign the usual nondisclosure agreement if you'll tell me what I need to know." It 's possible I could make an offer to buy your company, that is if the price is appealing and your company's board approves," Bessert stated. "Do you have any other parties expressing an interest?"

"Yes, but I can't say more about it, as I'm sure you can appreciate. By the way, how did you find us, me, our program? You have to know more than you've told me in order to feel the interest you have expressed," Ramsley asked.

"Word about your work here is likely to eventually slip out. You can't go on forever doing what you all are doing without people finding out something. It's just a matter of time before this becomes public. Once word spreads, the element of surprise is gone. Anything else your company may try to do won't have the same effect it would have had if you could have announced your own plan on your own timetable. If you offer stock for your company, timing will be everything. If you sell the company, you won't have to worry about it. It would be someone else's problem."

"I'm curious as to what brought you to me, Gordon. If we can have a trusting relationship, if you can bring yourself to tell me what you learned and how you learned it, I'd feel better about this meeting. I don't want to hold you at arm's length and I think you need to not want to hold me at arm's length either. We aren't breaking the proverbial ice here. How can we do that, you and I, get to understand each other better, to be able to relax in each other's company, not hold back secrets from each other? You asked me to tell you whatever it is you want to know about our business by offering to sign an agreement to keep the information secret."

"I understand how you feel," Bessert said, seemingly ready to give a little bit of ground and not resist having somewhat of a two-way give and take discussion.

"So, if you already know enough to bring you here to see me, then you know a whole lot more about what we are doing than I know about your reasons for making this trip."

"Well, okay. I learned a bit about you because someone slipped up and mentioned your name and that you were working on finding one of the largest gold discoveries ever made. I also learned what that project was about and to some degree where. I'm aware that you've been working on this for a couple of years and that you had to change your corporate name some months back because you thought your plans had been discovered, or were in danger of being discovered. I know what you have done in your lifetime and that your accomplishments speak for themselves. I know that you have a board of directors who hired you away from your last job. How they convinced you to take on this project, I don't know. But I'll assume that what you are working on would be a huge crowning moment for you if it all works out. The accomplishment would go down in the history books with your name right beside it in perpetuity. How am I doing, Wayde?"

"I am very impressed," replied Ramsley as he surmised that Consultants International's board member, the CEO of Becklen Mining, may have had something to do with Bessert's knowledge about everything.

"This is my point. I'd like in."

"I'll have to run this by my board," Ramsley lied.

"Call them now. I'll be at the Foothills Hotel in Golden, just west of Denver, waiting to hear back from you. I have other business here in Denver and I'll be here for a couple of days," Bessert said. "You and I know that this project of yours could become well known throughout the mining industry at the drop of a hat. It would be premature. I am under no agreement with you. Not now anyways. I am at liberty to discuss what I know with anybody. But I am willing to sign a nondisclosure agreement that would prohibit me from talking with anybody about what I know and learn," Bessert said.

Wayde Ramsley took Bessert's last comment to be a veiled threat. Bessert was at liberty to tell anyone he wanted to about what he already knew. Ramsley felt he was being shook down, extorted. He wondered if Bessert would try the same if he were negotiating a dollar figure for Consultants International or any other financial pitch that would clearly line Bessert's pockets to the disadvantage of Ramsley, his board, and his employees.

"I'll let you know," replied Ramsley. "It won't happen overnight. This could take quite a while. The board may want to meet to discuss the matter. It would help if you had an offer to make."

"How can I make an offer when I don't have access to all the details," Bessert countered.

"A fair point, but if the board wants to consider your request in person this could take a while," Ramsley said.

The two men stood up and said goodbye to each other. As Gordon Bessert departed, he left his business card containing his cell phone number with both Wayde Ramsley and his receptionist.

Bessert walked to the parking lot, pulled out his cell phone and called his lawyer saying, "I want you to call Becklen Mining's Robert Mendelson and to tell him that I want him to temporarily relinquish his board seat with Consultants International and to designate me as his interim replacement. I need it done today. If he balks, remind him that he owes me. Just say the word 'China.' He has something to hide and he knows that I know all about it. Then call a Wayde Ramsley at Consultants International and tell him the same thing. The board could refuse to acknowledge Mendelson's temporary designation of me as his stand-in. I'd like to get on the board but I realize that they can reject me in favor of anyone they choose. My objective here is to force the board to have to come together as soon as possible for another reason, and any good reason, such as this one, will suffice. Next, prepare a letter of agreement for nondisclosure and have it e-mailed to me."

Wayde Ramsley sent a brief e-mail to his headquarters staff and field supervisors. He told them about his meeting with Gordon Bessert and that it was possible Bessert could go public with what he already knew about the ongoing project if the company did not provide him with the information he was demanding. Ramsley implied that extortion was at play in that Bessert wanted to know everything about the company in case he was to make an offer to buy it out. Failing that, Bessert could retaliate by revealing their exploration secret. Ramsley warned that Bessert was well connected and could employ tactics that could seemingly seem inconsequential and that everyone should be especially on their guard to do their best to keep their work private.

Before ending his e-mail, Ramsley thought for a while about Bessert's motives. He was very skilled and confident. He seemed to usually get his way in his business world. But could he ruin Consultants International, LLC, if he didn't have his way? Could he notify other big mining operations, tip them off, get them to suddenly start exploring, or throw up road blocks for what was yet to come? The possibilities were endless. Bessert could resort to unscrupulous methods for whatever he was really after. Ramsley then included in his e-mail that perhaps it was time to press for a decision about their phase two and that he would communicate the outcome of the board's wishes. In the e-mail, he asked Stu Bergman to meet with their two field supervisors once again in Las Vegas to get all of their thoughts about phase two. He wanted Bergman to be ready to be able to answer any and all questions that board members would ask at the upcoming board meeting.

———⚬⚬⚬⚬⚬———

Larry McGray and Dalton Trindall read their e-mails from Ramsley and immediately made plans to drive to Las Vegas for the upcoming Sunday morning meeting with Stu Bergman. Trindall called Emelina Black Coyote's cell phone number. She had given it to him previously on one of their two recent dinner engagements in Tonopah. He felt attracted to her. He enjoyed their brief times together and he hoped to try to meet up with her once again on his way to Las Vegas.

———⚬⚬⚬⚬⚬———

Later that day, Wayde Ramsley got a call from board member Bob Mendelson, who said, "I have a problem and I want your advice, Wayde. I got a call from a Gordon Bessert's lawyer who urged me to temporarily step down from the board and to nominate Bessert as my stand-in. Do you know who Bessert is?" Mendelson asked.

"Yes, I certainly do," replied Ramsley. "Do you plan to tell me that you'll be taking a leave of absence?"

"That's what I wanted to get your opinion on."

"Do you know why he wants to orchestrate this move?" Ramsley asked.

"Knowing him, he has something he wants. He wants to position himself so he can get it."

"What do you think you should do?" asked Ramsley. "Obviously he sees you as a pawn in whatever chess game he is playing. Are you beholden to him? Does he have any control over you?"

"Something, yes. In a way, I suppose I owe him."

"What do you want to do, Bob?" asked Ramsley.

"Look," Bob Mendelson explained, "Bessert is powerful and successful. He wouldn't be doing this if he didn't have a plan that would make him far richer than he already is. I don't know what he has in mind, but whatever it is, it will probably serve his interests before anyone else's."

"Well, he was here earlier this morning. He wants me to share with him everything we have about the Mega Trend. I put him off saying that I'd have to put the matter to our board, of which you are but one member. As a board member, how would you vote on Bessert's demand?" asked Ramsley.

"I'd feel that I'd have to recuse myself from voting because one of his own employees is on my mining company's board of directors. It could be seen as a conflict of interest."

"Well, Bessert said he'd like to make an offer to buy out the company. He said he needed to sign a secrecy agreement with us so he could learn what he needs to know to help make a final decision."

"You are the chairman of the board, Wayde. What would you want me to do under the circumstances?"

"It would be up to the board whether to accept Bessert as your stand-in. I would vote against it because of Bessert's own conflict of interest in having already expressed an interest in buying out the company. On one hand, you have just said that you would recuse yourself from voting on something that you saw as a mere potential conflict of interest. On the other hand, Bessert has expressed a desire to engage in such a conflict of interest, without reservation. Your ethics win over his and I ask that you not leave our board, that is, if you can deal with whatever it is you owe Bessert," Ramsley replied.

"Thank you, Wayde," Mendelson said. "I'll see you on Tuesday morning at the board meeting."

"Does that mean that you won't be stepping aside?"

"Yes, it does. Bessert could have come to me personally. I've had a financial setback recently, not of my own doing. Bessert tried to loan me some money but I declined. He has been trying to get me into a position of vulnerability. He thought he had it until I turned his loan down. Now he is trying this tactic. I think I can vaguely see what he is after, and it is for his own net worth. Sooner or later, he's gonna cross that proverbial bright line, he'll be flying too close to the sun and get burned. It will be his own undoing."

"I like your decision. You can recuse yourself, as you said, when the board decides on Bessert's request to be given the keys to our headquarters. No explanation will be necessary."

Ramsley liked the way Bob Mendelson handled what, no doubt, had to be a difficult thing for him to do. He was glad Mendelson decided to stay on the board for what was quickly becoming a very serious time in the company's future. The choice was easy for Wayde Ramsley. Mendelson's definition of ethics was not a part of Bessert's vocabulary.

On the following Tuesday, Wayde Ramsley gathered Stu Bergman and Alice Harrison into his office to have a final discussion prior to the various board members' arrival. Ramsley was unusually animated, seemingly tense, as he went over some of the detail of the agenda they had drafted. No less tense were both Bergman and Harrison. This was going to be a critical day for them and their company.

Ramsley had been under increasing pressure for months. They were trying to maintain their corporate facade and their corporate covert mission. New worries kept surfacing, it seemed with each passing month. The field work had gone better than expected. That wasn't what bothered Ramsley. It was the unknown, the sublime, the occasional surprises pertaining to the corporation's existence, its reason for being, its goals, and its continued need for secrecy.

"Well," Ramsley said, "if those Senate hearings don't kill us, something else could. I suppose we are at the precipice. It is here that we either decide to race forward with all the momentum we can muster, continue as we have been, or retreat backwards and fade into the fog. In any event, the work we have all done is worth something. In the worst case scenario, the result of all of our efforts has a value attached to it. In the end, what we have will be wanted by someone. One way or the other, we will persevere. The question today is what is the road we will take moving forward?"

Ramsley continued discussing what would be discussed at the meeting when a phone call came in from Gordon Bessert. Ramsley was interrupted by his receptionist saying, "Mr. Bessert needs a moment of your time. He said it's urgent."

"Tell him that I am busy at the moment and that I will get back to him about the board's decision with regard to his request for a nondisclosure agreement."

A moment later, the receptionist interrupted, saying, "He won't wait. He said what he has to say will only take one minute."

Ramsley then took the call and Bessert said, "For the purpose of your board meeting, I'm thinking that after my experts get to see everything, and if they are satisfied, we could be talking about perhaps a hundred billion dollars. That's preliminary. It's not set in concrete. But it's a starting point if your board is interested. My people would need a few days with your people to go over things and then we could talk about a possible firm offer."

Ramsley replied, "I'll take that to the board, Gordon. They will be interested, I can assure you."

After the conversation, Ramsley contemplated that after Bessert learned that Bob Mendelson would not step aside from his board position with Consultants International, Bessert had decided to try an all or nothing approach. Bessert likely realized that he had nothing to lose by sweetening the pot with a preliminary purchase number. By doing so, Bessert could keep his hand in what he had hoped he could control and benefit from. There was more to Bessert's proposal but Ramsley could only guess at what obstacles Bessert would use to try to put Consultants International at a disadvantage. Bessert saw Consultants International as prey, to be put on the defense, so that Bessert Resources, Inc., could take control of the developing North American Mega Trend for pennies on the dollar.

The board meeting was lively and remarks made by the various board members were punctuated with both unusual observable and verbal expressions of their positions.

On the issue of Bessert's request and preliminary offer, Bob Mendelson did as he had said he would do. He recused himself from discussing and voting on the matter. The board decided to give Bessert one opportunity. Grant the nondisclosure agreement, set the sale price at two hundred billion dollars, nonnegotiable, good for fourteen days from the day the nondisclosure agreement was signed. They felt that such terms would put Bessert on notice that they were in no mood for bobbing and weaving delaying tactics. It would send him the message that they were not hard up to sell, that they knew they had other options, that they were confident about what they had and where they were going, and that Bessert wasn't the only fish in the sea.

Then the board turned its attention to the most important issue—should they proceed with phase two or not?. This was it, a momentous event like no other. The time had finally come to make the most important business decision they had ever made. It would require a stunning financial commitment. A several million-dollar war chest of funds had recently been set up to pay for lobbyists, lawyers, public relations, and other costs associated with trying to preserve their advantage and goal. Now a much more significant cost commitment would be needed. They had estimates for what it would cost to survey the most promising lands first. Following soon thereafter would be the need to secure their second-tier land claims of interest. The filing claims costs were going to be unprecedented. Combined, the amount was enough to make each board member weigh their vote with unease and trepidation. There was even fear on a couple of the board members' faces as the reality of their upcoming decision sunk in.

Bob Mendelson said, "As one of you said earlier, it's time to fish or cut bait. Are we going to realize a gain out of all this for our respective companies and our own individual corporate shareholders, go for the big fish, so to speak, or are we going to cut the bait for a host of others to reap the rewards from all of our efforts? Yes, there are risks, ones we are all well aware of. Either we move forward or we don't."

Wayde Ramsley, hoping to build a consensus, sensing where Mendelson was going with his preliminary remarks, asked, "Go on, Bob, what do you propose?"

Mendelson dropped his head for a moment, collected his thoughts and replied, "First, we give both the Chinese sovereign investment group and Bessert Resources a finite-time deadline to submit their best offer. If we set a deadline then we would be signaling that we did so because we were about to implement phase two. We know they will try a variety of tactics, the kind that any of us have employed in the past, in our own careers, to try to get the best deal possible. They don't know our timetable, nor should they.

"Secondly," Mendelson continued, "we get prepared to issue stock, an initial public offering, an IPO, for forty-five days from now. Each company represented here gets an equal sum of shares commensurate with the IPO's opening stock price offering to the general public. That will open up the secret to some degree, but we don't have to give away the farm with information that will tip our hand, at least not just yet. Wayde can issue a press release. That will support the opening share price, create investor interest and, if we are reasonably lucky, the share price will react favorably.

"Third," Mendelson continued without missing a beat, "on that very same day, Wayde sends out all the surveyors he can find, even if they have to be brought in from the east coast. We try to get the land posted with markers and then, as that is done, we have people march in to file the claims and pay the necessary fees. Again, Wayde issues another press release, making public that we have started building something the world has never seen before. Not hyped, but just exactly what it is. The facts will speak for themselves. The sheer magnitude of this whole project will seem to some incredulous. Others will see it as something that was inevitable. Then there will be the crowd who will want to try to ride into this thing on our coattails. That should juice up the share price.

"Fourth, while that is being completed, and hopefully within another six weeks, we deploy three or four large contract drilling companies and we assign the most promising locations, one to each company, all concentrated in either Idaho or in Nevada. Once that is underway, and as the first core samples are being extracted from the ground, Wayde issues yet another press release announcing the initiation of one of the largest drilling campaigns ever attempted. In that news release, Wayde can promise further public updates about the assay results and the amount of gold being found for each hole. Successive news releases would be announced in batches of assay results, something like twenty or thirty different drill hole assay results. Depending on those results, our share price either skyrockets, if the results are good, or it begins a gradual decline pending further press releases containing new assay results. We will need to claim the best land first and put our drills to work on the most promising land almost at the same time. If we start this process in about forty-five days, six weeks from now, it will be mid-May. We could get many months of drilling done before winter interferes with our driller's work. If we start in Idaho, then the drillers may have to shut down in December. The government won't want us clearing trees and land to create dozens of drilling pad locations during the soggy and snowy periods of the year. Old logging trails and dirt paths would become impassable for the duration of the winter and the authorities would halt our work if they thought the public lands were being unnecessarily torn up. So I opt for focusing our major thrust to be in Nevada, the southern part. We could use the town of Tonopah as our first regional headquarters, get the buildings we need, hire the people who either have the experience or who can be trained, and do our first heavy work south and north of the town.

"Additionally, and concomitantly, perhaps we can acquire a significant existing claim in Idaho where a lot of drilling has sufficiently proven that the gold is there. It would save us a lot of time and expense if we could buy some other company's prior hard work and decent assay results. Maybe fold the holding company into our own operation. Sweeten the pot for their shareholders. Scoop up all the existing claims we can buy and then file for new claims where none exist. Doing so would allow us to drill on existing claims where drilling permits have already been obtained from the Bureau of Land Management or US Forest Service, without losing time before winter sets in.

"As I said, if we start phase two with an IPO, immediately followed by deploying the surveyors and the claim filing in mid-May, we could be able to start drilling on certain land by July first. The results from that drilling, if we line up enough independent assay laboratories, should start coming in by late August or early September. If we can't get the assay results quick enough, then we contract with a lab to treat us as their only customer. We'd have to pay a premium for that.

"Gentlemen, this will require a substantial financial commitment. We will need to fund the first year's work ourselves now and not months later. Consultants International will have no other source of income to pay all these expenses. They will need a fat checking account. We can figure our contributions into our share allocations to our respective companies. After this initial building up of the check book for the first year's expenses, it will be up to the markets to fund the money needed to continue operations. Hopefully, then we can begin the process of building a mining operation in a couple of places, which can take years to complete as you all know. If the project is viable, we can participate in raising venture capital through private placements or debentures. While using the usual methods for raising new funds for our projects, our investors will know there is gold in the ground worthy of the continued funding of the ongoing project.

"I know that without announcing all of these plans prematurely that the opening IPO share price will be low to start with. But as each successive stage of phase two is implemented and announced, that share price could well increase significantly. Your own corporation's shareholders would benefit. And your corporations would be at liberty to sell your shares in Consultants International to take what profits you think reasonable for all the risks you have taken and the funds you have invested in this venture."

Mendelson paused for a moment once again and slowly continued his closing argument.

"If you are anything like me, this should be the hallmark of your careers. It should make you feel like you have been a part of something bigger than you or me, something bigger than our respective companies combined, because it will be, when it is said and done. However this project progresses in the coming years, the Mega Trend will dwarf the Carlin Trend. The Carlin will be engulfed in the overall border-to-border gold field. It will one day make many people and companies very wealthy. It will provide for a magnificent boost to local economies all along the line. It will cause new hospitals to be built, new housing developments to be constructed, an untold number of good paying jobs, a huge new source of revenue for local and at least two state governments. It will be your doing or your undoing. Your decision today is to either terminate this project or to take it to its intended destination. The choice is ours, and ours alone."

Mendelson finished by saying, "I remember hearing John Wayne say many years ago, 'Courage is being scared to death but saddling up anyway.'"

There had been complete silence as Bob Mendelson made his presentation to his fellow board members. Wayde Ramsley thought to himself that there were many hurdles yet to be crossed, ones he had nagging at him in recent months that could cause serious problems, ones which he still had to address. They would not be easy. One or more of them could wholly or partially bring phase two to a halt. They were the kind of issues he was paid to resolve. Yet there were ones whose outcomes he knew he could not guarantee.

Given the tenor of the moment, wanting to strike while the iron was hot, Wayde Ramsley asked with a slight chuckle, "Well, Bob, I guess the first vote to move forward was already made by you. How about everyone else?"

Wayde asked the corporate secretary to record the votes of each board member and to add them to the record of the meeting she had been making. It was a unanimous vote in the affirmative. The process of implementing phase two, of what had originally been referred to as Project X, and now merely referred to in-house as Our Clients, so as to couple the words with the company's new name of Consultants International, would be set into motion effective immediately. History was indeed being made as a result of the board's decision.

After the board members had all departed for their corporate jet planes at Stapleton International Airport, Ramsley thought to himself that the funding up to this point was less than the collective value of the airplanes they flew in. But that was about to change. There would be an influx of significant new funding for all of what he knew he and his staff would need to accomplish.

Ramsley e-mailed Alice Harrison and Stu Bergman, with a copy to their two field supervisors. In the e-mail, he told Harrison to be sure to update their two field supervisors with the board director's decisions and to tell them to stand by for further instructions. Then he told Stu Bergman and Alice Harrison in the e-mail to go ahead and hire the additional people they had identified they would want for the increasing workload they would experience at their Denver headquarters location and at their soil sample storage facility. Important to the launching of their stock issuance IPO would be the hiring of the people who could handle the added functions of a publicly held corporation, namely an investor's relations office. Stu Bergman was told to get with his staff and to figure out what would be needed in Tonopah to start up a regional headquarters for field drilling operations and other needs in the southern half of Nevada. Ramsley hinted that he would be working on some existing claim acquisitions in central and north central Idaho to be coupled with filing for new claims.

After reading the sudden influx of messages received from his headquarters, Dalton Trindall was pleased for a great many reasons, one of which spelled a better future for the rundown old mining town he had always disliked. *Tonopah*, he thought, *could have a future after all.*

Conversely, Larry McGray envisioned Elk City Idaho's second coming replete with an influx of new people, the employment of some people already there, new construction, a revived economy, and old men's opinions reaching a fevered pitch at the Elk City coffee and gossip shop.

CHAPTER 15

Sacramento, California

It's better to be on the offensive rather than the defensive.

Zachery Cameron leafed through the presentation he planned to make to a group of Native Americans later the following day at an Indian Reservation in north central Idaho. He was a recent law school graduate who served as an assistant to one of his prior professors, while waiting to take his bar licensing exams, the passing of a bar background check, and, he hoped, the receipt of his license to practice law.

Cameron had spent much of his law school years immersing himself in Native American causes. He claimed to be a Native American, but no one believed him. He was fair-skinned and did not have the usual features of an Indian. He liked to wrap a bandana around his forehead to hold back his long black dyed hair. At his law school, he often told students and professors that he was a descendant of the Apache and that his lineage traced back to eastern Arizona where his great-great-grandmother had been the wife of a cavalry soldier at Fort Apache. Few people believed his story but his obsession with the subject caused some people to think that perhaps there was some truth to what he claimed.

On many prior occasions, Cameron had given the same speech he intended to give the next day. He would tell his small audience of reservation onlookers that they were in need of a great many things. Given the right issue, he would try to file legal actions to draw attention to the issue and hopefully win some sort of concession or ruling that would benefit the reservation. In particular, he wanted to address reservation's rights and boundaries. The concession part of his efforts was to shake down others into agreeing, at a minimum, to a compromise, one perhaps that included a cash settlement from which he could be paid for his services. The court ruling portion of his two-pronged approach was what he used to threaten his adversaries with in order to obtain a concession.

Cameron seemingly meant well, and had the basic skill to do some of the legal work he claimed he could do. His pitch had increasingly been to focus on corporation debts he felt were owed to Native Americans. He painted a picture of companies and governments robbing Native Americans of their fair share of distributed local and state tax dollar-supported government spending. He argued, for example, that Indians paid sales taxes when they made purchases off the reservations. The sales taxes were used for local, county, or state expenses, none of which were directed towards the Native American communities from which some of those sales taxes originated. Further, he liked to create anger in some of his audiences by giving example after example of businesses buying up land that had previously belonged to the Indian. The businesses bought land and built warehouses, office buildings, shopping centers, gas stations, and housing developments. Some mined the land. Governments used the land for building roadways. All such development resulted in some land owner selling land to a purchaser. The purchaser would pay a sum of money to the seller. None of the money nor subsequent economic benefits would go to original owners of the land, the Native American community.

Zachery Cameron's argument made sense to some of his prior listening audiences and he had often aroused some of his listener's passions sufficient to cause them to join him in going to one location or another to demonstrate. They would make up signs to carry while walking in a circle, while looking to some passersby like people on strike at a construction site. He would notify any local news media outlets as to the event's particulars. Most often, however, he had been unsuccessful in having much of an impact.

Cameron's approach, this time, had some meat on the bones. The prior fall, he had taken a hiking trip up through the Clearwater region of the northern mountains in Idaho. He had been walking down a logging trail when he heard voices back in the US Forest Service's public lands and he paused to try to hear what they were saying. He carefully wove his way into the woods where he could see who was talking and hear what they were saying. He was sure he had heard one man say to another, "If we claim all this land, the Nez Perce may present a problem."

As he carefully drew closer, he saw in the distance two men who were speaking to each other. Each was bent over backpacks they were carrying, placing something into small white bags, sorting them and writing something on them as they occasionally spoke more loudly than normal so each could hear the other. In their conversation, he heard the men mention Denver, Consultants International, gold, how "the surveyors will hate staking out this rough land," mention of the need to finish their work before the first snow, their hope that they would be reassigned to southern Nevada, and the need to show that the work they had done would "connect the regions into one long string of discoveries." Cameron had then sneaked back to the logging trail and continued his hiking trip. Over the winter months, he had thought about what he had heard and, if what he surmised was true, the possibilities it could present to him.

Zack Cameron arrived at the Nez Perce Indian reservation and went to the reservation's community center where he was to talk about issues he cared about. He met the potluck dinner's host and together they spoke for a while about his upcoming presentation. He mentioned the need to organize Native American communities in a united approach. By doing so, he explained, they could bring their continuing grievances to the attention of those who seemingly did little unless prodded by legal actions requiring concessions or court ordered solutions.

Cameron asked his female host, "I have something that maybe you know about. I've heard that there could be some kind of new mining effort going on not too far from here. Has anyone here on the reservation mentioned it?" he asked.

"There's always one thing or another that we hear. Ever since we were placed on this reservation, there have been a great many miners who have come to our old lands ever since the mid–1800s. We've always been a peaceful people and we haven't caused much of a problem. We have our own land now. They can't do their mining work on our land," his hostess replied.

"Yes," Cameron said. "Let me read you something here and get your impression. Your treaty framework says, and I quote, 'The jurisdiction of the Nez Perce shall extend to all lands within the original confines of the Nez Perce reservation.' Now, here is the important part, 'and to include extra-territorial jurisdiction for the purpose of protecting the rights of the Nez Perce Indians of Idaho.'"

"Which means?" she asked.

"Your treaty with the United States includes language that extends, enlarges, expands your tribe's boundaries for the purpose of matters that impact the tribe, to protect the tribe's rights and interests."

"How far from the reservation might that be?" she inquired. "We used to be called the Nimi Ipuu people when we roamed and lived throughout what is now Idaho, southeast Washington, northeast Oregon, and parts of western Montana. That's about twenty-seven thousand square miles. Then we were confined to less than 1 percent of our former land."

"From a legal perspective, it's possible that a case could be argued that your 'extra-territorial jurisdiction' could extend to areas of land outside of the official boundaries of the reservation. The treaty only says that extra-territorial jurisdiction is a part of the tribe's reservation for the purposes of ensuring and protecting the rights of your people."

"And," she asked, "you think that mining in the state could be interpreted as infringing on our rights?"

"It's possible," he answered. "Maybe."

"And this possible new mining business that you said could be close by, do you think our tribe could benefit from it or are you saying we could oppose it?" she questioned.

"The law is not precise, although one might think that it is," Cameron explained. "It is subject to varying interpretations, as your people have learned all over the US with regard to treaties followed by revised treaties and even new treaties. I'm saying, if the proper convincing argument could be made on your tribe's behalf, it is possible that your tribe could benefit. I'd like to pursue it for a while without any legal tactics, to see what I can find out. I'd need your tribe's approval to research it."

"One of our tribal officials is here today," she replied. "Maybe you should talk to him. I'll introduce you to him. He's sitting at that table over there." She pointed in the direction of the man she had just referred to.

In a hushed tone, so as to not disrupt the ongoing presentation, Cameron introduced himself to the tribal leader, explained that he was one of those who would be making a presentation, and briefly explained that he believed a major mining effort could be launched just to the east of his reservation. Cameron said that there were significant issues that would impact the Nez Perce. He related the same information he had just told the hostess. He told the tribal leader, "I'd like to research this for you at no cost."

After the brief discussion with the tribal leader for "Natural Resources and Land Enterprise," it had been agreed that he would forward the necessary representation authorization to Cameron. With that said, he opened his laptop computer saying, "Give me your e-mail address. We have Wi-Fi internet for all of our people here on the reservation. I'll type something out and send it to you while you're making your presentation."

Zachery settled back in his chair at the tribal leader's table and listened to the current speaker who was addressing the Native American problem associated with obesity and diabetes. The speaker was saying, "And the foods that cause the epidemic are associated with sugars of all kinds, the kind that you know to be sugar and the kind that you usually don't consider which turn into sugar in your bodies. Foods that are generally white or tan in color are the primary reasons why our Native American population is predominantly overweight and the reason why early death happens due to the diabetes it causes."

One attendee raised her hand, asking, "What about honey?"

"That too," the speaker replied, "because honey is known as a sugar. It doesn't get converted into a sugar. It already is one." The speaker continued, "Things made from wheat and corn flour are the ones most responsible for our early deaths, our metabolic syndrome, our rampant type 2 diabetes, our rapid deterioration, and our inability to continue to physically thrive at an early age."

As the speaker finished her presentation, Cameron glanced down at the sheet of paper containing the potluck dinner's suggested menu of items for the listeners to bring and share with others. He noted, smiling to himself, that the speaker would not rub salt in their wounds and risk offending those who brought carbohydrate food items nor those who consumed them. The plate that had been brought to him as their guest consisted of all the food items that could eventually annihilate much of the Native American population at an early age.

Looking further down the agenda of presentations, he noted that the featured speaker was named Tiponi Isaw from The Indian Plight Charity Organization in Las Vegas. He thought he had heard of her from somewhere before. She came a very long way to make her presentation to a few dozen listeners, and carbohydrate addicts, he mused.

Next on the agenda was his name and the title of his presentation. It read "Attorney Zachery Cameron, Native American Rights and Treaties."

Upon finishing her speech, Tiponi Isaw took a seat at a table where she sat sipping a cup of coffee. She had been briefly distracted by a couple of people at her table who quietly whispered questions to her about substitutes for corn flour, bread, pasta, and various other foods considered to be taboo. Then she focused on the new speaker who was addressing tribal jurisdiction and infringements on Indian past and current land. He briefly mentioned that a company had been working just to the east of the Nez Perce reservation, for example, scouting out possible new places for exploring for precious minerals, ones that he felt should be considered partly owned by the Nez Perce. Tiponi Isaw's attention drew sharper as she listened, suspecting that the speaker was possibly addressing something he knew about, possibly involving what she had come to know as the existence of what was being referred to as the new Mega Trend. Her suspicions were confirmed when she heard him say that a company in Denver might try to build mining operations one day alongside of the reservation land.

"Close proximity and the attendant noise, dust, and disruption to the environment was one thing," he said, "the taking of precious metals was yet another."

Tiponi Isaw waited for the young speaker to finish and then approached him, asking if he had a business card. She told him that she enjoyed his speech and said that perhaps they would run into each other again.

For his part, Zachery Cameron told Tiponi Isaw that he had heard of her. He told her that he was aware that she had made similar presentations and that he had heard of her charity work on behalf of the Native Americans.

Cameron marveled at the many advances that had been made on Native American reservations over recent years. After his presentation, he went to his car, checked his own laptop for e-mails and found the tribal leader's authorization "to represent the tribe for research purposes only and not for the filing of any legal actions without the expressed authorization of the reservation's tribal council."

Zack Cameron returned to his home in Sacramento and began to outline the position and argument he would present if he could make contact with an official of this Consultants International in Denver. He would keep it short.

Cameron planned to introduce himself as a legal representative of the Nez Perce, state the concern, offer one or more possible resolutions, and provide his point of contact as his law school's address and phone number. That, he knew, would imply that the law school was backing his efforts to address a legal matter that the law school and its myriad of known professors of law felt worthy of pursuing. It could be seen as an academic exercise with merit for learning and one that would provide a service to a community that would benefit by the law school's expertise and learned staff.

Zachery Cameron came from a Sacramento upper class family who could afford to pay for his education and from which he received an income through a family trust fund. Through his Sacramento family's connections, he had been able to get accepted for admission into the law school even though his law school admissions test score had been substandard. Yet he had done well because he had found a cause that interested him. He felt that he didn't want to focus on establishing the kind of usual law practice that would pay handsomely, if successful. Rather, because of his steady source of trust fund income, he was able to think of practicing law in terms of serving others for less pay.

Cameron visited with three of his law school's professors to talk about what he thought might make a reasonable learning experience for him and any students who wanted extra credit for helping him with research. The professors had agreed that the matter he had raised about the words "extraterritorial" rights of the tribe had not been made clear in all situations. For that very legal reason, it opened the door for arguing its interpretation, as it applied to that tribe, by lawyers and perhaps eventually a court of law.

Cameron contacted his first year law school students by e-mail with a blanket offer to participate in his new legal project. He advised that he would only select two students to work on the project and that their participation would require research to be done upon the conclusion of the current semester and likely at times throughout their upcoming summer vacations.

When he was ready, Zachery Cameron placed a call to the number listed for Consultants International. He asked the receptionist if he could speak with the president or chief executive officer for a moment, explaining he was a "professor from the University of California School of Law."

A moment later, Cameron heard a voice answer his phone saying, "Wayde Ramsley."

Cameron said, "Mr. Ramsley, I'm Zachery Cameron and I am the legal representative of a Native American tribe in Idaho. I'm calling to ask you if you can tell me whether your company is planning any kind of mining operation in Idaho."

"Which Indian tribe?" Wayde anxiously asked.

"Can you say whether the information I have received is accurate?" Cameron asked.

"We don't disclose information about our clients. We are consultants, as you likely know," Ramsley lied, hoping to deflect his caller.

"Are you saying that you have no mine-related business ongoing in Idaho," asked Cameron as the two sparred with each other.

"No, we don't, you have the wrong company," said Ramsley.

"I think not," said Cameron, not willing to give up the reason for his call just yet. "Let me explain the reason for my call—"

Ramsley interrupted saying, "My receptionist said you're a professor with a law school?"

"Yes, that's right," Cameron lied in kind, knowing he was only an assistant to a professor, as he tried to continue, "let me get to the point. We are aware that your company has either directly or indirectly—"

"We don't mine," Ramsley interjected once again, wanting to sound impatient. Ramsley already knew enough from what the caller had said to know that his business activities had somehow been discovered yet again, this time by an Idaho Indian tribe who had retained legal counsel. *For God knows what*, he thought to himself. Further discussion, he feared, could lead him to accidentally saying something he would regret, disclosing something, anything that the caller was hoping to confirm or discern. If the caller persisted, Ramsley decided he would just say nothing, listen, fend off the caller, deceive him, dodge his questions and turn the tables on him to see what he could learn without giving up anything in return.

"Our law school has taken up this issue as one of concern. If your company is planning any kind of mining activities, you need to know that there are Indian ancestral burial grounds all over the state. Plus there are certain tribal rights for one tribe where the treaty extends to jurisdictions outside of the reservation itself. The tribe is aware of your interest in developing the land adjacent to their reservation. They would prefer no such activity for several reasons, including those pertaining to environmental concerns." Cameron paused to see if Mr. Wayde Ramsley was still on the phone.

"I'm listening," Ramsley said.

"Your company has shown its intention to contravene the treaty the Nez Perce have with the Unites States," Cameron was saying as he was interrupted once again.

"We have no such plan," Wayde Ramsley tried to interject.

"I believe you do, Mr. Ramsley," Cameron persisted.

"I don't have time for this," Ramsley objected.

"Perhaps you'd rather that I talk to someone else, maybe one of your legal representatives," Cameron said, fishing for any kind of response that would indicate that Consultants International was what he thought it to be, a mining company.

"I don't need a lawyer for this, we aren't who you think we are," Ramsley protested.

Cameron thought that Ramsley would have ended the phone conversation by this point if he had indeed called the wrong company, then he continued by saying, "In short, our options for stopping your company, or any other, are many. We can file different kinds of civil actions that would bog down your company, perhaps for years. Regardless of who wins in the end, your company will be delayed, at the very least, and at no small expense to your company."

"Well, this is all none of my concern," said Ramsley, now wanting to end the conversation as quickly as possible.

"Your own people in Idaho were unmistakably clearly overheard discussing your plans for a large mining operation that encompass both Idaho and Nevada," said Cameron. "There are plenty of tribes in both states who would want to be a part of any action we plan to take to halt your company."

"Look, Mr. Cameron," Ramsley said with finality, "if you want to talk to someone about what troubles you, I suggest you call our law firm, Chase, Bitterson, and Clark, and ask for Arthur Mercer."

"I know that law firm, Mr. Ramsley. They specialize in mining matters and they represented a company we had to deal with in another one of our cases," said Cameron, almost gleeful over his sudden discovery. "They have major clients in Vancouver, the Mecca for exploration and mining companies, as well as in Denver," he said as he surmised he had caught Ramsley in a lie trying to dodge the purpose of his call. "They have had clients who had similar problems with Native American tribes," Cameron stated.

Ramsley mentally kicked himself for having said too much. "Look, Mr. Cameron, you'll need to talk to someone else. I have a lot to do today and I can't spare any more of my time."

After the phone call ended, Wayde Ramsley quickly contacted Arthur Mercer, filled him in on the phone call, saying,

"Dear God, Arthur, if we can only expedite this process. We're going to need that public relations firm you mentioned before this is all over with. Hopefully a firm that has inroads with the Indian community."

Mercer responded, saying, "We are making progress on your IPO plans. Have you heard back from the Chinese or Bessert yet on a possible offer?"

"Not yet. When I notified Bessert that we would go ahead with a nondisclosure, he sent in his people to meet with Stu Bergman and our two supervisors. They're evaluating everything. We'll just have to wait and see. I don't trust the Chinese company or Bessert, but we'll see what each has to offer, if anything."

Mercer asked, "Are you serious about getting a public relations firm?"

"I'm thinking we might need it before all of this is over," Ramsley replied.

"Maybe more than one," Mercer thought out loud.

"You think that's necessary? I'd rather only have to deal with one person for everything," Ramsley replied.

"You have a few complicated issues that need to be dealt with. The sooner they begin to get addressed, the better. Maybe it would be better to compartmentalize the issues with one for each separate firm," Mercer said.

"How much do you think that will cost?" Ramsley asked, then added, "We already know that the lobbyists in DC are going to cost a couple of million or more this year alone."

"I suspect much more," Mercer added. "As for the public relations people, it will all depend on how much time and effort they have to put into it. Depends on how much worse things get requiring them to do more. You know how it is. The bills can stack up, like with the lobbyists," Mercer explained.

"You mean like our legal bills," said Ramsley, only half kidding.

"It's part of the cost of doing business, Wayde," he replied.

"The costs of our PR, lobby, and legal expenses could easily exceed what we've spent so far this year on exploration," Ramsley begrudgingly stated as a matter of fact. "Damn all these parasites and shakedown artists," Ramsley said.

"You need to have these pending problems addressed," Mercer replied. "And there likely will be more before this is all over with. It's an ongoing process. They raise a roadblock and we try to take it down. Remember, Wayde, you called us, we didn't call you," Mercer said, sounding slightly offended.

"I didn't mean you, Art. I meant the people who cause all these problems. The damn people who make us have to use people like you and the others. Please don't take offense."

"None taken. Remember our discussion. It's better to be on the offensive rather than the defensive. Think about the PR solution and let me know. I was thinking of using one or two major firms plus a couple of charity types who have connections to the people we will need to soothe, get next to, and persuade."

PART 4

CHAPTER 16

Las Vegas, Nevada

The gospel according to the Devil.

The Indian Plight Charity's office received a visitor. He appeared to be Native American, in his forties, casually but expensively dressed, and he had been dropped off in front of the charity by someone driving a BMW. He announced to the charity's receptionist that he would like to talk to Tiponi Isaw. The guest was asked his name but he declined by only saying, "My employer wants to become a contributor."

The receptionist said that Ms. Isaw was not in but that he could talk to her deputy if he wished. The guest agreed and he was escorted into the charity's conference room where he was introduced to Tony Rappaport.

Rappaport offered his hand and the guest took it while saying, "My employer asked me to see if Ms. Isaw was in. He'd like to meet her and discuss the charity. He is interested in making a donation. He's up the street in his car. I can call him to come in if Ms. Isaw is here."

"Can I get your name?" asked Rappaport with a smile.

"Yes, I'm Lewis Flores," he replied.

"I'm sorry, she isn't here at the moment. We can arrange an appointment," Rappaport offered. "What is your employer's name?"

"He likes making contributions anonymously until he signs a check. But Ms. Isaw might recognize him when she sees him," Flores said, smiling.

Rappaport thought that the person might be someone who had contributed to the charity in the past, as he said, "She's in town today. Can I contact her for you and arrange to have her meet your boss here?" Flores nodded in agreement with Rappaport's suggestion.

Tony Rappaport called Tiponi at her condominium and asked if she would be available to meet with a donor who was waiting to see her, and if so when. While Tiponi Isaw was still on the phone, he asked Flores, "How about in fifteen minutes? She is on her way here." Flores nodded yes, and walked back out of the conference room door, out onto the sidewalk, and up the street to tell his boss about the delay. Isaw told Rappaport she would leave right away for the office.

Arriving a couple of minutes late, Tiponi Isaw parked her white Lexus in a vacant parking space near the front of the office, walked in, and asked Tony, "Did he leave?" as she set her purse down on the conference room's table.

Tony answered, saying, "A guy came in named Lewis Flores. He said that his employer wanted to meet with you. No one has come back yet. It's been about fifteen or twenty minutes since he left. Hopefully they should be back shortly."

Both Rappaport and Isaw heard the front door open and both turned to greet who they hoped would be someone who would make a substantial contribution. The man stopped at the receptionist desk, smiled, and said "Tiponi, it has been a long time."

Tiponi tried to maintain her composure. The man standing before her was a person she had hoped she would never see again.

"Tony, excuse us, please. This gentleman and I can use the conference room. Feel free to leave if you want," she said while giving Tony a very brief glance before turning her attention back to her visitor.

The man was of Indian ancestry, had longer than usual black hair, had a sun-weathered leathery complexion, darker skinned than the usual, and seemed slightly attractive to Tiponi. Yet his facial gestures were hard, threatening, and conveyed a certain kind of menacing command. Tony thought he recognized the man but couldn't remember from where. As he left the room, Tiponi closed the door, turned to her guest, and asked him to sit down at the table.

Tiponi asked him if he would like a cup of coffee. After he said yes, she asked if he wanted to accompany her across the street to a coffee shop for some excellent coffee or would he prefer the coffee she could make for him there in the charity's office.

"I don't want to put you to any trouble," he said.

"It is no trouble. I'll have our receptionist make us some," she said.

Tiponi excused herself for a moment, asked for fresh coffee to be made, and then sat down at the conference room table.

Sitting across from her was Leonard "The Devil" Moreno. Nearly twenty years earlier, he had been a part of a petty crime group of fellow wayward local Native Americans. Raised in Tonopah, he had learned that crime could pay if it was done the right way. Initially, he had referred to his group of street thugs with the poorly named and amateurish "Band of Indians," followed eventually by the more ominous name "The Devils," a name that local residents used whenever they referred to the misbehavior and typical crimes that members of the group committed. They were a street gang whose notoriety had become feared. Moreno had taken control of the

gang and he had become whispered as "The Devil." For those
who didn't know Moreno, his infamy spread over time to other
towns, cities, and even to a few Native American reservations.
He had become a bit of a legend. Some of the young teenage
Indians, ones having a propensity for engaging in illegal activity, who lived on reservations, talked about him with a kind
of misplaced reverence and respect. Some dreamed of meeting him one day and joining his growing organization which
some liked to refer to as "The Devil's Indian Mafia."

Tiponi knew that on occasion, Leonard Moreno's people
had sometimes made mention that their organization was
also a charity. Such references had confused some people who
had wondered if they were connected to The Indian Plight
organization. Conversely, Tiponi Isaw had studiously tried
to remain under the radar while truly working for charitable
purposes. The only thing charitable about the Indian Mafia,
as Leonard Moreno enjoyed knowing his organization had
became known as, was that his charity was self serving in that
it lined his owned pockets and those who did "the devil's bid-
ding," as he was fond of saying.

Tiponi tried to smile slightly as if not caught off guard by
Moreno's visit. She knew that his presence would not merely
be a social call. He had something to say and she might as well
brace herself for whatever was coming.

"Well, Lenny, I can't imagine why you are here. I was told
that someone was here to make a donation to my charity."

"And I do want to make a donation, Tiponi," Moreno
interrupted. "Your people in their many places, including on
some of the reservations, occasionally get in our way. Yes,
there is plenty of room for both of us. But my organization
has grown."

"Yes, I know," Tiponi said. "But we try to benefit the reservations and we try to not raise our money from among our own people."

"There are a lot of casinos out there. Our reservations have hundreds of them. We want to expand our operations to include some of those places," Moreno said.

"You'd be taking a risk," Tiponi replied. "We have on occasion used a casino to stage something or another, but to set up business based on the casinos could eventually draw the attention of the authorities both on and off reservation. Lenny, you're known as the Devil who is always watching. You have eyes and ears everywhere stretching from Tonopah in all directions. You see opportunity as we do but you seek it for a different reason and in a more obvious attention getting way. That doesn't make me superior to you. But it makes what I do safer. Lenny, you're like a lightning rod. Your name and activities attract unwanted attention. Sooner or later, you're going to get zapped. It's not a question of if, but when. It's just a question of time. It's the way you operate."

"I know," said Leonard Moreno. "That's why I'm here. Your method has worked for you. There are times when my people's work lands them in jail. That's bad for business, bad for my people, and it makes my organization vulnerable."

"You mean it makes you vulnerable. Someone arrested might make a deal and reveal all that they know," Tiponi admonished.

"That's a part of it, but like you, I've tried to insulate myself from my people and their various activities."

The conference room door opened and the charity's receptionist entered, carrying a small tray with two hot cups of coffee and packets of imitation cream and sugar. Tiponi reflected about the kinds of activities Moreno's people had been rumored to have engaged in. There had been allegations of every kind of crime imaginable, including even a murder or two in Los Angeles when a drug deal went bad.

Moreno continued with an authoritative tone of voice, "I want to donate a sum of money to your charity. In exchange, I want you to join with me in my organization. Be my second in charge. Be my adviser. Shield us both from the cops. Create a barrier between us and everyone else. I'll give you one hundred thousand dollars now if you agree. Cash. You can do with it what you want. Give it away or keep it. But if it were me, I'd keep it. As my second in command, you would be paid a percentage of our take that filters up to me. Again, you could do with it what you want. Your charity would make a lot of money. I'm guessing half a million a year or more based on our earnings as of now."

Tiponi was not shocked at the proposal. It wasn't the first time Moreno had suggested uniting their organizations. But this visit from him had been totally unexpected, especially at a time when Tiponi was about to embark on the most complicated task of her lifetime. Tiponi had never entertained agreeing to Moreno's prior suggestion. Now, with Moreno coming to her in person to make such an offer once again, she knew that he was serious and that his response to a rejection by her would be extremely dangerous. She knew she had to be careful with what she said.

"Lenny, that's a lot to digest on such short notice." Tiponi tried to stall, to buy some time to think about the ramifications of what could happen if she declined the offer, which she surely intended to do. But not now. Not here.

"You could still operate your charity. We'd meet often, work out issues, problems, make sure that whatever we do that we were protected. But I sense you could decline my offer. If that's your decision, then you and I would have some problems between each other. I want to absorb your people and I need you to help me make my organization bigger. I'll accomplish that with or without you."

"You make that sound like you would move me out of the way if I didn't agree," Tiponi stated. "If my people were to end up working for you then I wouldn't be able to raise nearly as much money for the charity. The money you offered wouldn't be enough to make up for what would be lost."

Tiponi thought that she would need to mislead Moreno into thinking that she was considering his demand, as if it were only a negotiable offer. She was being put in the position of having to choose between the more dangerous self-independence that would come with declining Moreno's offer, or the safer more peaceful slave like submission to his will. She knew the second option, in the end, would likely eventually erode and evolve into a more dangerous environment, no matter what. It would be inevitable. Sooner or later she would likely become dispensable, sacrificed in some way to shield Moreno from competitors or the law.

"Give me an example of how you envision I could be of help to you, Lenny," Tiponi asked.

"Right now, there is a truck stop outside of LA. I want my people to set up some of your girls to make the truckers happy when they stop to rest for the night. Have the girls ask the guys if they want a date, you know. But I want the girls to also find out what truckers are hauling. If it's good stuff, we can hijack the trucks and trailers while the guys are busy being distracted. If it works, we can move the girls to other truck stops."

"Yeah, Lenny," Tiponi countered, "and if anyone's caught, it would result in a lot of jail time. If the person caught snitches you out then you'd be toast too. There's a way to do this right and there are a lot of ways to do it wrong. But it could not be done often nor in the close proximity to each theft. It's the kind of crime that will draw in major law enforcement efforts. If there is a pattern, they will see it as organized crime and racketeering. They'd set up a local, state, and federal task force. It would only be a matter of time before they got you and a lot of your people. You know I'm right, Lenny," Tiponi said, hoping that she was coming across sounding as though she was possibly interested in joining forces with Moreno.

"Join me and you can have it all. The choice is yours, Tiponi. Decline my offer and you will be out of business. Totally. We've grown mostly in Los Angeles. I hate the desert. I'm living in Santa Barbara now. You could move there too. One way or the other, get out of Las Vegas. I'd prefer that you merge with me. Work together," Moreno said.

"I apologize, Lenny. I have to be somewhere later tomorrow and I need to pack and get on the road. Let me think about it. I'll get back to you in about a month. How can I get in touch with you?"

"There isn't a whole lot to think about here," Moreno said more sternly. "Don't make a problem for either of us. I came to you respecting you. Return the favor. This is just between you and me. None of my people know what I have said to you here today. Keep this between us. You can call my man Lewis Flores. He is usually with me. Here is his cell phone number. We can arrange to meet. I'll be back in Las Vegas in a few weeks. Don't discuss this with Flores, me, or anyone else on a phone. Only discuss it with me in person."

Leonard Moreno sat staring at Tiponi for a few seconds while she boldly returned the eye contact to show that she was not intimidated. It was all Tiponi could do to maintain the appearance of calm in place of the fear and defiance she was really feeling. She didn't want Moreno to see the hatred and anxiety she was suppressing. Then, without saying another word, Moreno got up from the conference table, turned away from Tiponi, left the office, and walked up the street to his car.

Tony Rappaport came into the conference room and asked, "What was that all about? I know that guy. Isn't he Moreno?"

Tiponi looked at Tony Rappaport briefly, smiled as confidently as she could, and replied, "Better days may be just around the corner. I gotta go. I have work to do at the condo before I leave on my trip."

Tiponi knew that what she had been told had been emphatic. She didn't want to reveal just how potentially dangerous the proposal could be if she made the wrong decision or merely said the wrong thing. Tiponi wanted to hold back from telling Tony about Leonard Moreno's ultimatum. She didn't want to alarm him.

Moreno had the power to harm, and would likely resort to treachery, if she said or did the wrong thing. Violence was second nature to him. It always had been. He had used money, drugs, fear, threats, and physical harm to silence his critics, certain local officials, a reporter or two, a pharmacist, and a long list of others. He would do so against Tiponi and her people if he didn't get his way. He had as much just said so. Knowing Moreno as she did, she knew that he would stop at nothing to protect himself, eliminate threats, cause competition to disappear, and to acquire his illicit fortune.

Back at her condo, Tiponi sat in her living room thinking about the morning's revelation, and the option she had briefly thought about when ending her conversation with Moreno. She remembered the previous time when she had a similar discussion with him. He had flashed menacing expressions towards her as he tried to convince her to join with him. He had said that his golden rule was to "do onto others before they do it to you." He had brazenly said that his ten commandments were just the opposite of the biblical ones, and that some day someone would write a "gospel according to the Devil." Tiponi knew that Moreno was egomaniacal, easily offended, retaliatory, and a threat to even his own followers. He was a loose cannon, often reckless, and unrepentantly revengeful. He completely lacked feeling any human compassion and was absolutely devoid of having a conscience.

There were many considerations to be worked out and little time, a month perhaps, to set certain things into motion. Moreno's entrance into the picture complicated things. Tiponi knew that he would have to be dealt with one way or another. He couldn't just be ignored. She wouldn't be surprised to learn that Moreno was having her followed. Worse, it wasn't beyond Moreno to try to set up people. He could plant some illegal substance in her car and tip off the authorities so that she would be arrested and convicted. Easier yet, Moreno could choose the path of least resistance, one that guaranteed finality. He could have her kidnapped, driven out into the desert, killed, and buried.

Moreno had his blind spots, but he had risen to his level of criminal prowess and success through all kinds of tactics, some surprisingly shrewd, properly calculated, and executed to have the desired effect and outcome.

Tiponi made a call to her contact at a Native American reservation where she was to have made a presentation and canceled it, saying, "It will have to wait for another time. I'm coming down with a cold or the flu."

Next, she called tribal leaders of four other Native American reservations, delaying indefinitely visits she had meant to make on the same trip.

Tiponi sat back and made a list of things she now needed to do. It was lengthy and incomplete, she was sure, but it was a start. On the list was a note for her to cancel an upcoming annual physical and her biannual dental appointment. Also listed was a reminder to pay any bills that needed to be paid, check her post office box for new mail, renew a prescription, fill up the gas tank for her Lexus, buy some new professional looking clothes and shoes, make a hairdresser appointment, among many other things which she needed to get done as soon as possible. She also wanted to take out a temporary one million dollar term life insurance policy on herself while revealing the beneficiary's name, in case of her death, only to her attorney.

Next, Tiponi placed a call to Consultants International to try to make an appointment with Wayde Ramsley, saying that it was regarding some public relations work he needed to have done. The receptionist quickly checked with Ramsley to see if he wanted to meet with the person calling. Ramsley had replied, "Yes, go ahead, the day after tomorrow in the afternoon. She's probably someone Art Mercer found for us."

CHAPTER 17

Denver, Colorado

Would you consider a joint venture offer?

Two days later, Tiponi Isaw landed in Denver, rented a car, and drove to the address where she had an appointment with Wayde Ramsley. She entered Consultants International's suite of offices and introduced herself to the receptionist.

Tiponi was wearing her new business clothes consisting of a pinstripe lady's suit with a scarf around her neck. Her shoes were leather short heels and her hair had been redone so that she had more of a professional appearance.

The receptionist escorted Tiponi into Wayde Ramsley's office and after a brief introduction between the two, he motioned her over to the two wingback chairs in the corner of his office.

"Tell me, Ms. Isaw, what your charity thinks it can do for us," Ramsley said, initiating the conversation.

"I've overseen a small organization that has contacts all over the western states. I'm personally well known by tribal leaders particularly in Idaho, Nevada, California, and Arizona, places you have a special interest in."

"So, you've been briefed," Ramsley replied.

"In a roundabout way. I'm aware of perhaps a few problem areas you might want solved and that you are on a short time schedule," she stated.

"It can't all be solved anytime soon. It'll likely take longer than we want, depending on the issue. So, your public relations strength is with the Indians?" he asked, noting that she had the appearance of possibly being of Indian decent herself.

"That's but one," she answered. "You have other concerns and I think I can help with those as well."

"How many people do you have working with you?" Ramsley probed.

"I can pull together at least a few of my best people and likely more. It depends on what you authorize us to try to fix for you."

Ramsley thought for a moment. He had hoped he could find but one public relations person he would have to deal with but his lawyer had suggested more than one, each focusing on its own problem. "We have to have you sign a nondisclosure agreement before I continue. If we do retain you for your services, each person you assign to this task will also have to sign the agreement."

"Understood. It's customary, I know," said Tiponi.

After reading and signing the document presented to her, Ramsley set it aside and looked up at the ceiling wondering where to begin. At that moment, his secretary entered saying that Arthur Mercer was returning his call. Ramsley asked Tiponi if she could wait out in the receptionist's area for a few minutes.

Ramsley picked up the phone and thanked Mercer for sending him a public relations person so quickly. He asked what he knew about Tiponi Isaw and The Indian Plight Charity Organization from Las Vegas.

Mercer replied with a little alarm in his voice, "Wayde, I didn't send anyone to you."

"Her card says she is Tiponi Isaw. She's the chairwoman of the charity. She gave me a list of her references consisting primarily of members of tribal councils. Looks like three or four dozen names from as many different reservations."

Mercer asked Ramsley to stall the meeting while he did some quick checking. He wanted to see if the charity had a website, to call the number on her card to see who answered, and to call a few of her references to see if they were real and to verify her potential for helping to solve upcoming possible problems with the Native American community. "Don't tell her anything just yet, Wayde," Mercer stated. "Not until we know more about her. Telling her everything could be like giving a teenager a bottle of booze and the keys to the family car."

Ramsley agreed, saying, "I thought you sent her to me and that she was already vetted." Mercer assured Ramsley that the checks could be done in an hour or two. Mercer suggested that Ramsley make some business excuse, that some kind of urgent problem had come up, and to ask the lady if she could come back to the office in a couple of hours. Ramsley agreed, thinking, *There goes another thousand dollars for two hours of Mercer's time.*

After Mercer did some verifications, he called Ramsley back, saying, "She may have value in heading off more than one of our problems. "I think she can arrange a lot of tribal support. She's highly regarded by those I was able to contact. Not a one had any hesitation. One reference wanted to know the nature of my inquiry. I explained she could assist us in employing Native Americans at a great many locations. The tribal council leader said, 'She's always been looking out for our people. If anyone can help, she can.' Try to get her perspective on a time line," Mercer continued, "how long she thinks it could take to handle one or two of our issues related to possible resistance we might encounter. Any idea as to cost?"

"Not yet," Ramsley replied, "but it's probably going to be as much as what you're charging us." Both men chuckled and then ended the conversation.

Tiponi had gone back to her rental car to call Tony Rappaport to see if there had been any messages or unusual phone calls. He had told her that there were no phone messages but that they had received a phone call from a lawyer who called from Denver wanting to verify the charity's existence, how long they had been a nonprofit organization and the name of the person who directed the charity, among other questions. Tiponi had replied to him not to worry about the call, she knew what it was about. She explained that it pertained to something she was working on. She told him that she would inform him more about it when she returned back to Las Vegas.

Tiponi Isaw reentered Ramsley's reception area just as he opened up his door to see if she had returned. With a warmer greeting than he had extended to her before, he invited her back into his office, apologizing for the delay.

Tiponi presented Wayde Ramsley with a Native American gift, saying, "It is yours whether you decide to use my services or not. I buy these things made by the recipients of our charitable gifts. I like to support their work and to expose others to their artistic creations," she said.

"It's beautiful," Ramsley said as he opened a small box containing a silver desktop business card holder containing a dark red colored gemstone on its front.

"The gemstone is one that Native Americans sometimes like to use in their lapidary work. It's a Mexican fire opal. They're fairly unique, and occasionally found at reservation retail stores," she said, smiling at Wayde Ramsley's reaction.

"Thank you very much," he replied. "Okay, let's get started. It's getting late and I don't want to hold you for too long."

"I had a late lunch and I'm here for the duration, for whatever we need to talk about. I have a plane reservation back to Las Vegas tomorrow morning," Tiponi explained, knowing that Ramsley had his attorney verify her charity's presence and location.

"All right then, there is this project we have been working on for a couple of years, preliminary stuff. But we are at the stage where we need to move quickly. We seem to be drawing unwanted attention and we are afraid our project is slowly becoming known. So, we have a timetable when we need to take certain actions. We are a private company owned by a few others who have shareholders they have to answer to. I realize that the kinds of issues we'll talk about here are the kind that can bubble up to the surface at any time and I want to try to stay ahead of the curve, if that's possible. I also realize that we could be talking about months of work, maybe even much longer, that you and other PR people, our lobbyists, and lawyers will have to spend addressing these issues." Ramsley droned on for half an hour talking about his company, its structure, its relationship to the consortium that had given birth to his mission, and the breadth, indeed the enormity of what was at stake.

Tiponi listened carefully, making notes on her legal pad of those things she didn't know and questions she intended to ask Ramsley. There was much she already knew from the e-mails she had read on Dalton Trindall's stolen laptop computer, but Ramsley was filling in a lot of blanks that gave her a much clearer picture. Tiponi intended to try to not reveal her knowledge about what she already knew. But she also wanted to use her advance knowledge in such a way that it gave Ramsley a sense of her ability to quickly grasp new complex information, to get him to have confidence in her.

"Tell me your timeline for important matters you will be implementing," Tiponi asked.

"It's not set in concrete," Ramsley answered. "We have about six weeks for best offers to have been made by two interested parties. We may have another interested party, but that's just a guess. I have to return a phone call to someone tomorrow morning. They're on east coast time."

"And so that deadline is flexible?" Tiponi asked.

"Maybe. If so, not by much. It will depend on circumstances. Then we hope to launch an IPO within a couple or a few days after that deadline if we have no solid offer to purchase our project."

"And that would be sometime around the middle to the end of May?"

"Yes, as close as possible to mid-May," Ramsley replied. "Next is the assignment of surveyors and the filing of land claims. It will be an ongoing process. It could take months, but we have to have the element of surprise. It would take any other company just as long or longer to try to file for claims adjoining ours, hoping to beat us at our own game. So we'll have to hit this phase hard. Do it as fast as possible. Once that is done then we can relax a little. We'll have land tied up in many prime locations from Canada to Mexico. It will be ours to explore in more depth with drilling rigs. Essentially, as major gold deposit claims are filed, we'll begin to assign them to various drilling companies."

"And that would be about when?" she asked, already knowing the answer.

"Sometime in early July, if all goes well," he answered. "And after that, there will be news releases along the way in our phase two initiative. I expect we will pretty much be finished filing for a majority of the claims that we will want by fall. Others will be added, I'm sure. But once this process kicks off, there are some problems that could raise their ugly heads to try to derail us, slow us down, prevent us from making progress. And," Ramsley said with added emphasis, "that's where you and other PR people come in, along with our lobbyists and our legal team. We want to try to be on the offensive instead of on the defense as much as possible.

"Let's talk about the issue you may be able to help me with," Ramsley said. He described the information that he had received about a young lawyer in Sacramento who seemed hell bent on stopping the entire operation in Idaho using "legal shenanigans," as he called it. He explained that their lawyers would have to deal with whatever legal challenge the Sacramento lawyer tried to throw their way. "In addition," he further explained, "this guy apparently has inroads to some of the Native American community, certainly on a couple of reservations that we should be concerned about.

"I think I can solve that problem for you. I have friends with the reservation's tribal council in Idaho. Much more than that, I think I know of a way to neutralize this lawyer in Sacramento. Just give me what you know about him and let me research it," Tiponi confidently said.

"How?" Ramsley asked almost incredulously.

"I know what makes such people tick," she replied. "especially with regard to the Native American causes. I might be able to make this person understand that his intentions are honorable but his methods and results would be contrary to the needs of the communities he hopes to help."

Ramsley just stared at Tiponi. His eyes were wide open, wider than usual and his mouth was partly open as if he was about to say something. The look on his face was one that said that he had just observed how successful this Tiponi Isaw could possibly end up being. Ramsley thought to himself, *Wow, such a simple approach with so much potential.*

THE PROMISCUOUS PUPPETEER 265

Ramsley asked how long she thought it might take to begin, and possibly finish, solving that particular public relations and legal problem.

She replied, "If we are lucky, within a month or two. That's why I asked you for your timeline for implementation. I'd like to solve this problem and maybe another or two before, and not after, your D-Day. I can assign one of my best people to this with confidence that there will be a good chance, but not an absolute one, that this could be fixed so that you could cross this one off your list of worries. But, and I caution, there are many reservations that could express alarm over your project. They could organize and try to sway public opinion and politicians or interfere at any number of your locations."

"That happened to also be on my list of things that I wondered if you could help us with. My lawyer said he thought you might have the connections," Ramsley said, still somewhat surprised with this lady's simplicity, directness, and apparent talent for problem solving.

"That is a very difficult one. There can be no promises or guarantees that no Native American or small groups won't spring up here or there, you know, spontaneous emotional combustion situations. But, as I said, I do know a lot of the key people. I know what's important to them. They have repeatedly told me that perhaps the most important thing, and one of the most elusive problems for them, is to get major companies to build whatever a company can build that will provide medium incomes or better for their tribal residents. Their economies depend mostly on money flowing into reservations. Then that money gets spent by reservation residents. That creates yet more jobs, more businesses, more professional opportunities. So I feel confident I can help with this issue as well. The only problem would be the unforeseeable situation or circumstance that could flare up for one reason or another and spread too rapidly for tribal leaders to be able to exercise their influence. In time, I think such flare-ups could be defused. Again, no guarantees."

Ramsley sat back in his seat, still soaking in the ease with which she explained her thoughts, the depth of her reasoning, and the confidence she exuded as she spoke.

"What else do you have on your list for public relations?" she asked.

Ramsley looked over his list while saying, "I think they probably will require some other kinds of expertise maybe we should just leave good enough alone. If you can handle these two issues, I'd be very pleased."

"Please tell me all of the issues. It would help me immensely to know what else you are having to deal with, even if you don't ask me to help solve them," she asked.

Wayde Ramsley studied the paper on his lap and said, "Well, we have these two entities who want to make an offer to buy Consultants International. I worry because there have been some actions on their part that smell like possible trouble as we draw close to our IPO deadline. I'm not sure what to expect. My experience tells me that there will be some last minute roadblocks, perhaps insurmountable ones we won't be able to address until we learn the nature of them, if there are any."

"Tell me all about them, please," Tiponi asked, positioning herself now at the edge of her chair leaning forward as if eager to hear more.

Ramsley explained what he knew about the two possible buyers and the problems they could present.

"But you want them to make their offer, right? To see a good offer, one which they would carry out, see through to completion, if it was good for your company."

"Yes, of course, but—"

"I have some ideas. I know that you're thinking that I couldn't possibly be capable of having my people help in these two cases, but I think there is a strong possibility of that happening. Let me think about this for a few days and get back to you. If they become a problem for you, it likely won't happen in the next week. As you said, such problems usually pop up at the last moment when they think you're eager to complete a deal, when they think they can back you into a corner, wear you down, cause you to make last minute concessions. Give me just a few days and let me brainstorm this with my staff. I have many talented people whose expertise would surprise you." *Yeah*, she thought to herself, *the kind he wouldn't want to hear about. The kind of problem solving that involves tactics that he would not approve of if given the chance.*

"And the other significant problem?" she asked.

"It's one for the lobbyists. It involves politics, upcoming hearings in the House and Senate. They could result in legislation that could stop us dead in our tracks. Even without new legislation, the public sentiment could shift against us and make our company's future goals seemingly impossible, if not very difficult to achieve."

Ramsley explained the problem that the lobbyists had just begun to work on. He said that it would likely take months, if not well past the next year's elections causing delay after delay for perhaps as much as a year and a half or longer.

Tiponi Isaw reached across to touch Wayde Ramsley's wrist, in the calculated manner she had learned many years ago that would lower his guard by some degree. "I can solve that for you, I think. Would you be surprised if one morning you woke up to learn that this senator had canceled his hearings, had decided it would be better if he didn't pursue his environmental agenda in favor of winning over the Native American people, and others, so that they didn't ruin his upcoming reelection chances? After all, that's what's most important to him. I think we can cause the senator to worry more about being defeated."

Tiponi knew how to cause Senator Maxwell and his staff to think twice about their own agenda. She knew she could cause busloads of Native Americans to demonstrate against him at every speech he gave, arrange demonstrations in front of his home, have Native Americans call their own press conferences to announce their support for more jobs, more companies, and not less, as the senator's approach would result in.

"I believe it's possible that we could get the senator to drop the whole matter if it is handled right," Tiponi continued. "Imagine the scene we could create, the cameras, the reporters scurrying around not knowing what to make of it all, other than having a new story to broadcast or write about, one which would hurt the senator and his desire for another six years of power and people bowing at his feet. It would be a public relations nightmare for him to continue down his current path. Again, no guarantees. But I feel confident we would have some impact. I'd like a stab at solving this one also," Tiponi said.

"This could take a year or two. The lobbyists are expert—"

"This could only take a few weeks, if I can fix it for you. If I can't, then you still have the years, as you say, to have your Washington, DC, people try to run interference for you. They will slowly, at a snail's pace, chew away at your check book, with small successes, if they are lucky. I'm asking for you to consider my approach. We are quick and we are usually successful. If I can't make some real headway in addressing these concerns for you, I will tell you. I don't waste people's time. I get results. The way I see it, I'd have about four to six weeks to try to address some or all of these problems for you."

"Not only are you reassuring, but you're also convincing. We never talked about what you would charge. I assume your profits go to your charity, after expenses, that is," Ramsley stated.

"Yes, they do," she replied. "In this case, my charges would be result-based oriented for any of the problems you have mentioned. I ask that we get paid accordingly. I can't predict whether the source of the problem comes back later using some other technique. My work on these problems would be based on what you know and what you have told me." She glanced at her watch and said, "It's almost 6 p.m. already. Let's both take a rest room break."

Ramsley replied, "I need to think about this for a while. I'll make some coffee. If we go forward with part or all of this, we'll need to hammer out an agreement, a contract which I can have prepared tomorrow and sent to you in Las Vegas."

"I have a much easier approach," Tiponi said. "Let's take that short break. When you're ready, I'll tell you my thoughts. All you really have to think about is whether to entrust me with about six weeks to see what we can do about each of these issues you raised. Let me provide you with an easy solution to paying for our charity's services. Meet you back in here in?"

"Fifteen minutes," he said.

After their break, the two returned to the chairs in the corner of Wayde Ramsley's office and Tiponi said, "Will you give me about six weeks to see what I can do for you, if our charge meets with your approval?" She knew that this was it. This was the moment she had been preparing for. She had been thinking about this slowly developing set of facts, piece by piece, for months, ever since she first learned that there was some kind of geological exploration work being done in more than just one location and that they were likely interrelated.

"Yes," Wayde Ramsley said.

"You can negotiate with me on cost, if you like. I won't be offended. I suggest that I would then, in a sense, be a partner with you, with your company. Something more than merely an endless stream of hourly bills from lawyers or lobbyists and public relations firms. I suspect you'd be paying out many times more over a very lengthy period of time. I propose that I receive two hundred thousand dollars for each of the five problems I can reasonably solve for you. That could come to a maximum of about a million dollars, if I am successful. I propose that my charity receive five million dollars, if I solve all of the issues, which will be distributed to all those I have to make payment to for their help. I'll have to make significant donations to various causes in order to ensure the help I need from the Native American community. I'll tell them that they will only receive our charity's funds if and when we are reasonably successful. That's a maximum of about six million dollars."

"How would we define, your words, 'reasonably successful'?" Ramsley asked.

"That would be for you and me to work out when the time comes," Tiponi answered. "I will be honest and I think you would be too, given the amount of money we are talking about here. Next, if there is an IPO, or if your planned IPO is canceled and you are bought out or if you decide to not go public, I would want five hundred thousand dollars worth of stock in your company. If you don't do an IPO, then I ask for the same amount in the companies that comprise your board of directors. I would earn this bonus if I can only complete my work within forty-five days. If you agree, I can tell all those whose help I will need to enlist from the Native American communities that you will be making a very significant donation to the charity which I will dole out to the various reservations in exchange for their help. My work for you is free if I fail to accomplish what it is you want accomplished. Compare that cost to what the lawyers, PR people, and the lobbyists would charge, regardless of whether they failed or succeeded. I promise success or you don't have to pay me or the charity. I think we both know that you'd likely pay out several times the amounts I suggested, and over a very lengthy period of time, in order to just *try* to solve the kinds of issues you've told me about."

"Somehow, Tiponi, you have managed to persuade me. I suspect that you could persuade the feathers off of a duck. It's a deal. What do you want in writing from me?" Ramsley asked.

"Just one page. That we have five issues to reasonably address within, let's say, eight weeks, and the terms for payment as I described. You sign it. That way, if anything happens to you in the interim, God forbid, I still have something convincing I can submit to try to be paid," she answered.

"I wish I had a dozen people like you, Tiponi. Keep me informed. Here is my personal cell phone number. Call me day or night. I'll want to know what kind of progress you and your people are making.

"Deal," she simply said as she stood up and shook his hand, then turned, walked out of his office and headed out the front doors.

When Tiponi got into her car, she reached into her purse and turned off the miniature tape recorder she had been using. Then she rummaged to the bottom of her purse where she found the first used tape cartridge which she had changed for a fresh one during her suggested bathroom break a half hour earlier.

The next morning, Wayde Ramsley was feeling more hopeful about at least a couple of the problematic issues he had been worrying about as he prepared to return a telephone call to

Harry Seckinger, the founder and CEO of Future Strategic Holdings, Inc. Seckinger had founded what had become one of the most successful privately held investment companies in the world and was known for his sharp eye in seeing long range opportunities. His company's successes were numerous and made for interesting, and envious, conversation among corporate leaders. He had met Seckinger and many of his senior people at various industry-related functions over the years. Seckinger was younger than Ramsley and had become one of the wealthier people in the world. Yet Seckinger had not been known to flaunt his status nor his wealth. He was seen as an unusually gifted man with a warm personality and a great sense of humor.

Seckinger and his company were based in Singapore with offices in London, New York, and, of all places, Denver. Ramsley thought briefly about Seckinger's kingdom consisting of partially- or fully-owned companies around the world.

Since having been in Denver, Ramsley had kept a very low profile. He had been trying to not draw any attention to his secret work and continuing connection to the precious metals industry. If circumstances had permitted, he would have maintained contact with many of his old cronies. Ramsley had been unaware of Seckinger's announcement months earlier that they were expanding their minerals-related portfolio of companies and that he had begun increasing his stake in the gold and silver exploration market. Future Strategic Holdings, Inc., had steadily increased its investments in its Minerals Division which now exceeded thirty wholly-owned and forty-seven partially-owned precious metals companies. Seckinger's companies controlled the largest exploration and mining land mass, hands down, with over three million acres on four continents.

Wayde Ramsley dialed the private cell phone number which had been left by Seckinger's personal assistant. Seckinger answered and Ramsley stated who he was and that he was returning his call.

Seckinger said, "Hello, Wayde. I don't have much time at the moment. My plane just landed in Denver. I guess I'm just an hour's drive away from you. I'm on my way to my Denver office to meet my people there. They have a hunch that you have been working on something big. In fact, very big. You didn't know this, of course, but I secretly set up my office in Denver to pursue something that needed a cover. People thought it strange that I'd open a major division of my company in Colorado, so we gave it responsibility for overseeing our oil, gas, routine metals, and precious metals companies. In addition to that ruse, I had a team of people begin researching a large gold field last year. I think my people and your people are working on the same thing. We suspect that you are well ahead of us in researching geographic areas that we have been interested in. I'm sorry for this quick explanation. My people think that you are about to go public. If that's true, it's imperative that I, and some of my Denver staff, meet with you. The sooner the better. Are you available? Can we meet later this morning or afternoon?"

Ramsley was shocked at what he had been told. This was totally unexpected. All Ramsley could say was, "Tell me what time you want to visit."

"Let's try for noon," he replied.

Ramsley cleared his day's schedule. This would be another very long day, he knew, and the shock of Harry Seckinger's words was still sinking in. Another company, a private one, no less, had been working on the same concept as he and his board had been working on. *But*, he thought to himself, *we are likely well ahead of them if we are lucky*. Ramsley weighed whether he would divulge anything at all about what his company was up to. He couldn't lie about it. But he wondered if he should only say nothing and just listen to what Seckinger had to say. It sounded as if Seckinger had come from almost halfway around the world from Singapore just to meet with him.

Harry Seckinger and four others entered Consultants International's office suite fifteen minutes early. He and his staff were introduced to Stu Bergman. Then Seckinger said, "Can you and I talk privately for a while, just you and me? I know we'll need to execute secrecy forms. They're already done. I have them here in my briefcase, the usual format." Seckinger opened his briefcase and handed Ramsley the forms and said, "Here is one for you to sign as well. I'll be telling you some things that we want to remain private."

Ramsley was caught off guard once again by Harry Seckinger and he led him into his office, closed the door, and showed him to the two wingback chairs he and Tiponi Isaw had spent a few hours in the day before.

"You'll need to hear me out, Wayde, before you come to any conclusions," Seckinger said. "The reason for my hurried arrival here was because my people learned from a source a week ago that you have been exploring the existence of what we call the 'the golden cradle,' a string of gold deposits that lay along a fault line from somewhere up in Canada to perhaps the middle of Mexico. For the past year, we have been exploring both the Canadian and the Mexican side of this concept while working our way towards the middle close to the US border from the north and toward the US border from way south in Central Mexico.

"We have identified a northern point perhaps several hundred miles north of the US border. But this past winter's weather kept us from finishing our work up there. We've also decided on a southern point way down in the interior of

Mexico. We believe these northern and southern points are, in reality, shall I say, infinite. In other words, we don't know how far south or north the gold deposits actually go, but we had to start somewhere. Meanwhile, we learned you've been exploring this same fault line within the continental US. Are you following me so far?" he asked.

"Yes," Ramsley replied, while trying to look relaxed and wanting something for his growing indigestion.

Seckinger continued, "I'm not looking to compete with you. I'm not looking to buy you out. What I am looking forward to doing, if we can arrange it, you and me, is to join forces, to become one major company. Our efforts in Canada and Mexico are slowly becoming known and it is only a question of when before our project becomes public knowledge in both countries. The same goes for you. When that happens, every guy with a shovel will be out there filing claims before we have our chance to finish our preliminary exploratory work. We decided to set into motion a large claim staking operation maybe later this year. We'd do it sooner if we could arrange the logistics. We were contacting assayers, surveyors, drill rig companies and found that most of them had already committed themselves to some other work starting in May or June. Soon, with a little help from a couple of big mouths, we were able see that your company was lining up major contracts, tying up the people we would also need. There's more. A lot more that we learned." Seckinger paused to take a sip of his coffee.

"I'm here today to propose we share with each other everything we each know. Our charts, our assay results, our records, our test results, everything. I propose that we allow a week or two for getting up to speed on what each of our companies has and has been doing. Then, if we are still interested in what you have been doing and you are still interested in what we have been doing, perhaps we can merge our resources and become one. If you and I decided to do what I propose, then we would be one giant formidable force with the resources to accomplish what has never been tried before. Once we drill and prove up the precious metals, we could lease the land to other mining companies, never giving up ownership, or we could sell individual sections to other miners while requiring a mining operation be set up within a certain timeframe while requiring them to immediately pay us an annual fee, with royalties to follow, once production got underway. If the fees or royalties go unpaid the claims would revert back to us."

"That's a lot for me to absorb all in one sitting," Ramsley said.

Seckinger continued, "Well, in short, that's our business model for what we'd like to try to do. There's a lot of gaps in what I've just said, but I wanted to give you the short version first to see if you might be interested. I know you could choose to go it alone. So could we. But I suggest we could both reduce our risks and increase our success potential by joining forces. If we work apart, we'd be reinforcing the definition of playing both ends against the middle, our Canadian and Mexican work being the two ends and your US efforts being in the middle. If we don't join forces, we'd be competing for talent and everything else you can think of. Then, in the end, we'd be competing for the same customers, the same companies to buy into our discoveries. We could avoid all of the bullshit we'd each have to contend with, much of which would end up being against each other, draining each other's time and efforts that could be better utilized working together."

Ramsley thought for a moment. "We're also a private company, but we're owned by a few public companies, each of which has their own publicly traded stock with retail and institutional shareholders. How would you reconcile that?" Ramsley asked.

"I'd prefer that your company merge with mine but I realize that can't happen because of your public status. But there is a way where we both get our cake and get to eat it too, as they say. Your company, Consultants International, that is, and my Denver subsidiary would set up a new company. We each merge everything we have into one. The new private company can issue non-public shares to both my Denver resources corporation as a 50 percent owner, and the new company would do the same for your public companies, issue them 50 percent of the private inside shares. Not tradeable as public shares on the open market. Each could sell their shares in the new private company to each other or to anyone else we choose, or could grant private shares to employees or contractors in lieu of cash, or whatever.

"Your company and my Denver company would be overseen by a new board of directors who would choose a president and chief executive officer, and the board would be independent of the new company's executive management. It can be done with relative ease and none of all the costly processes a publicly held company has to deal with. We'd be free of the constraints a public company has to adhere to. No shareholders breathing down our necks trying to influence our decisions," Harry Seckinger said.

Wayde Ramsley took a deep breath and gazed down at the office's carpet. Seckinger said nothing, knowing that Ramsley needed to think about all of the ramifications of what had just been presented to him. Ramsley then said, "I'd need to call for an emergency board meeting."

Seckinger added, "If you were planning to do an initial public offering to make your company a publicly held one, then yes, this totally turns everything around. I suspect you are close to some kind of launching of some major new initiative. Call your board together. I'll present my proposal to them, and then leave the room and go back to my company's Denver offices and wait for your board's decision. This would be a win-win for both of our companies. It would solve some huge hurdles we'd each have to forge independent of each other. Together we'd become the largest exploration and mining company in the world, all wrapped up into just one decision, the one your board would need to make quickly. Instead of playing both ends against the middle, to use the metaphor again, I'd rather that we didn't play against each other at all. I'd rather that we worked together. If you know anything about me and my companies, we don't fail. We have the track record. In that regard, we would have each other. Fifty-fifty."

"I'll have to get back to you," Ramsley said weakly. He had been caught totally off guard with Harry Seckinger's proposal. This truly was unexpected, especially now when so many buttons had already been pushed, so many proverbial juggler's balls were already in the air, at a time when he needed to concentrate his every skill in moving his company into their phase two initiative. His world had been turned upside down, but not in a bad way. Wayde continued, "Let's allow each team to look at each other's data while I contact our board members. Perhaps I can do this preliminarily by way of a conference call with them instead of having to bring them all here to Denver," he said. "I'll try to arrange a time for later today or perhaps tomorrow, depending on when I can get everyone together on the phone. If I can arrange that, I'll call you to come on over here so you can use my speaker phone to brief my board and to answer any of their questions. Once that is done, you'd have to leave so our board members could talk with me in private. How does that sound?"

Seckinger and Ramsley then spoke to their own people giving them the go ahead to both receive from, and to divulge information to, each other.

After Harry Seckinger's departure, Wayde Ramsley made notes of the conversation he had just had with Seckinger. Then he called in Stu Bergman and Alice Harrison into his office and he briefed them with the proposal that had just been made, asking that their two field geologist supervisors be briefed and told to cooperate with Seckinger's Denver team. Ramsley then asked his receptionist to make contact with all of the Consultants International board members' offices. She was to only say that there was an urgent need for a telephonic board meeting suggesting the time for 9 a.m. mountain standard the next morning.

Ramsley wondered what his board's reaction would be. No doubt at least one board member would ask, "What's in this for us? How do we gain from such a proposal? Let them have Mexico and Canada. We'll take the US," and other related points worthy of the board's deliberations.

The last matter Wayde Ramsley had to deal with before he went home for the day was the rejection of an offer he had made to buy out an exploration company that had miles of claims where gold and silver had been hand mined by prospectors long before he had been born. He knew that millions of ounces of gold had been previously extracted and his Idaho field geologist supervisor had carefully reviewed all of the existing exploration company's drill results. They had hit "pay dirt."

But given the fickle market place and poor investor sentiment, because the price of gold had been in a temporary slump, the Idaho company had slowed down their activity while waiting for the market conditions to improve. This in turn had made the explorer's stock price decline to what Ramsley had thought was perhaps a desperate level. The company would need cash and Ramsley had made an extremely low offer. The letter before him from the CEO said that the company's board of directors had rejected the offer.

Ramsley placed a call to the explorer's chief executive officer. After briefly exchanging friendly greetings, Ramsley asked, "What kind of an offer would you entertain?"

"You know, Wayde, we likely have tens of millions of ounces. Your two million dollar offer was just not acceptable to me nor to our board."

"Would you consider a joint venture offer?" Ramsley countered.

"We would, of course. Just put it in writing and I'll take it to the board for their decision."

Ramsley probed further by asking, "You're also the chairman of the board of your company. Can't you give me some kind of idea as to what you think would be of some interest to you and your board?"

"I know that you know what our claims are possibly worth," he replied. "In just one location we've proven up over a million ounces of gold in less than one mile. There are likely a few million ounces of gold just at that one small location."

"I know—" Ramsley tried to interject.

"And we think we will have dozens more of that to come," the CEO continued.

"I know, but—" Ramsley tried to continue but was again cut off.

"Wayde, this property here in the north central mountains of Idaho is only the tip of the iceberg. There's likely far more here than you realize."

"I know," Ramsley said again, "I agree with you. Likely much more gold than anyone realizes. Yes, yes, I can see it." Ramsley held back from revealing his thought any further. Ramsley knew that the gold stretched for a thousand miles or more from border to border.

The two closed their conversation with Ramsley saying he would sharpen his pencil and come up with a better figure. Ramsley then quickly sent an e-mail to Alice Harrison, Stu Bergman, and his two field supervisors, filling them in on the offer he had made based on Larry McGray's research and recommendation. He explained that the gold deposits this company likely had at their disposal could be worth billions alone. It would take money to prove it, "but," Ramsley closed in saying, "if we don't get this property someone else might do so" and that he would make another try at it with a better offer.

The e-mail Ramsley sent was also read by Tiponi Isaw from Dalton Trindall's stolen laptop computer.

CHAPTER 18

Various Locations

A lot of loose ends to tie.

In Las Vegas, Tiponi Isaw reviewed the list of issues she had agreed to try to help resolve for Wayde Ramsley. It would take all of her time in the coming weeks to try to address those issues and the success for doing so weighed heavily on her shoulders. She called Tony Rappaport from her condominium and told him to come over at the end of the day. They had a lot to accomplish and she knew she would need his help.

Upon his arrival, Tony had told her that they had a visitor that morning. It had been one of the people who worked for Leonard "The Devil" Moreno. The visit was unpleasant, the kind she had feared could begin to happen in an attempt to put pressure on her. He was sending a message for her to capitulate to Moreno's suggestion to either join with him or to face some sort of unspoken consequence. Rappaport explained, "I recognized the guy, but didn't show it."

"What happened?" Tiponi impatiently asked.

"He just walked in, walked past the receptionist's desk, came into the conference room, and sat down. I asked if I could help him and tried to shake his hand. He just glared at me for a moment and then reached under his shirt and lifted it. He had a gun. He said to tell you that you would know why he was there. Then as quickly as he had come in, he got up and walked out. I didn't go to the door to see where he went next."

"Who was he? I mean, do you know his name?" she asked.

"No, I just recognized him from somewhere but I don't recall other than I think he is with Moreno's organization."

"I'll take care of it," Tiponi replied, trying to change the subject.

"Then do you know what it was about?" he asked.

"A mistake on their part. Moreno has his people shaking down businesses around Vegas," she lied. "This guy wants small businesses to pay for protection. He thinks we're just a charity that has money to spare. I can fix it. He won't do anything worse. Don't worry. If he comes back, tell him that I have to be the one he talks to, that only I can make decisions regarding insurance and that I'll discuss it with him in our office any time he wants to talk with me."

Next, Tiponi slowly and carefully briefed Tony in detail with all that had been happening in recent months and, more importantly, in recent days. She told him that she had an overall plan that they had to execute quietly and successfully and that she would need his help to do it. After a couple of hours of discussion, Tony Rappaport went home.

Tiponi checked Dalton Trindall's former computer for any new e-mails and saw one that caught her by surprise. Wayde Ramsley had sent out a thank you note to Dalton for his service, saying, "We understand your reasons for not wanting to complete an additional year. You have been a valuable member of our team and I thank you for all of your sacrifices and dedication over the past two years."

Tiponi wondered why Trindall was leaving. Had something gone wrong? Maybe something he disagreed with? Then it occurred to her that his stolen laptop would be of no further use to her and she decided to have it destroyed as soon as she could. She would be partially blind in knowing some things that had been routinely provided to Trindall and his colleague. But she had opened the door to Wayde Ramsley just in time to ensure another avenue for knowing some of what she needed to know. He, she believed, had been open with her, forthcoming with answers to her questions, and seemed to be showing a willingness to keep her informed of things she needed to know about.

Tiponi then called a lawyer she had known for many years. She instructed him to prepare an offer, one that could be revoked at any time up until ninety days from the date of acceptance, in which the buyer-lender would agree to purchase 25 percent of an exploration company in Idaho for one million dollars at market price on a specified date. In addition, the buyer wanted a debenture issued by the company, payable back in five years at 10 percent interest. The buyer-lender would lend the company two million dollars for overhead and operational expenses to be used for continuing their drilling. It was a sum she had learned should be sufficient until market conditions improved which would put the company back on sound financial footing. The debenture would have to have a guarantee for a 50 percent interest in a lien against all of the company's assets, including the miles of claims they held. The attorney said he would work up the agreement and get it to her within a few days. "No," she quickly answered in return. "I want to have it express mailed to the company right away. I can't afford to wait. I want the offer to expire in two weeks. That should give them enough time to weigh it with their board and to get back with an answer. Payment, if they accept the offer, would be made ninety days from the date they agree. I have the right to cancel, to back out of the offer, at any time up until the ninetieth day. I'll need you to keep on top of this, time-wise. Nothing can fall through the cracks. Put it on your calendar, if they accept. Cancel the agreement if I don't get a certified check to you a few days before the deadline."

"Do you want all this to be in your name, or maybe in the charity's name?" the lawyer asked.

Tiponi thought about the question for a moment. She didn't want to risk Wayde Ramsley finding out about her involvement in the offer or the possible subsequent transaction. He would likely not react kindly to it. "No," she answered. "Can we set it up in a trust or something that would shield my name and the charity from being involved?"

"I know what to do," he replied. "What are you up to, Tiponi?" he asked with a chuckle.

"Never mind, I'll tell you later," she said.

The lawyer said he'd take care of it and then asked, "What the hell are you gonna do with a gold exploration company, Tiponi?"

"I'm not going to do anything with it. If we can close the deal, the shares and all papers will need to be convertible to someone else's name. I will never own any of it nor will I benefit from it. It is for something special, it will be a part of the charity's work, nothing more."

"Anything else, Tiponi?" her attorney asked.

"Yes, tell them in the offer that this would be a one-time offer, that there would be no negotiations, and that the offer will expire, if not accepted, with no future offers. I want to make sure they understand that this is not something they can play around with."

After her conversation with the lawyer, Tiponi hoped that the offer she was making would be accepted. The amount was for as much as what Wayde Ramsley had been willing to pay for the entire Idaho operation controlled by the company. Her offer, on the other hand, would allow the company to continue their exploration activities at a time when gold prices and mining sector market conditions should be improving. Further, she hoped Ramsley would buy the remaining 75 percent of the company, or all of it including the shares she hoped to own. If he didn't, she felt that this company's better days, and higher share price, could be just around the bend when Consultants International announced what they had discovered and started staking new claims including those bordering the Nez Perce reservation.

She had to move quickly before Wayde Ramsley learned of a new pending offer. She knew that the company in Idaho could call Ramsley and try to use the pending offer to see if he would raise up his own offer, but that was a chance she had to take and she hoped Ramsley would be too busy in the next couple of weeks to give the Idaho company issue any of his limited time. Perhaps when that day finally came, she mused to herself, if Wayde Ramsley wanted the Idaho company, he would have to pay a whole lot more for it, and she could possibly benefit, perhaps immensely.

The Idaho company would likely have to do a news release saying that they had just completed a deal that would provide them with enough money to significantly advance their exploration efforts into a category that could result in advancing a portion of their claims for the purpose of developing a mine on the property. Such a news release would likely come to Wayde Ramsley's attention, prompting him to move quickly if he wanted to sew up that stretch of land in north central Idaho. Tiponi smiled for a moment, realizing just how much she had learned in the past several months about the precious metals exploration and mining industry. This would be an investment, she knew, that had some potential to fail. In any event, she felt that the property had gold for the taking, if anyone had the backbone to finance the needed operation. The gold wasn't going to go anywhere. It was there, where it would remain until some company decided it was time to dig it up.

The next morning, Tiponi received information that Leonard Moreno had called for a meeting with his senior people. The information had originated from one of the ladies who occasionally did some night work for one of Tiponi's field people. The lady had decided to work for one of Moreno's senior people. While with him, she overheard him take a cell phone call from Moreno agreeing to meet on a certain upcoming day at a specific seaside location in Santa Barbara, California. Moreno's underling had been told that they would sit out on the beach where they couldn't be heard.

Tiponi typed out and printed a letter to various federal agencies showing on each copy the names of all those the letter had been addressed to. In it, she wrote the location, date, and time of an organized crime meeting where various criminal activities that they were engaged in would be discussed out of microphone or earshot of anyone. She spelled out that this was their opportunity to make a significant case against the up and coming Indian mafia, comprised of those who, although Native Americans, were the undesirables who had once been a part of various reservations from around the western region of the US.

Tiponi included in the letter Moreno's full name and those of a couple of people who she knew worked for him. She mentioned that they were involved in a host of crimes on a routine and continuing basis, including robberies, murders in the Los Angeles area, drug deals, and other various activities.

In closing the short letter, she wrote, "I can't reveal who I am for fear of retribution. Please know that Leonard 'The Devil' Moreno insulates himself very well from detection and that you better bring your parabolic microphones and set them up all around the area, disguise them if you have to get close. This may be your one and only chance to break up this new crime family before they commit untold devastation wherever they choose, including on Native American land making Native Americans their victims as well."

Tiponi handled the printed letters that came from her printer, and the envelopes she put the letters into, using latex gloves so her fingerprints wouldn't be on them. She wanted desperately to stop Moreno, but given the time she had available, this plan would have to do for now. If the authorities were interested they could begin a significant criminal investigation, if one wasn't already in progress. She planned to tell Moreno in three or four weeks that she had decided to close up shop, to shut down the charity and her fundraising operations. She would ask him for a contribution to her charity, a small one, something insignificant, a token of his appreciation for her work and her dedication to his fellow Native Americans. Moreno would be angry and retaliate for Tiponi's rejection of his offer.

Tiponi decided she would have to close the charity's office. Move everything out, donate the furniture and equipment to a local reservation, make a generous payment to her organization's board members, the fundraisers, those who had helped raise money for her charity. For now, she needed to have her people and herself assume a low profile. The charity's post office box could still be used, but nothing else. To Moreno, she had to appear as having vanished, as she would tell him she would, to Panama perhaps where she could operate without being in Moreno's way. Fearing that Moreno likely knew where she lived, Tiponi decided on a location where she and any of her people who wanted to join her could go to be safe, away from Las Vegas.

In Vancouver, Gordon Bessert and his people had been denied access to Consultants International's data. Wayde Ramsley had changed his mind after he weighed Bessert's tactics with regard to Bob Mendelson's board seat on Consultants International and other things Bessert had said and done that made Ramsley feel that Bessert's methods were unscrupulous.

Bessert was angry at being shut out by Wayde Ramsley and also because Bob Mendelson had failed to step aside from his board position. He was planning to expose Mendelson in a roundabout way and he had his legal staff preparing a lawsuit against Wayde Ramsley and Consultants International for having denied him the usual secret agreement arrangement offered possible suitors to a joint venture or a purchase agreement. Bessert had his lawyer communicate their intentions to Ramsley's lawyer Arthur Mercer, hoping it would intimidate Ramsley into providing Bessert with what he wanted.

At Bessert's office, his secretary received an envelope in the mail addressed to him. On the outside was typed the words "Personal. To Be Opened By Gordon Only." Bessert's secretary pondered for a moment whether she should open the envelope, as was her usual routine. She decided to leave it unopened and to place the envelope on her boss' desk. Tiponi Isaw had sent the envelope and had taken the extra precaution to place another envelope inside the one Bessert's secretary would receive. On it she had written simply, "Gordon, here is the private information you asked for." Tiponi had hoped that the envelope, within an envelope, would prove sufficient to give Bessert's secretary a second pause to consider that if the contents were personal, that her opening it might make her boss angry.

Gordon Bessert sat at his desk going through papers that had been placed in his inbox. When Bessert came to the envelope marked "Personal. To Be Opened By Gordon Only," he opened it and then opened the second envelope. Naturally, he was curious. Inside was a nicely typed letter which said: "You have been caught, Gordon. The evidence is clear. There are recordings. My private investigator and lawyer both are aware. I am asking you to back away from the Denver matter, in its entirety, and anything that has to do with the people involved. Make your intentions known quickly or I will send the evidence to the British Columbia Securities Commission, the US Securities and Exchange Commission, the RCMP, and to the FBI. The tapes show your attempt to bribe, to blackmail, to purchase insider information and to violate other criminal statutes both in Canada and in the US. If you continue your corrupt intentions, using legal strong arm tactics or otherwise, I will also mail copies of the tapes to your board members, to your senior executive staff, the heads of your subsidiaries, a few of your industry friends, among many others."

Bessert's hands began to shake as he finished reading the anonymous letter. He folded the letter back up, and placed it, and the two envelopes, into his briefcase. "Mendelson," he wondered to himself. "Was this Mendelson? It has to be. He's the only one who could have secretly recorded our dinner conversation when I had offered Mendelson a check." Bessert searched his mind for details of who he had talked to. One of his subordinates? One of Mendelson's subordinates? Mendelson had to be involved somehow. He had tried to get Mendelson to step aside as a Consultants International board member so he could try to take his place.

Bessert contemplated that the only way the letter writer might know whether he had declined further interest in Consultants International, as the anonymous letter had instructed, was for him to have his lawyer tell Wayde Ramsley's corporate lawyer and Ramsley himself. He would use the same lawyer who had called Mendelson, on Bessert's behalf, asking him to take a leave of absence from Consultants International's board and to recommend Bessert as a temporary member. Bessert pondered his mistakes in the whole matter. He had tried to move too quickly and in doing so had made errors in judgment. Now, he had to extricate himself. Failing to do so could mean that he would be black-balled by industry leaders, held at arm's length by the key people he had to deal with in his corporate world, and perhaps investigated and charged by government authorities.

⎯⎯⎯⎯⎯ ∿∾◦◖◗◦∾∿ ⎯⎯⎯⎯⎯

Tiponi e-mailed Wayde Ramsley telling him that he might soon receive word that Bessert Resources would no longer be pursuing its interests with Consultants International. She added, "I believe Bessert has been cautioned that if he ever brings the matter up again, it would ruin him, if not his businesses. He would be committing career suicide."

Ramsley replied to her e-mail asking, "How did you arrange this so fast?"

Tiponi responded, "I've learned that some of my happiest moments are those where I accomplish what others thought couldn't be done. Trust me, it didn't take much to get Bessert to pray for absolution. He'd been caught and he knew it. He was going to slip into a downward spiral. Which reminds me, Napolean Bonaparte once said 'never interrupt your enemy when he's in the process of falling on his own sword,' or something like that."

Wayde Ramsley knew he had underestimated Tiponi Isaw. His respect for her grew exponentially almost instantly. He was excited by her reply. She was a dynamo, someone to be admired, who knew, unlike almost all others, how to checkmate her opponent before he even learned who he was playing against. Ramsley was in awe at her choice of words. He suddenly felt confident and even entertained by Tiponi's bold self-assurance. She was an authority and a power not to be taken lightly.

While Wayde Ramsley and Tiponi Isaw were congratulating each other on their success, Bessert took an additional step to ensure his sudden lack of interest in Consultants International became known by the author of the letter he had received. He had his lawyer also call Bob Mendelson to thank him for his friendship and to say that he was no longer interested in the Denver matter.

When Mendelson got the call, he notified Wayde Ramsley to tell him that Bessert would not be a threat to the company. Ramsley sat back in his chair and smiled, saying, "I know. I got the same word from our lawyer and from someone who is in public relations. I wonder what gave Bessert a change of heart?" What he didn't say to Mendelson was that his new prodigious public relations firm headed by Tiponi Isaw had skillfully and quietly orchestrated the unexpected outcome. Ramsley hung up the phone and wondered how Tiponi would handle the next issue she had accepted to try to resolve. Suddenly, Ramsley thought, what had been a small list of potent distractions that had caused him to lose sleep had become something to look forward to, something to which he had a ring side seat.

———✸———

In Washington, DC, both the Chinese Ambassador and Quon Zhong received an envelope containing a CD. A note that accompanied it merely said. "This is for what you tried to do to an American mining executive when he was in Beijing. Drop the Denver company interest immediately or these pictures that are on the CD, and the story that goes with it, will be mailed to various high level officials in China, including Mr. Zhong's family members, and to various international news organizations, intelligence services, and embassies around the world."

Prior to mailing the two envelopes to the Chinese embassy in Washington, DC, Tiponi Isaw had received an e-mail from Wayde Ramsley saying that he had received a phone call from the Chinese delegation's leader, a Mr. Tai Shi. Ramsley said that the offer he made was significantly less than had been previously mentioned. The caller had also said that the offer would be received in writing by Ramsley shortly. In completing the conversation, the caller had reminded Ramsley of when he had last been in Ramsley's office, when they had discussed one of his board members having already been to China. He had said to Ramsley, "I'm sorry to have to inform you but it has come to our attention that your board member got into some trouble while he was here. I think we can keep his trouble from becoming an embarrassment."

Ramsley further wrote in his e-mail to Tiponi that he was concerned that the Chinese delegation might be trying to signal their intention to blackmail Consultants International into accepting their offer. "If not," Ramsley wrote, "I wonder if perhaps the Chinese delegation is using Bob Mendelson's gambling debt matter as leverage."

Tiponi suspected that the Bob Mendelson issue with Gordon Bessert had been solved for good. But now there was an additional issue that was related to the Chinese interest in Consultants International. It seemed to her that the Chinese embassy's Quon Zhong played a major role in trying to compromise Mendelson, which Gordon Bessert had somehow found out about.

Tiponi planned to try to use her suspicion to her advantage, to take the lead, the offense. The Chinese were hinting at the same incident that Mendelson had somehow gotten himself caught up in. The ploy had all the earmarks of some of the methods her people had used. The ploy, in this case, was the delegation's apparent attempt to use the Mendelson affair as a part of making an offer to buy the Denver company. They were trying to put pressure on Consultants International to win a major low price concession in their effort to buy the company.

Tiponi Isaw had in her possession the salacious pictures of the embassy's official Quon Zhong. He had answered a Las Vegas AD for males seeking males. The photographs depicted the subsequent meeting that transpired.

She had known that Mr. Zhong was vulnerable, that he had likely played an integral part in the Mendelson affair. The Chinese officials were trying to pressure Wayde Ramsley and Consultants International's board of directors. It was yet another shakedown, a form of blackmail, one done with the hope of extorting a favorable decision from Consultants International. Wayde Ramsley had indicated that if the price wasn't right, he wanted to convince his board to reject it without making a counteroffer. The Chinese had previously been informed that the starting price would be at about one hundred fifty billion dollars and would only go up higher as the company implemented certain parts of their phase two plan. Ramsley had been worried that a rejection of the Chinese offer could result in something that could become deeply troubling, something which would put Ramsley and his company at a severe disadvantage. Ramsley's instincts had been correct, but he had no idea about the forces that were at work, the players who were involved, and the seriousness of the game they wanted to play.

Tiponi Isaw took advantage of an opportunity to try to get the Chinese to back down. She used a countermeasure maneuver which she had observed, learned, and successfully used many times in the past. She was adept at her craft and her success spoke to that skill. She e-mailed Ramsley saying that the Chinese embassy's interest in his company would likely be a thing of the past, "a flirtation for which they had been made to feel embarrassed."

A few days later, after Tiponi Isaw had mailed the two revealing CDs to the Chinese embassy, Wayde Ramsley e-mailed her saying that he had just received a call from the Chinese delegation's Mr. Tai Shi who merely informed him that the Chinese offer was being withdrawn. Ramsley finished his e-mail by simply writing the two words "thank you."

———⁓⁓⁓———

Towards the end of the first week of April, while walking to her car, Tiponi received a call on her cell phone from her lawyer who said that the company in Idaho had accepted her offer. They would sign the necessary papers and send them to him as quickly as they could.

Tiponi had wanted to use some of whatever money she would earn for the charity through her work for Wayde Ramsley to make a gift, a donation. The stock shares and debenture, if ever finalized in about ninety days, would be presented to the tribal council of the Nez Perce. It would give them access to some of the land that had once been theirs. They could use the shares, if the Idaho company, or anyone else, ever began to mine the property, to pay for whatever needs they deemed appropriate. It would give them an incentive to support the company and its work. It could provide many jobs to the reservation's people and, importantly, it could also help to gain their support for the help she planned to ask of them in solving yet another problem which Wayde Ramsley had asked her to think about. She planned to eventually meet with the tribal council leader, who she knew from the reservation, and who had been present on the day she had given her diabetes presentation. She would show him documents pertaining to shares and a debenture guarantee, if her efforts to help Ramsley were successful. She didn't plan on telling him everything. She would only mention the particular matter that he and his tribal council could help her resolve within the coming month.

In mid–April, Tiponi met with the tribal leader. She explained that she intended to transfer the shares and the debenture over to the tribe once she had resolved a specific problem. She explained, "In other words, I will have to go through a checklist of matters needing to be addressed. Then I will be paid a donation. After that, I can close on the deal with the exploration company. But I will need your help. If we are successful, and if luck is with us, this could turn out to be worth many millions of dollars more than it will cost."

The tribal leader listened intently to Tiponi's explanation and proposed plan. He knew she could be trusted and he understood what was at stake. He assured her that what she was asking of him and his tribe could be arranged.

Tiponi asked the tribal leader to send an e-mail to Sacramento lawyer in training Zachery Cameron in which he would be politely told that at the request of the tribe, he was withdrawing the tribe's letter of authorization for Cameron to represent them.

Cameron had wanted to research possible options pertaining to what legal actions could be taken to try to get a court some day to review the tribe's claim for more land. Tiponi Isaw had explained to her tribal leader friend, "This isn't going to go anywhere. We both know that. Reservation boundaries do not get enlarged. If anything, they get shrunk. More than that, my plan here will give some of what used to belong to the tribe back to the tribe. As a shareholder, the Nez Perce will not only own a significant part of a company that controls the land, but it will guarantee you the right to continue to have some control of the land should the company go out of business or get bought out by some other company. In addition," she reasoned, "the precious minerals beneath the surface would essentially be proportionately yours as well. If the shares rise in value, the tribe would benefit. It would behoove the tribe then to do what they could to help *your* Idaho company to succeed."

Tiponi made clear to the tribal leader that the Sacramento lawyer was to be under no illusion that his service on behalf of the Nez Perce was to continue. He had to understand. Plus, Tiponi requested, that Zachery Cameron be asked to respond by e-mail that he would take no further action. She asked that a copy of both e-mails be forwarded to her as soon as they were sent and received. Tiponi Isaw then e-mailed Wayde Ramsley saying that the Sacramento kid was about to have the Nez Perce welcome mat pulled out from under him. She related that it would be done gently because an injury is forgotten much sooner than an insult. In this case, she did not want to have the lawyer's feelings hurt. He could prove useful in some other way in the future. He would be flattered and not made to feel embarrassed, demeaned, or unappreciated.

Tiponi stayed the night at a guest facility on the reservation and the next morning she found both e-mails from the reservation leader waiting for her in her laptop computer. After reading them, she forwarded them to Wayde Ramsley saying, "I'm up in Idaho meeting with a tribe who may be able to help us with that senator issue. Meanwhile, the attached two e-mails should allow you to cross one more problem off of your list. The legal obstacles that this Zachery Cameron had planned to throw up to block your company have been dismantled. He is a threat no more. Compare this result to the results you would have received from having your law firm battle Cameron for a year or three. The costs would have been monumental and the outcome would still have been in doubt."

Tiponi added in her e-mail to Ramsley, "Please know that at some point, perhaps very soon, I will need you to pay me and my charity for the work I and my people have accomplished for you. A good portion of those funds will have to be donated to those who have helped me to help you. It is as I explained before. This isn't something that can wait two or three months. The funds will need to be available for us upon request. Failure on my part to make certain donations would result in new problems with certain entities equal to, or worse, than the kind you thought had gone away." Tiponi had known that by wording the last sentence as she had that it would cause Wayde Ramsley to wonder what Tiponi could be capable of doing if the tables had been reversed and she had been employed to work against Consultants International, instead of for it. What she had written wasn't as much a veiled threat as it was a hint that her talents could be used to ensure that the company would be brought to its knees if she wasn't paid what was owed to her.

Ramsley read her e-mails and just shook his head in amazement. Tiponi Isaw was one of a kind, unlike anyone he had ever worked with. Ramsley smiled to himself. He felt more comfortable than before and he hoped he could talk her into other future problem solving projects, as she liked to call them. Ramsley couldn't believe his luck. Isaw was unbelievably talented and her dry sense of humor tickled him. But, he cautioned himself, the job was far from done and the more difficult issues still lay before them.

Tiponi returned to her home in Las Vegas after discussing her need for the tribal leader's help with another matter, one involving politics. With mid-April came increasing pressure for her to try to resolve what she knew would be the most difficult part of her plan. It would have to be a multipronged approach and it would have to be well-coordinated.

Senator Henry Maxwell had to be persuaded to cancel his announced initiative to slow or stop the use of federal land for the purposes of prospecting and mining. He had said that environmental groups and citizens supported a legislative initiative that would preserve federal lands, to leave them undisturbed for generations to come. The federal lands were not national parks, but the land consisted of almost 80 percent of all land west of the Rocky mountains, on nearly one-third of the entire continental US.

Tiponi's plan was simple, but it would require many tribes to help pull it off. The tribal leader with the Nez Perce had agreed that Tiponi's views paralleled those of many in the Native American communities. He had said that he agreed with the need for a better economy, one that didn't almost wholly depend on reservation casinos.

The tribal leader had agreed to contact many other tribal leaders from many other western reservations and ask them to send a formal request to Senator Maxwell's California headquarters and to his Washington, DC, office. They were to request that Maxwell not pursue his initiative as had been described because it would only satisfy the environmentalists, whose work they none-the-less respected. They were to write that they wanted their reservation's people to have access to funds that were earned and not just the kind of funds that were disbursed by the federal government, sufficient enough to merely keep the reservation's economic status as it had always been. Instead, there was the competing interest for Native Americans to become more self-sufficient, to be able to become more dependent on their own efforts and not those that resulted in the arrival of more and more sacks of flour to feed their growing diabetes epidemic. The various tribes were to be asked to address this issue with their reservations and nearby off-reservation news outlets. It was believed that by doing so, the Native American's views would mirror those of the communities away from the reservations where economies would suffer and potential new jobs would not materialize.

Next, Tiponi asked for and received support for having a few busloads of Native Americans to demonstrate outside of Maxwell's California Senate office as well as outside of his campaign headquarters, and to inform local, regional, and national major print and broadcast news organizations about the demonstrations the day before the demonstrators arrived. The goal was to have about one hundred demonstrators, with signs, on the two sites early on the first morning so that any interested reporters could get their story prior to their daily deadlines. The demonstrations were to last for three days at most.

Another part of the plan was for Tiponi's charity to arrange to offer a campaign contribution to the senator's campaign. One hundred thousand dollars would be the pledge. One million dollars would be raised through various campaign fundraising efforts if the senator canceled upcoming scheduled hearings. It would be suggested that the senator could say he and other members of Congress wanted time to re-study the issues pertaining to the economic impact his proposed legislation would have on all communities. He could also add that he wanted to show his concern for the impact his proposed legislation would have on Native American communities that were near or next to Federal lands.

As a last part of her plan, Tiponi Isaw planned to bring tribal leaders from a variety of reservations together for a conference with local mayors, county administrators, state legislators, and other elected representatives. They would arrange a group thought to be sympathetic to her and the Native American's point of view. The meeting was to take place in Tonopah, Nevada, a town in need of revival, new businesses, new employers, new streets and sidewalks, everything. The meeting would only last for three hours and news organizations would be invited to cover the meeting, live, if they wished, or by way of internet broadcast. She arranged for the news media to be made aware of the unsightly conditions of the town, asking them to come and see for themselves a town in need of help, the kind of help Senator Maxwell was intent on preventing.

In her plan was the threat to have hundreds of unpaid volunteers from California and elsewhere shift from wanting to help Henry Maxwell's candidacy to instead help raise funds for his rival. It was calculated that the million dollars that would have been raised over the next twelve months for Senator Maxwell would instead go to his challenger.

The first day of the demonstration had arrived and, right on schedule, buses unloaded in front of Maxwell's campaign headquarters. Some of the demonstrators wore traditional Native American clothing while others did not. One of the demonstrators sat on the ground just outside of the headquarters' door beating a large, deep-sounding drum. The demonstrators joined in a traditional Native American dance. A few news media people showed up to record the event. It was colorful and effective. The campaign manager was asked to come outside amongst the demonstrators for an interview but he declined, favoring one inside the headquarters instead.

Tony Rappaport, who was present, tried to remain inconspicuous. The demonstrators had their own leadership and they knew what to do. In between the drum beats, the demonstrators chanted "Maxwell kills jobs." After a short period of time, the chant was changed to "Maxwell kills economy." As a third alternative, so as to not sound too repetitive, they chanted, "Defeat Maxwell." The demonstration leader used a bullhorn to lead his people. At some point soon after having started their drum beating and chanting, a decision was made, probably by the campaign manager, to call the police and ask that the demonstrators be asked to leave since they were demonstrating without a permit. The ensuing discussion between a sergeant and the demonstrator was perfect for the news media. "The constitution guarantees the right to assemble in public, but Indians don't have those same rights" said the demonstration leader, who clearly appeared to be a Native American.

"Not here," said the sergeant.

"You want to force us off the sidewalk and back onto the reservation," the leader replied.

Then a lieutenant chimed in, saying, "The Constitution is for peaceful assembly."

The leader said, "We're not running around here with tomahawks threatening anybody. We want people to know that Senator Maxwell is proposing to keep our reservations poor, to prevent us from having a better standard of living." With that, other people, who had been walking along the street, joined in with the demonstrators.

"Disperse or be arrested," said the lieutenant.

"We won't leave," said the leader.

Then the lieutenant ordered the Sergeant to call for three prisoner transport buses.

"We have three buses if you want to borrow ours," said the demonstration leader, hoping to expedite the arrest process while the news media was still present. The leader's comment brought some needed laughter from onlookers and some of the demonstrators.

Tony Rappaport called Tiponi to fill her in on what was about to happen. She told Tony to use the money she had given him to pay for any fines or bail fees, should the police make the threatened arrests. Then she said, "Walk inside the campaign headquarters and tell whoever you encounter that you have a major campaign contribution to make. Ask to speak to their campaign manager. Then tell him that he will be receiving mail containing the contribution compliments of a Mr. Leonard Moreno and that the envelope will be marked for the campaign manager's attention only so that he knows who to thank. I'll mail the envelope. It'll be sanitized. No prints. Then leave and stay back a distance. Watch to see if you can help our friends but don't get involved."

The police arrested the demonstrators, Tony Rappaport paid their fines, and Tiponi Isaw mailed the envelope. Instead of containing a campaign contribution, it contained pictures of Senator Maxwell's staff members having a party. She included a note that merely said, "What happens in Vegas doesn't always stay in Vegas."

Tiponi had planned to have Maxwell's campaign manager learn that the Senator's press assistant, his legislative aide, his communications director, and his director of constituent services had engaged in a night of lewd and lascivious behavior at a Las Vegas hotel. The embarrassing event happened when they were supposed to be attending a brainstorming session when they were actually partying, all at taxpayers' expense. No threat or promise had been attached to the envelope's contents. There was no mention about Maxwell's pending legislation. Maxwell's campaign manager would fear that the photos could be distributed to the news media, to Native American tribal councils, and to Maxwell's challenger's campaign headquarters, for them to use as they saw fit. The timing for this last part of Tiponi's initiative couldn't have been better.

The past two weeks had been difficult and Tiponi only gave herself a 50 percent chance of succeeding. If Maxwell didn't bow to the pressure that was being laid on him, then he was not a typical politician—one where getting reelected was more important than the cause he was faking, hoping that he would benefit from another six years in office.

After mailing the envelope, Tiponi Isaw called Wayde Ramsley and told him that he should have his lawyer in Denver monitor certain news outlets for a possible change of heart by the vulnerable US senator from California.

Tiponi arranged for a nearby truck to come to her charity's office in Las Vegas to pick up all of the furniture and she canceled the charity's phone and internet services. Leonard Moreno, she believed, would be angry to learn of her departure from her home base instead of joining forces with his organization. She knew that Moreno would be blamed for the pictures she had sent of Maxwell's staff's indulgence in sensual pleasures. On the other hand, she hoped that the federal law enforcement agencies she had tipped off would succeed in eventually dismantling the Indian mafia. She surmised that once a few of Moreno's people were in custody, one or more would tell everything they knew. One way or another, Moreno would exchange his new Santa Barbara residence for a prison that would house him for a good portion of his life.

On April 10, Tiponi read on Senator Maxwell's website a copy of a news release he had quietly issued. The press release said that the senator would be canceling upcoming hearings concerning federal lands usage. The only explanation given was that he and his staff planned to travel to various California and out-of-state localities to further learn of the concerns of those who would be most impacted by any new restrictions to federal land access and usage. Tiponi copied the web page containing the press release and attached it to an e-mail to

Wayde Ramsley. In her e-mail she asked for a day and time when she could visit him and receive payment.

Tiponi called a local real estate agent she knew and listed her condominium for sale. She instructed that all matters pertaining to the listing and eventual sale were to go through her attorney. Then Tiponi purchased a new car for herself and had the two cars that were in the charity's name sold with the proceeds deposited into the charity's bank account. There was much to do, a lot of loose ends to tie, but few would ever know anything more than she had simply packed up and left Las Vegas.

CHAPTER 19

Denver, Colorado

You will have made a lot of people very happy.

Wayde Ramsley received Tiponi's e-mail and set an appointment for April 17.

Ramsley was elated. There was a new bounce to his step. Very significant obstacles to his company's plans had been quickly and quietly removed. Instead of it taking a year or two, or even longer, with no guarantee of success, it had all been resolved in about a month's time.

On the seventeenth, Wayde Ramsley cheerfully said "Welcome" to Tiponi as she was escorted into his office. It was early in the morning and she had hoped to catch an afternoon flight back to Las Vegas.

"Please, sit down," Ramsley said, motioning with his hand as he led her to the same wingback chairs they had sat in when she first met with him nearly a month previously.

"I wanted to meet with you one last time, Wayde, to see if there were any last minute issues you needed to have addressed," she said.

"And to be paid, I'm sure," Ramsley said, still smiling. "But I have a proposition for you. Come work for us here, or from your home, if you wish. We could put you on a retainer and pay you a monthly fee for just being available to us to handle any new public relations issues."

"I'll consider it," Tiponi lied. "Thanks for your kind offer. It's gratifying to know that you have faith in my people and me."

"How did you do it all? I mean, how did you solve the issues?" Ramsley asked with an inquisitive expression on his face.

Tiponi beamed. She was obviously pleased at Wayde Ramsley's compliment. "Trade secret," she said almost inaudibly, as if speaking in a hushed voice about something that couldn't be revealed. "I'm kidding. I have a lot of contacts. A lot of talented people, smart people who know how to get things done. They are expert at putting pressure where it's needed. The right kind for the right occasion," she said while thinking to herself about how Ramsley would recoil in horror if he really knew what she had done and how she did it. They consisted of methods she deeply hoped she would never have to employ ever again. "Understanding human nature and what people respond to most. It is a kind of psychology to which we apply a special kind of therapy," Tiponi said as Wayde and she both chuckled in unison.

"I suspect there will indeed be more problems as we move forward. So, can I sign you up as being on retainer," Ramsley pressed, "maybe twenty-five thousand a month? You can always say no to any issue you feel uncomfortable taking on."

"I'll need to give it some thought. But right now I have a lot of people waiting to be paid and I have to take care of them, and my expenses are extensive, as you can imagine."

"I'd like you to consider a change in the terms we agreed to," Ramsley asked.

"That's not possible, Wayde. My expenses exceed what I originally calculated they would come to. I'll have some left over for myself, but not nearly as much as I had hoped," Tiponi said firmly, as she thought about the tape recording she had made of her first meeting with Ramsley during which the costs had been agreed to. As a last resort, she could force him to pay the agreed amounts by telling him some of the things she had done on his behalf. He would fear repercussions if her methods, employed at Ramsley's behest, ever became public knowledge.

There was a moment of silence as Wayde Ramsley thought about what Tiponi had just said. "I didn't mean it the way you took it," Ramsley said. "I'd like to offer you more in stock shares than in actual dollars. I'd be able to preserve some cash and you'd be able to realize more if the share prices rise."

"Thank you for the offer," Tiponi said. "But I have very large debts to be paid as a result of the work I did for you. I must first take care of all those who helped me to help you."

"One million made out to you, five million made out to your charity. And five hundred thousand dollars worth of stock," Ramsley thought out loud.

"Yes," Tiponi said. "I know there is no graceful way for me to ask you this, and for that I apologize in advance. May I have the five hundred thousand dollars that would have come to me in stock shares given to me in a check instead? I'm afraid my expenses will require that I have the cash instead of the shares."

"I think that would be a mistake on your part. I believe those shares will be worth far more than you dreamed possible," he said.

"I know, Wayde. I would gladly take your thoughtful offer. However, it's as I said. My people were promised certain sums of money. I keep my word. I must take care of all of them before I take care of myself."

Ramsley studied Tiponi's face for a brief moment as if deep in thought. "Very well then, I'll be back in a few minutes."

Ramsley got up from his chair and left the room. A while later, he came back with two checks, one of which was for the charity. The other, Tiponi's check, had been increased by the five hundred thousand dollars she had asked for in lieu of the stock shares. Then he handed her a brief typewritten letter on his company's letterhead that read, "This is to promise that Consultants International will provide Tiponi Isaw with one hundred thousand dollars' worth of stock in either Consultants International or it's successor, or in shares of the companies comprising its board of directors, said shares to be delivered immediately upon either an IPO or the cancellation of an IPO by the board."

"This is for you. You deserve it. We would have been wrestling with those problems that you solved for me for many years. It would have cost us far more than you realized. You deserve this because you were willing to sacrifice your own income and bonus in favor of paying your people and your expenses. I respect you more than before, if that's even possible. We are about three weeks away from resolving the IPO issue. Once that is done, my vice president for administration, Alice Harrison, will forward to you your stock certificates.

"Oh, Wayde, I'm so grateful." Tiponi scribbled out the name and address of her Las Vegas attorney and gave it to Ramsley, asking that any correspondence to her pertaining to the shares that had just been promised be sent to her lawyer. "You will have made a lot of people very happy," she said as she kissed his cheek before departing his office.

Tiponi's work was done. After depositing the two checks, the smaller amount into her personal checking account and the larger one into her charity's account, she made plans to pay her immediate staff, her charity's board members, the people she had promised money to for their help, and to finalize the deal she had made with the exploration company in Idaho. While waiting at the Denver airport for her flight to depart, she made notes of everything she needed to do to conclude her charity's, and her own, affairs in Las Vegas. Tony Rappaport would be waiting for her at the airport in Las Vegas and she would fill him in on her plans and decisions. Then she would offer Tony Rappaport the opportunity to follow her to the Nez Perce reservation in Idaho where she planned to stay indefinitely, where there was safety, and where she could be among the people she had helped and served for a good part of her life.

The following day, Consultants International's board of directors met in Denver. Wayde Ramsley presented the board with their two options for the company. Either form a new company, one that would remain private, in conjunction with Harry Seckinger's proposal, or stay the course and make Consultants International a public company and to proceed with the initial public offering of shares to the retail and institutional market.

The board grappled with many concerns and issues, one of which was the disappointment that Seckinger's geologists had not been able to accomplish much in Canada because of the long winters and snow-covered ground which prevented their geologists from making much headway. The other issue was similar. Seckinger's geologists had been unable to make much progress in Mexico because of the ongoing extremely dangerous Mexican drug cartel violence against the Mexican people, institutions, businesses, and the Mexican government itself. That violence included thousands of random murders and demands for very large payments for protection from the cartel. Kidnappings for ransom often resulted in murders with increasing frequency.

The decision was made for Consultants International to go public. An IPO would be made on May 1, sooner than had been expected.

On the appointed day, it was formally announced that a new company, called the Mega Trend Gold and Silver Corporation, had been formed. Its stock was available for purchase by the general public. The announcement included substantial information about the company's work and what it planned to accomplish with invested shareholder money. The stock was issued at thirty cents. Within days, it climbed to forty-six cents a share.

Mega Trend Gold and Silver's CEO Wayde Ramsley then ordered the deployment of hundreds of surveyors and staff to stake out and file land claims on land stretching from northern Idaho to southern California. Within weeks, Mega Trend Gold and Silver announced their control of a land mass previously unheard of anywhere in the world. Assay results and the results from all of the prior tests that had been done were released in the news release which had to be lengthy to accommodate all of the information that the public and their shareholders needed to know. The share price rose to three dollars and eleven cents before settling back down to a lower amount.

Then two weeks later, the company announced the deployment of thirty-three drill rigs with the promise of more to come in the coming months. The goal was to concentrate the rigs on three locations where it was believed three new mining operations would be built. Among the three locations was one that was just west of Tonopah, Nevada, where the company was already making progress in establishing its new regional headquarters for the southern two-thirds of Nevada. The share price rose even higher where it fluctuated on average in the six dollars-a-share range. Those who bought, or were issued, shares upon the IPO saw their investments rise by nearly twentyfold, or by about 2,000 percent. Tiponi Isaw's one hundred thousand dollars' worth of the new company's stock became worth nearly two million dollars in a matter of weeks.

All of the original geologists and staff of the former Mining Engineers, Inc., who initiated Project X and those who worked for its successor, Consultants International, had been awarded shares in the new company as had been agreed to in their employment contracts. Although not large, the resulting share price made sure that each could enjoy a worry-free retirement.

Wayde Ramsley had made a successful once and final offer for the existing Idaho exploration company's land claims that were along the route he had an interest in acquiring. The exploration company and all existing shareholders were issued new Mega Trend Gold and Silver stock which then skyrocketed in value, making the Nez Perce Tribe richer than they had ever imagined possible, increasing their share value to nearly twenty million dollars.

One problem that briefly surfaced on Mega Trend's new Idaho acquisition pertained to a request by the Nez Perce reservation's tribal council to search for any obvious possible ancestral burial grounds on the claims now owned by Wayde Ramsley's company. A tip had come into the reservation's tribal police department saying that there was a burial site that had been discovered. The exact location had been provided. The reservation's elders had decided to have some of their people visit the property and the location of where one burial ground had been reported. Ramsley granted the request.

What was found instead of an old burial site was a poorly dug recent site. Local police were called in to investigate the fresh remains of three bodies. The autopsy had revealed that the three had been shot and quickly buried in a shallow grave. Wolves had found the location and partially dug up the bodies. The bodies had not yet fully decomposed and a fingerprint had been discernible enough for possible identification.

Dental remains of the three were also used to try to help identify the murder victims.

Then a rumor spread on the reservation about three men who had been planning to kill a woman and a man on the reservation. Instead, the result was the death of the three men. The woman who was to have become the victim was whispered as safe, although no one seemed to know her name.

The Idaho police authorities eventually learned that the fingerprint they had taken was from a man named Leonard Moreno of Santa Barbara, California, previously from Tonopah, Nevada. The other two bodies could not be identified. Moreno, the local authorities were told, had been recently indicted by California and federal authorities for murder and for running an ongoing organized criminal enterprise. California police said that they believed Moreno had murdered two other people who planned to testify against him in an upcoming trial.

The investigation into the death of Moreno and the other two men went unsolved. There was no evidence. The scene of where the shootings had taken place had not been discovered. There were signs that four-wheel drive all terrain vehicles had been to the site, but rain had washed out the tread marks in the soil which seemed to lead in no one particular identifiable direction. Interviews of those few people who lived within a few miles of the location revealed nothing new. None reported having heard gun shots in recent weeks.

Wayde Ramsley was given a full briefing by Art Mercer, the newly appointed chief counsel for Mega Trend Gold and Silver, of what had been discovered. The request for looking for any discernible ancient burial sites had been replaced with an agreement to notify the authorities and the Nez Perce Native American reservation if any remains were ever discovered on the land owned by Ramsley's company.

As the summer months came to a close, Wayde Ramsley announced his retirement. He had personally capitalized on his own success through the new company's share price. In the news release, the new company's board of directors announced the appointment of Robert Mendelson as their new chief executive officer for what would eventually become the largest exploration and mining company worldwide.

CHAPTER 20

Kingston, Washington

It's kind of a hidden secret.

Dalton had sent a notice to Ramsley and Bergman saying that he would not be renewing his annual contract. On his last day of work, while driving north, he smiled as he thought that the best view of Tonopah was through his rearview mirror, however, he knew that the town would soon be revitalized. He would avoid the worst of the coming hot summer sun which could cook an egg, make a pot of coffee, and, as he had often done, heat bottles of water for taking a shower.

The dusty, dirty desert field work had primed him for the more civilized comforts of his home. He thought about how the old-time prospectors from a hundred to a hundred fifty years ago were true pioneers, hardened adventurers, ones who risked any manner of death from day to day. Many others ended up disheartened after having failed to find their sought after treasure. Many such prospectors eventually surrendered to an irretrievably broken spirit, depression, and oftentimes a self-imposed exile and early death. Confronting the desert and its many hazards and discomforts required proper supplies, a proper frame of mind, and a proper body capable of the inhumane demand that would be placed on it. More than that, surviving the desert required perpetual optimism, a dream, and the belief such dreams would be achieved. Some men, who qualified for the nomadic desert life, if not honorable, were often cutthroats, high stakes gamblers, or violent men. Mining sometimes drew the worst mankind had to offer, along with the good.

In the past century, some things had changed in his industry while some things remained the same. Dalton had helped make history. He had been a modern-day prospector. His lifetime achievements had helped to discover and unearth many millions of ounces of invisible gold with the promise of far more to come in the decades ahead, long after his life would come to an end. He was proud of his efforts and the results. Although not the kind of subject that would become well known by the general public, his name nonetheless would be among the likes of industry famous Dr. Keith Barron who had been credited with making the largest gold deposit discovery in the past quarter of a century. Many segments of the new Mega Trend were believed to contain gold deposits equal to or greater than the Carlin Trend, such as the one in the mountains of north central Idaho.

As Dalton Trindall drove north, he wondered if Emelina Black Coyote would ever be able to put the decades-old loss of her husband behind her. Perhaps the passage of time hadn't allowed her painful memories and her mind and soul to sufficiently heal. He had hoped that she would have been able to accept him into her life. There had seemingly been some kind of unspoken imperceptible transitory barrier between her and him, a certain mild reluctance, something that held her back, that made her seem preoccupied, cautious, mildly distant, a prisoner of her thoughts, her past, possibly her life's experiences. Perhaps it was nothing more than her devotion to her family and her seeming preference for a modicum of privacy or solitude.

Dalton drove up to a high point along the highway leading north from town, pulled his truck off the road, and got out to look over the landscape he had been working on for so much of his life. The air was warm, still, and had the pleasing aroma of the desert. The scenery lay tranquil with its vastness which he found beautiful in its own unique desert way. He felt a sense of loss which came with the passing of but another adventure, a part of his life gone forever, while a new one, he hoped, awaited him in the times ahead.

Dalton removed his old truck and trailer from the Nevada desert for the last time. Upon returning back to his home in Kingston, Washington, he promptly sold both and bought a new truck and top-of-the-line camper, one with a built-in shower. Dalton intended to resume his own prospecting more as a hobby, as he had done many years previously while young. Of particular interest to him were the last Colorado and Washington state prospecting locations scouted out by a recently deceased geologist friend who had retired from a career as a professor and a respected mineralogist for the US Geological Survey Service.

During the summer months, Dalton rejoined his local rock club in Port Townsend, Washington, where he renewed old cherished friendships. He also once again was able to reunite with the informal group of local friends who had also retired from the geology profession and the mining industry.

Dalton loved the spring and summer seasons at his home on the Kitsap Peninsula, visiting the various seaside villages, smelling the saltwater air, seeing the trees once again full with new green leaves, the very tall cedar trees that ran right up to the edge of the sandy beaches and the high rocky cliffs that surrounded the area.

To the west of him was the nearby snow-covered Olympic Mountain range. Across the Puget Sound, he could see the northern Cascade Mountains stretching for over a hundred miles, from his vantage point, with the towering Mount Baker to the north and the even taller Mount Rainier to the south. Both mountains seemed as if sentinels guarding the lesser string of mountains that lay in between them.

Dalton wanted to investigate various boat dealers to see if he could be interested in a boat which he could keep at a nearby marina. He planned to take time during the summer months to see what was available and to allow his interest in a boat to either fade or intensify.

In his garage and basement were literally dozens of five-gallon buckets containing rocks as small as a golf ball and ones as large as a cantaloupe. They all awaited his practiced eye and potentially a rock saw during the winter if he felt they were worth the time and effort, to see what was inside of them. He often liked to think and tell other people that when he cut open a rock it made him realize that, aside from the creator of the heavens and the earth, he was the very first human being to see what was inside. That very thought had always stayed with him. It was what drew him to geology both as a curriculum and later as a career and was one of the under-pinnings of his personal faith.

Dalton spent some of his Summer and Fall back in Kingston fixing up his home. He arranged to have his roof re-shingled and his home repainted. He enjoyed his newfound freedom and rose early each day. He occasionally walked down to his beach to scout out places where he could harvest shellfish for the taking when they were in season. During the summer, he rowed his rowboat out a short distance from the shore and caught large Dungeness crabs in his crab pots.

On one occasion that Fall, Dalton joined his retired geologist friends for a luncheon at the Fireside restaurant at the Port Ludlow Inn. While seated at the windows that over-looked a marina and the waterfront, his eyes caught a glimpse of a lady walking from the water's edge towards the hotel's front door. She looked familiar, but from another place. He excused himself from the table and went out into the lobby and froze in place for a second when he realized the woman was Emelina Black Coyote. He was overwhelmed at the sight of her and he sprang forward while calling out her name. She turned towards him and upon recognizing who he was, she quickly opened her arms, saying, "Oh, my God." They hugged briefly and Dalton took her to his restaurant table, introduced her to his friends and quickly paid for his meal.

"Let's walk for a while," he suggested to Emelina, almost pleadingly.

As they entered the lobby area again on their way to the front door, Emelina's son Rodrigo, daughter-in-law Susan, and her grandson Xavier got off the elevator. The greeting was warm and one of welcome surprise. They all tried talking at the same time, each with their own competing questions and replies. Rodrigo said, among other things, that he was selling his turquoise mine and ranch house outside of Tonopah, saying that a new mining company had opened offices and an operation in Tonopah and that the real estate market had suddenly come alive for the first time in decades. It was the perfect time to try to sell his mine and home. He had asked, "Is that what you were there for when we first met?"

Dalton, now able to talk about his work, said, "Yes," with a big smile.

Together they sat down and talked for a few minutes. Dalton learned that they were visiting for a couple of days and that Rodrigo, Susan, and their son were on their way to the marina store to get ice cream cones.

Emelina sat and listened as Dalton and Xavier peppered each other with questions relating to rocks and geology. Dalton promised to give Xavier some of his minerals which he had collected over the years. Then they all agreed to meet later that afternoon at a place called The Point, a new S'Klallam Native American tribe entertainment destination.

After Rodrigo and his family said goodbye to go for ice cream, Emelina's eyes welled up with tears.

Dalton asked her if she was all right, asking, "What's wrong?"

"Nothing is wrong," she answered. "I'm happy to see you. This was so unexpected. I didn't know if we would ever see you again."

Dalton took her hand and said, "Come on, Emelina, lets' go for a short walk." They held hands as they approached the bay that was ringed with homes, sail boats at their anchorages, a Cedar-forested shoreline, and the marina.

"I've thought a lot about you," Dalton said. "I've missed you, more than you know."

Emelina slowed their pace, saying, "Me too."

"You were always so busy helping Rodrigo with his jewelry art shows. It was hard for us to schedule time together," Dalton said. "Are you all here for a show? Is there an event you all will be attending? I'd like to see it."

"No, no, we are just here to visit a pretty place. They have a saying here 'come for a day and stay for a lifetime.' With the selling of the ranch house in Tonopah, our lives will change. That part of our life is over. I want to put the past behind me. Start over with what remains of my life. I like this place. It's kind of a hidden secret, this Port Ludlow. The best part of being here was finding you here. We're thinking about moving to this area or some place nearby, Dalton," she said.

"You know," he interrupted, trying to bring a little humor to the moment, "you need to stop calling me Dalton. Some people call me Dale."

Emelina took his arm in her two arms as she turned him towards the beach and the totem pole that stood ahead. "You know, I also have had another name that people referred to me as for nearly thirty years. I should tell you it in case we ever run into someone who calls me by my old name," Emelina explained as they approached the totem pole at the water's edge. "I was known by an Indian name. It is from the Hopi tribal language. It's roughly translated as 'child of importance coyote.' The Hopi name is Tiponi Isaw."

END

AFTERWORD

Thank you for acquiring my new book, *The Promiscuous Puppeteer*.

If interested, my prior publication was titled "Jeremiah's Tale," available on the web at Lulu.com.

In *The Promiscuous Puppeteer*, a reference was made to a poem that Tiponi Isaw had found while reading some of the contents on Dalton Trindall's laptop computer. So as to not leave you with yet another enigma, I thought the poem I wrote might be of interest. To explain the title, "A Chesapeake Skipjack Skipper's Dream," a Chesapeake skipjack is a kind of small commercial shellfishing boat. They were usually propelled by wind and sail. In later years, skipjacks became motorized and the boat's marine architecture grew in popularity, spreading from the shores of Virginia and Maryland to all parts of the US. The poem references a man who had lived alone while performing a difficult and lonely job. The man often wished for someone who he could love and who would love him in return, someone with whom he could share what remained of his life. Then, that day finally came.

A CHESAPEAKE SKIPJACK
SKIPPER'S DREAM

Moving with life's daily pace,
rising fresh with each new morn',
wishing for time from the race,
safe passage through each storm.

Shoulder always to the wheel,
focused on each day,
Losing that which time would steal,
That time would take away.

Weathering perilous subtleties,
riding out life's role,
holding to a vision,
of an unknown blessed soul.

"On thee, my dream, I cast my gaze,
my respite from the gale,
the calming of white capped waves,
The seas on which I sail."

The energy, the force, the might,
unleashed with each new morn,'
"Ready I for each new fight,
As I weather out each storm."

"Your pristine shore is on my chart,
your road I know alone,
your warmth I carry in my heart,
Your love could guide me home."

"This dream's a dream," the skipper thought,
"'Tis time to sail for home,"
Where the dream's fair lady that he sought,

would be dreamed anew alone.
And dream he did, as seasons went,
he labored every day,
and wondered what his life had meant,
as his years slipped away.

And then by chance his dream took form,
one summer she appeared,
By Fall she promised her devotion,
That winter she would hear...

"On thee, my love, I had cast my gaze,
You were the respite from the gale,
You were the calming of white-capped waves,
The seas on which I sailed."

"Your pristine shore was on my chart,
your road I knew alone,
your warmth I carried in my heart,
Your love is now my home."

"I dream no more," the skipper said,
the dream I held so near,
the dream's fair lady that I sought,
the one I hold so dear."

In spring he asked her for her hand,
He offered her his life,
When she reached out and took his hand,
His dream became his wife.

Although I wrote about Tonopah from a first impression perspective, while exaggerating my view of the town, my wife and others who have visited there felt that my description was partly warranted. Yet, I feel it only right to say that I understand the history of Tonopah and I realize that a great many people have dedicated themselves to resurrecting the town.

To those who have worked hard to this end, in initiating the town's gradual growing new appearance, I salute you. I don't regret for one moment the time I spent in Tonopah. It is one of those historical places that makes its own impression, a place I would like to revisit some day. I chose to begin this story with Tonopah and to end it with Port Ludlow. Should you visit both locations, the contrast between the two, in the way I described, would then be understood.

GLOSSARY

BLM: US Bureau of Land Management agency.

Carlin Trend: The largest (invisible) gold discovery ever made in North America. It is located in northeast Nevada outside of Carlin, Nevada, known as the place where "the train stops and the gold rush begins." It was named after a US Civil War general. Found and mined in the early 1960s, it is now about five miles wide and sixty miles long. Multiple mining companies have produced about sixty million ounces of gold, or almost 80 percent of the gold produced in the US, along the Carlin Trend. It is considered one of the largest gold discoveries in the world and its eventual north-south endpoints have yet to be determined. Some believe the Carlin is but a small segment of an overall larger discovery that is being slowly identified by small exploration corporations such as the thirty-kilometer (plus or minus) long Oro Grande Shear Zone in central Idaho.

G/P/T or g/p/t: Grams per ton.

GPS: Global Positioning System.

Mickey: A drink laced with a drug.

mineral: Various natural substances, including chemical elements, including precious and base metals, coal, oil, or other inorganic substances taken from the ground for economic activities.

patented claim: Land that was converted from being government-owned to privately-owned. Conversely, patented land claims are those that are owned by government but are leased upon the filing of a claim, payment of an annual fee, and the initiation of some kind of work on the land.

POG: Price of gold

USFS: US Forest Service

USGS: US Geological Service

ABOUT THE AUTHOR

Below is the incredible and previously unknown story of a destitute, homeless, street person who became a self made financial and career success. Author Walt Biondi's privileged upbringing was suddenly terminated when his parents divorced. Upon moving to California, he was soon a homeless, young teenage street person, in and out of jails, a petty thief, facing serious malnutrition, illness, assaults, robbery, and hypothermia. He had become a total failure who was on the brink, unable to thrive both physically and emotionally. Then, after hitting rock bottom, he fought his way out of destitution and near life threatening poverty. In time, he became a comparatively storied and unimaginable success. Here is a small portion of that story in his own words:

"I began my life in Pennsylvania and was raised in relative luxury and privilege thanks to my business owning grandfather. I was too young to have an appreciation for the lifestyle that was afforded us as a result of my grandfather's benevolence. By the time I was about twelve years old all of that began to change when my parent's marriage fell apart and my mother's parents demanded that the marriage not end in divorce. My family was subsequently quickly disinherited and disowned.

After the divorce, I went with my mother, brother, and sister, to California, for a new start. During the previous years' turmoil my school grades had plummeted. A school counselor had strongly advised my mother that I be enrolled in the school's "shop" curriculum to become a printer's apprentice typesetter.

I recall one particular teacher in my eighth grade who, to this day, had a profound impact on me. Ronald Smoyer taught biology, later to become a successful physician. He instilled in me a temporarily renewed passion for learning. That one experience would later prove to be a life changing event. He recognized my desire to write. He assigned me as a student journalist for the school's in-house newspaper.

I never progressed beyond the ninth grade in high school. I was labeled as "incorrigible." While in California I lied about my age so that I could work. After having saved some money, while fifteen years of age, and as an act of teenage rebellion, I absconded, ran away from home, never to return. My bad decision then led me into a downward spiraling existence.

I joined up with a friend who owned a Volkswagen Beetle. Together we made our way east. In crossing the country we took a detour and navigated south through Tucson, AZ. We crossed the border into Nogales, Sonora, Mexico where we were falsely arrested and thrown into a Mexican jail. Upon release, we proceeded north back into the U.S. and once again headed in an easterly direction. We feared that our return to our homes could result in being sent to a juvenile detention facility until we were eighteen years old.

Gasoline, and what little food we could afford was purchased with small amounts of change we received from turning in stolen empty soda bottles. Occasionally, we took milk and bread that had been delivered to the front door of homes.

Soon, my California friend grew homesick and decided to drive back to his home. I never heard from him again. I was broke, penniless, and no one would hire me unless I could produce a (false and forged) parental-school work permit. I looked younger than my age and what little work I could find resulted in being significantly under paid. A common tactic a few small business owners used was to hire me for a week, and then to fire me without paying me what I was owed.

I found it impossible to earn enough money to survive. I became sick, malnourished, faced near starvation, and weighed a dangerously low one hundred and fifteen pounds for my five foot ten inch height. I slept on park benches or in the woods of a nearby park. I had no blankets and no winter coat. I was occasionally frost bitten and suffered hypothermia from time to time. I was destitute. I was hitting rock bottom. I had been beaten and robbed of what very little I had on two occasions. I recall, one Christmas, renting a room for a night at a place where itinerant people could stay temporarily, for a very small fee. I shared the expense with another street person. Together we opened one can of "Spam" and shared a wooden utensil in consuming our meal. I roamed the streets for the most part. I was living life on the abyss. I'll never forget the absolute feeling of helplessness.

On one occasion, I consumed most of a full bottle of high proof liquor called "Vat 69," suffered alcohol poisoning, and was then beaten by thugs looking for money that I didn't have. Some time later, I was arrested by the police, jailed, and eventually released after the charge was dropped. The combination of these events caused me to realize that I was either going to remain a failure, risk a life of incarceration, incur a debilitating illness, succumb to an early demise, or, I was going to fight my way up from the cesspool of a life I was living. Knowing that things couldn't get any worse, and that I was living on the brink, I finally resolved that I had no where to go but up. It was like a sudden determination, an awakening, or an epiphany.

My metamorphosis from life on the fringe, vagrancy, as an off and on homeless street person, was underway. I obtained three part time jobs and celebrated my eighteenth birthday in a large rooming house, one with a shared bathroom and a pay phone down the hallway. I began to earn enough money to subsist on. I contacted my parents and promised that I would do everything in my power to never disappoint them again. Meanwhile, I remained independent.

I passed a GED high school examination and regained my health. I served in the U.S. Navy while working part time jobs. I was later hired as a police officer, followed by being appointed a Deputy U.S. Marshal. In the evenings and on weekends I attended college and graduated with Honors, using my memory of Dr. Ronald Smoyer as my inspiration. I went on, over time to devote myself, through public service, to helping those who were victimized by others. Ironically, I also ended up owning a franchise printing business. Over the years I eventually built a small landscaping, firewood, and a private home security business. Financial and career rewards also came to me by way of my public service.

I had been given not only another chance in life, but one which I could use to help others. In time, I became a Chief Inspector for INTERPOL, was appointed to a Presidential Appointee's position, and served as one of the heads of two different Federal law enforcement agencies in Washington, D.C., one with five thousand employees under my command spanning the globe. At the pinnacle of my career I was selected for, and received, The President's Distinguished Senior Executive Service Award.

I offer this very personal information about myself for the first time because I hope it will serve to help others, and motivate them to aspire to achievements. Both private and/or public service success is attainable through self improvement and accomplishment. Having experienced failure I feared its existence. I ran from it and never looked back.

As a result of my Biology teacher's assignments, I continued to write, whether it was poetry, short stories, text booklets, or books. If you have just finished reading my newest book, "The Promiscuous Puppeteer," I hope you enjoyed it. I also owe its creation, in part, to Dr. Ronald Smoyer's influence on me. In school I had been seen as a day dreamer. Later in life, I wrote that 'day dreamers often become night writers' It can be true, can't it? In my case it was. People can usually become, within reason, whatever they make up their mind they are going to be.

And so, one can go from absolute life crushing failure to success in life, while using lessons they learned along the way. I am living proof. Those who think they can't improve a bad situation, doubt their ability, or fail to make an unending commitment, to reach higher. I liken such a thought to something I wrote for myself years ago when I needed to inspire myself to aspire to ever increasing personal success. To me, 'Real aspiration is not the moth that is drawn by the light of the nearest light bulb. Rather, it is the moth that is drawn by the light of the most distant star.' And, there you have it. A part of my life never told before until now.

Blessings to each and every one of you."

Walt Biondi